McKINGLEY
Volume One

All the Wright Moves

The Best Thing Yet

McKENNA JEFFRIES and
ALIYAH BURKE

McKingley Volume One
ISBN # 978-1-78184-616-2
©Copyright McKenna Jeffries and Aliyah Burke 2013
Cover Art by Oliver Bennett ©Copyright 2013
Interior text design by Claire Siemaszkiewicz
Total-E-Bound Publishing

Published in 2013 by Total-E-Bound Publishing, Think Tank, Ruston Way, Lincoln, LN6 7FL, United Kingdom.

ALL THE
WRIGHT MOVES

Dedication

To my mom, who taught me that helping others is the greatest thing we as human beings can do. To my family, who gives with an open heart and are always there to support me. To Aliyah, whose wit and big heart is what makes her one of my closest and dearest friends.
— *McKenna Jeffries*

Many thanks to the men and women of our Armed Services who spend their time away from those they love. Thanks to my husband, who is ever supportive. And of course, thanks to McKenna, who took this journey with me.
— *Aliyah Burke*

Chapter One

Katiya Wright stopped only after a step into the open doorway. The sight before her made her breath catch and she leaned against the doorframe for support and to view the tight jeans hugging a firm ass. The man bent, stretching the already fitted jeans taut. She bit her bottom lip to stifle a whimper. Her gaze travelled from the ass to muscular legs that bulged enticingly as he stood. She retraced her path back up to a bottom that should be declared illegal to a tapered waist, and a back that rippled with muscles visible through his shirt across his broad shoulders. The man shifted to the side as he lifted the computer monitor onto the desk. Katiya snapped out of her daze, glancing away from his luscious body.

The large room, which had been empty a few days earlier, was now filled with over fifty individual oak desks, office chairs and a file cabinet with a printer on it. It was as she'd envisioned, each work area set up like an office. She walked over to the desk closest to her and touched the last item that she knew had arrived today. A complete computer system with all the bells and whistles sat on top of the desk. A look at the screen showed it was installing some sort of software. With another glance around the room she noted that the systems were almost all set up. She returned her attention to the lone man still installing the computers and wondered where the rest of the work crew was.

A flare of interest filled her as she watched him work. With efficient moves he hooked up all the cables. Moments later he flipped on the system, punched a few keys, and the Windows logo came up. The man moved onto another desk and bent to pick up another computer out of a new box. She tried to figure out why she seemed to be attracted to him. It had been years since she'd had even a minuscule amount of interest in anyone. She hadn't even seen his face nor had any interaction with him. Katiya continued to study him. She should probably let him know she was there, but she didn't want to break the moment and continued to watch as he set up another system and moved onto another.

Snap out of it. No dating, she reminded herself. Clearing her throat, she walked over to the man. He stiffened and straightened from the box he was unpacking.

"Everything is looking great." She glanced around again, pleased that her vision was finally taking shape.

Katiya turned to look at him again then stopped. *Damn, he's even more captivating up close.* His dark, brooding eyes studied her silently. Black shaggy shoulder length hair framed a tanned, craggy face. He wasn't what she'd call typically handsome, but something about him made her want to look at him more than once. With large blunt fingers, he pushed back his hair from his face. He dwarfed her five feet nine inches — he had to be at least over six feet tall.

"There are just a few more systems left to set up in here."

His deep, bassy baritone set off a clenching sensation in the base of her stomach.

Control yourself. Katiya took a calming breath. "Yes, I see that. I'm surprised that there aren't more techs helping to get it done."

"There were, but they are setting up the other systems for the centre offices," he replied.

Katiya frowned. "What? The donation was only for these systems." She motioned to the computers around the room.

"Miss?"

"Katiya. Katiya Wright. No need for the Miss." She paused. "I don't understand. Why are computers being installed in the centre offices?"

"Katiya Wright. You're the owner of The Oasis, I'm pleased to meet you." He reached out and shook her hand. "You're doing some great things with the community centre. As for the reason why the centre's offices are being set up too. Do you realise how outdated your systems are?" The man cocked his head to the side, studying her.

She ignored the flash of pleasure that filled her at his touch and statement about her work at the centre.

"I know they are but this" — she gestured to the systems again — "was more important to get than computers for our offices. What does — ?"

"Why didn't you just ask for a donation that included the centre offices?"

Katiya narrowed her eyes. She didn't appreciate his almost chastising tone, but instead of replying in anger, she put on her 'diplomatic mask'.

"We had thought we would have to get more than one donor to get everything here the way we wanted. But when I approached your company, the donation made was more than generous enough and we didn't need to seek any other donors. Taylor Bytes gave us all the computer systems, printers and provided techs like you to set it all up for us. That was what we needed. The centre offices having computers were secondary to that."

Although she had not met the man behind Taylor Bytes, the multibillion-dollar software company, Katiya was very grateful for his unselfish donation. When she had approached the company she had never expected them to donate everything she'd needed to get her computer classes up and running. The man continued to study her intently. Katiya shifted and tried to mask her wince. Her leg ached from the plane ride.

"So what they say about you is true."

"What do they say?" she asked, leery.

She knew people talked about her dogged determination to get donations for The Oasis—her community centre. They either respected her or called her a pest. She didn't care as long as The Oasis was running well.

"The Oasis and programs you have here come first," he stated.

"That's the way it should be. And this is why I still want to know about the installation of the additional systems."

"After we got here we were met by Rhianna and she mentioned that you had to go out of town unexpectedly. She showed us where things were to go, I set the men to work and asked Rhianna to show me where we would set up the wireless network. She ended up giving me a tour. From outside you wouldn't know how huge this place is, and the set-up is phenomenal. Rhianna mentioned the various classes, services and so on you offer. It is impressive."

"Thanks." She smiled.

"No, it is you and the people here this community has to thank. Your dedication to the centre and its programs are admirable, however you need good equipment to do the work you do. While we were in Rhianna's office, I noticed that her computer was a dinosaur. I asked why the donation hadn't included the offices and she said almost the same thing you had. I made a few calls and Taylor Bytes included the centre offices in the donation. The other techs are setting up the systems."

Katiya stared. She knew that Rhianna, who was her second in the centre, would not have asked for more donations and she had probably tried to dissuade him. From the look on his face, she could see he wasn't a man easily dissuaded. She wasn't either. This time, though, she would let him have his way. It was a benefit to the centre.

"Thank you and Taylor Bytes."

"You're welcome, Katiya."

She stifled a shiver at the way he'd said her name. It was almost like a caress. However, his face was expressionless She must have imagined it.

"Rhianna mentioned you were flying in today but I thought you would be in tomorrow. We planned to come back to set up your system then."

"I came straight from the airport. I had to check and see how things are doing." She smiled wryly.

"I know the feeling. I rush back to work after being away too."

They shared a companionable look. He glanced at his watch. Katiya looked at hers and noted it was almost noon.

"Do you have time for us to set you up today?" He crossed his arms.

"Sure. What do you need from me?"

"Access to your computer. We need to make copies of your hard drive files and programs you installed to put on the new system. Let me get one of the guys to work on it."

She nodded as he unhooked what looked to be a walkie-talkie from his belt. Katiya wandered over to another system and glanced at the screen. The system seemed to have finished loading whatever it had been doing.

"Calix will meet you at your office," he said.

"Okay." She turned to face him and gasped—he was close. He smiled. Katiya stifled a whimper. The dimples bracketing his lush lips made her want to lick them.

Down, girl.

"Ummm... I better go meet Calix." She backed away.

"Depending on what you have on your hard drive, it should only be about an hour or two to get your info off the old system."

"Okay. Thanks again." She turned then walked quickly to the door.

"You're *very* welcome, Katiya." His words followed her out of the door.

Again his words felt like a caress. *Just your imagination.*

Katiya walked down the hall to her office, absently waving at the various employees and patrons of the centre.

"Katiya, you're back." She turned and smiled as she saw Rhianna De'clare striding towards her. "Did you get Lissa Gayle to agree to teach the computer program?"

Katiya marvelled at how Rhianna could make the simple act of walking so graceful and sensual. Even though Rhianna would deny it, she still had a dancer's grace. Now she would just have to convince her to teach the dance class she had planned but hadn't told Rhianna about yet. As she got closer Katiya noticed that Rhianna's soft, honey coloured skin had a light sheen of sweat and her short curly dark brown hair was messy. It was a sure sign that Rhianna was agitated about something. Her light grey eyes still had that serious look they always did. Rhianna stopped and spoke briefly with a centre worker then came the last few steps to her.

"Yes I did. We were able to work out a fair salary. It will take a few months for Lissa to get things settled in New York before she can move here to McKingley."

"And she doesn't have a problem moving from such a big city to New Mexico?"

Katiya shook her head. "Nope. She actually said she is looking forward to not having winters anymore. Can't say I blame her. Even though it's spring there, it still felt cold to me. I am glad to be home."

"Glad you're back and everything worked out," Rhianna said. A guilty look flashed across Rhianna's face. "Did you check out the computers? The techs were here since yesterday—a day earlier than planned. They mentioned they had some wiring to do and so on. They came back to install today."

"They've been here two days? Yes, I've checked out the systems and spoke with..." Katiya's eyes widened as she realised she didn't even know the man's name.

"Spoke with…?"

"The head tech mentioned they are donating comps for the offices too. He filled me in on everything."

"Head tech?" Rhianna looked amused.

Confused, she gave her a look. "Yeah. He was in the room back there finishing up the installation."

"I tried to tell him it wasn't necessary," Rhianna said.

"I know you did. He looks like he does as he pleases. Besides, it works in our favour." She shrugged.

"So you're cool with them outfitting the space next to the computer area as a computer lab?"

"A *what*?" Katiya demanded.

"He didn't tell you everything." Rhianna winced.

"Explain, Rhia."

"It would be easier to show you." Rhianna sighed. "Come on."

Katiya followed Rhianna back the way she had come. She glanced into the computer room where the man was bent over lifting a computer. He glanced over his shoulder but Katiya looked away quickly, hurrying past the door. Rhianna stopped at the double doors a little distance down the hallway. When Katiya caught up with her, she opened a door and gestured Katiya to go in. Katiya stepped inside and gasped. The massive room had been empty prior to her trip. Now, it looked like a very well stocked computer lab. She'd intended for it to be that exactly, but never in her wildest dreams would she have imagined it would be so…perfect.

Long tables were lined with high backed stools bracketing each side. The wall held organisational units that filled the entire space. She counted. There were fifteen along the back wall and twenty long tables scattered around the room. Next to each table was a computer system on a smaller computer stand with a printer on the bottom. Although the set up was impressive, it was the other three walls that shocked her.

Five flat screen monitors hung on the wall, each one with a console below it. Eyes wide, Katiya walked over to the one of them. She ran her hand over the console. There were so many buttons and controls she didn't have a clue what any were for. She counted the consoles too and noted there were five on each wall for a total of fifteen. She turned to Rhianna.

"The...ummm...head tech had them set this up." The same amusement was in Rhianna's tone.

Katiya glared at her. She didn't see anything funny about this. There had to be millions of dollars of equipment here. She knew a little about computers but not enough to know what everything was. She glanced at the console again.

"When I gave him the tour he asked about what other programs we were planning. I... ummm..."

Katiya returned her attention to Rhia. Guilt was visible on her face.

"You what?"

"I got excited and started mentioning what we had planned if we could pull it off." Rhianna sounded defensive.

Katiya bit her lip, trying not to laugh. Rhianna was as bad as she was when she started talking about The Oasis and plans they had.

"He asked me to show him the room we wanted set up for training to build computer systems. Before I knew it, he had somehow commandeered the area and had people in here installing things. He said if people could build the computers, there should also be the option to program them too. Then he put those things"—she pointed to the three walls with flat screens—"in so they could design programs and software. I don't know how he did it. I was..." She shrugged, looking both bemused and sheepish at the same time.

Katiya stared at her in shock. The usually unflappable Rhianna had been steamrolled. Katiya started to chuckle and leaned against the console, careful to not touch any buttons. "I was trying to figure out what it was about him that was so..."

Rhianna glanced at her sharply. "So...? You're attracted to him." Shock was clear in her tone.

Katiya winced and straightened. Rhianna knew her too well.

"No. He's just so commanding. Like he is in charge or something."

Rhianna gave her a strange look then her lips twitched and she grinned.

"Yeah, yeah. He's in charge of setting things up." She waved her hand at the room. "And from the look of things has some major clout with Taylor Bytes to get all this for us and done in a day no less. But we don't have anyone to train on this stuff." She paused and looked around again.

Excitement filled Katiya. The computers she wanted were installed and the added bonus of the offices getting outfitted, too, was more than enough. Now this—a computer building, programming, and software design. She had only dreamt of setting up a lab. All of this was so much more.

"I'll have to call Carlson to upgrade our security system. With all this in here, we will need it. Stein will need to hire more security persons. Also we have to find someone who knows this stuff to train people well," Katiya said.

"Stein already is working on it. I know that tone. It is… Wow." Rhianna's usual eloquence had deserted her.

In this case, Katiya didn't rag on her. It was understandable.

Rhianna continued, "We already have plenty of people to teach."

"Really, so soon? How much it is going to cost us?" she asked, still looking around the room in awe.

"Nothing. They are volunteers," Rhianna answered.

"Volunteers?" She looked at Rhianna.

"The owner of Taylor Bytes and some of his other employees have volunteered to. Not only set up training programs, but the head honcho has stated that they will keep us supplied with whatever we need for this program—equipment, parts and knowledge." Rhianna had a grin on her face again.

"Really? Wow. I'll have to make sure and thank him. Wait a minute. The *Mister* Taylor was here. You met him. No fair, I didn't even get to meet him." Katiya pouted.

Rhianna started to laugh.

"What is your problem?" Katiya demanded. "I've never seen you grin so much,"

"Heeee…" Rhianna was laughing too hard to continue.

Katiya shook her head. "You better tell me."

Rhianna put her hand up, making the sign to give her a moment. She took a breath then seemed to gain control.

"You al—"

"Ahh…Rhianna. I'm looking for Miss Wright," a languid male voice said.

Rhianna stiffened and her face went cool.

Katiya blinked, intrigued, and raised an eyebrow at Rhianna, who gave a quick shake of her head. Katiya made a note to question her later. Curious, she glanced around Rhianna. She made a *hmm* sound as she took in his lanky frame lounging in the doorway. His lazy smile curved his full lips. His tanned skin highlighted his sharp features that came together to create an extremely sexy face. His dark hair rested over one shoulder in a long braid that almost reached his waist. She lifted her head, meeting his gaze again, and his smile widened.

"You've found me. Cut out the Miss stuff. It's Katiya. And you're Calix. Right?"

"Yep."

"Sorry, I was supposed to meet you in my office. We got a little sidetracked."

"No prob."

Katiya stood straight. "Let's go. I don't want to keep you from something else."

"I'm almost done with Rhianna's set-up. Just waiting for everything to download." Calix shrugged.

"Okay. Rhianna, I'll catch up with you later for you to bring me up to speed on what has been going on."

Rhianna nodded. Katiya walked over to Calix. He straightened and stepped out of the way as she passed him.

"Rhianna," Calix said.

"Calix." Rhianna's tone was cool and dismissive.

Surprised, Katiya looked between the two of them. Calix had a smile on his face and Rhianna was turned away from her so she couldn't see her expression.

"After you," Calix said to her.

Katiya walked with him down the hall. As they passed the computer room she glanced in. The man was still in there, typing on one of the systems.

"What is his name?" She gestured to the door they'd just passed.

"You mean Giga?" Calix asked.

Katiya frowned. "The man setting up systems in there? Giga, as in gigabyte?"

"Yep, that's Giga," Calix replied.

They continued down the hall, stopping briefly as she spoke with various people along the way. Finally reaching her office, she unlocked her door and went inside.

"Sorry about the delay."

"It's what you do. Being the head of a centre this large you're in high demand. I know the feeling. Wow. That's a beautiful desk set you have there."

Katiya looked around her spacious office. It was richly decorated in her favourite colours — pale yellow, burnt orange and dark brown. Two sofas were on opposite walls with lots of pillows. Her desk was massive and made of six different kinds of exotic wood, including ebony and Carpathian elm, and pieces of custom glass.

"Thank you, it was a gift from my good friend Iona — she designed it. Iona's a descendant of the family the town was named after." She glanced at the floor-to-ceiling matching credenza with hutch and bookcases built into the walls — all with the same design. It was the first thing most people mentioned about the office.

Going to her desk, she started to boot up her computer. "So what's your job at Taylor Bytes?"

"I run the Research and Development area of Taylor Bytes. The head honcho did it to punish me." He gave her a puppy dog look.

Katiya snorted. "I can imagine you probably did something to deserve it."

"Yeah, I did. At least that's what he said. It's a lie—he just likes being the big brother and messing with the little brother," Calix said matter-of-factly.

Startled, she glanced at Calix. "Taylor is your brother?"

"Yep, when I choose to claim him." Calix laughed then said, "Are you booted up?"

She glanced at the screen. "Yes."

"May I?"

"Oh, sure," she said moving from behind the desk out of his way.

Calix went behind the desk then sat in the chair and started typing. She leaned against the desk and watched his fingers move fast over the keys. When he started humming, she tried to make out what song it was. Calix attached an external drive to her computer.

"Okay. This will take about two hours. I'm downloading your files and any software you added to your computer onto this." He patted the drive.

"Don't I have to tell you what I did?"

"Nope, I checked your configurations and know already. Before we install the new one we'll double-check that everything is on this. Don't touch the computer while this is running." Calix stood.

"I won't."

"I'll be back in a bit to check on how things are doing," he said striding across the office to the door.

"Calix."

He stopped and looked at her.

"I want to thank you and Taylor Bytes for all you are donating to us. I plan on thanking your brother personally when I finally get to meet him. This is so generous of you all."

Shock filled Calix's face then a huge grin curved his lips. Katiya shook her head. It was similar to the one

Rhianna kept giving her. She didn't know what was going on but she would get to the bottom of it.

"Okay, I'm tired of these weird grins. What is everyone finding so funny?"

"Everyone?"

"Rhianna gave me the same type of grin you are. So, what is up?"

Calix bit his lip. "It's probably because —"

The walkie-talkie crackled. "*Calix, come in.*"

She recognised Giga's voice.

Calix picked up the walkie-talkie clipped to his belt. "Calix."

"*I need you in the comp room.*"

"Got ya. On my way," Calix replied. He clipped the talkie back to his belt then glanced at her. "Gotta go. I'll be back to check on things."

Before she could reply he turned and strode out of the door. She stared after him and sighed. She hadn't got the man's name or an answer to her question. The phone rang, interrupting her thoughts. She strode over to her desk and answered the phone. "The Oasis."

She sat and listened to the caller. Before she knew it she was busy. Throughout the next few hours she was swamped with work. Calix came and went a few times, checking on the download and bringing in her new computer system, printer, scanner and fax. He placed the boxes on the floor next to the desk. Katiya raised an eyebrow. She'd known about the computer but the rest was a surprise.

"We're a full service crew," Calix said cheerfully. He winked and left the room.

Katiya got up to check the boxes and whistled. All the equipment was top of the line. She had checked them out longingly but knew they were not part of the budget. She returned to her seat on the couch and went back to work.

"Ready to get your computer back?"

Startled, she glanced up at Giga, the man from the computer room. He leaned against the office doorway. She kept her gaze on his face.

"Sure, come on in."

He glanced around as he strode inside. "Nice."

"Thanks."

Giga went over to the desk and started setting things up. Katiya watched him and marvelled at how, for such a large man, he moved with an innate grace. He glanced at her and she quickly lowered her head, getting back to work. Absently she listened as he set up her system. He worked silently, the only sound was of boxes being ripped open, equipment being moved then set up.

"You're all set," he said.

She looked up then stood before walking over to him. Giga stepped back and gestured. She went to her chair and sat, seeing her system was up. She searched to make sure her files and programmes were all there. After ensuring everything was, accounted for, she glanced up and stifled a gasp. He was sitting on the desk close to her but she hadn't heard him move.

"Everything there?"

"Yes." *Why do you sound like a flighty teenage girl, Katiya?*

"Good." He studied her intently.

She returned his stare. Something about his eyes seemed familiar.

"Have dinner with me—tonight."

She raised an eyebrow. He hadn't asked, instead had phrased it as a statement. Almost like it was already going to be.

She opened her mouth to say no. "Yes." Katiya's eyes widened. She didn't date and hadn't in over fifteen years.

He smiled and cupped her cheek. His hands were soft and tender and the unexpected touch made her shudder. His eyes darkened as he looked at her lips. Katiya wondered if he would kiss her. She wanted him to, despite the fact they hadn't even gone out. She didn't even know his name but yet wanted to feel his lips on hers.

"Is six-thirty okay to pick you up?" His voice was husky and even deeper than before

"Yes, that is good. Here is my address." She looked away from his compelling gaze.

His hand lowered from her face and she almost whimpered at the loss of his touch. She quickly wrote her address on a sticky note then removed it and handed it to him. He took the information then shifted, putting it in the pocket of his jeans. The fabric stretched tight and she held back a sigh.

"Six-thirty," he stated.

"Six-thirty," she echoed.

He ran a finger down her cheek then stood, turned and strode across the room.

"Hey, why do they call you Giga? And what is your real name?"

He stopped and turned to her.

"I'm good with computers. You don't know my name?" An enigmatic smile curved his lips.

She got an uneasy feeling. "No."

"Call me Warwick," he said.

Shocked, she sat back shaking her head.

He nodded. "Six-thirty. It's too late to change your mind. I get what I want." His look was scorching.

He strode out of the door, closing it behind him. Katiya leant back against her chair and stared. After a few moments she started to laugh. No wonder Rhianna and Calix had looked at her like she was crazy. How had she missed the air of charisma and take charge attitude that was all around him?

"I'll be damned. Warwick Taylor in the flesh. The guru behind Taylor Bytes."

From what she had heard and read about him, he had started Taylor Bytes when he was eighteen. He was a genius—his IQ tested off the charts. Some had called him a brash young man. It didn't matter—in less than eighteen years he had taken a small, little known company and made it into a multi-billion dollar corporation. He'd developed cutting edge computer technology and software. She tapped her pen against the desk. In all the articles she had read and research she had done, none had had his picture. She had searched for it but it had seemed as if he was a ghost. After meeting him, she knew for sure he wasn't. No ghost would or could make her pulse race like that or have her break her rule and agree to a date.

"Why did you agree?" Her voice echoed in the office.

She didn't have any idea but it didn't matter. She and Warwick Taylor were from two different social circles. Yes, she could interact with the rich class to get donations but she knew where she belonged. Katiya glanced around room. She preferred simple things. No matter how much he enticed her, she would let him know when he picked her up that their dating would never work. She ignored the pang of sadness the idea caused and got back to work.

Warwick Taylor strode down the hall, his thoughts on the sexy woman he had just left behind. From his first look of her, her light, hazel gaze emanating sharp intelligence and—although she tried to hide it—attraction, he had been captivated. It was a startling feeling. The sassy sway of her walk was tempered by a slight limp. He had seen her wince. He had almost asked her if he could help ease her pain before he'd remembered they had just met. The way she moved had her hips swaying in a fashion that made his cock hard. He fought the need to bury himself inside her where he imagined it would be warm and wet. He shook his head. He usually had better control than this. Yet all he could think of was taking the sienna skinned enchantress on the closest flat surface.

The emotion and fire in her gaze as she spoke of The Oasis only enhanced her allure. The sexy tilt of those biteable lips beckoned, causing his tongue to ache for a taste. Her sculptured cheeks, full nose and round chin only added to her air of confident sensuality. The complete package—that lush curvy frame that made him think all manner of sins. He knew it was foolish to even contemplate it, much less act on what he was imagining. She made him feel primal.

Usually he turned attention away. Women threw themselves at him, trying to land his wallet and not him. He remembered the expression on her face when she had realised who he was. With her, he knew it would be the opposite. His money would be a detriment in winning the luscious Katiya Wright.

Warwick's grin widened. Yes, he wanted to lay her down and have her in every way imaginable but that wasn't all he wanted. He wanted all of her—heart, soul, mind and body. No matter how foolish it might seem, he already knew they would be more than lovers. Convincing her would be a challenge. He was just the man to change her mind. She would soon learn. When he set his sights on something, he was not dissuaded from his course. And winning Katiya was what he would do.

* * * *

As he stood in front of her door, Warwick took a breath for control. He pushed the bell. The door swung open. He forgot to breathe. Earlier her hair had been pinned up in a bun but now it hung loose in kinky curls that almost rested at the top of her cleavage.

Her yellow sundress hugged her bountiful breasts. It was tied at the waist with a dark brown and yellow belt made from what looked like the same fabric as her dress. The belt accentuated the lush flare of her hips. The yellow of the dress stopped at her hips and changed to white then just before her knees it became dark brown. Peekaboo flower cut-outs were scattered on the white and brown area. The dress kissed the top of her knees, exposing toned legs and dainty feet in strappy, pale yellow, heeled sandals. Her matching toenails highlighted by the shoes. God, he loved sexy toes. He raised his gaze to hers.

The stark desire in her eyes made him gulp. Warwick tried to remind himself that his parents had raised him as a gentleman. His body, on the other hand, was hard and ready to do lots of decadent things to her body.

Her expression went leery then resigned.

Chapter Two

The fog of desire cleared from Warwick's mind. Katiya bit her lips, straightened her shoulders then looked at him.

"War—"

"Before you list all the reasons why our dating would not work out or say that we are from different worlds and all that, let me just stay that we're both from the same world. Earth. And this earth man wants to go out with you, an earth woman." He looked her over again. "Among other things. See you as often as I can and get to know each other very well. So are you ready for that, Katiya Wright, or are you too afraid to give us a chance?"

Katiya's light hazel eyes narrowed, then a vixenish grin curved her lips. She turned and went back into the house. In moments she returned with a bag that matched her shoes over her shoulder. He bit back a harsh groan as her body brushed his.

"I need to close the door," she stated.

He stepped back. She closed, locked the door and turned to face him. Warwick's lips twitched at the challenge in her eyes.

"If you weren't planning to go out with me, why are you dressed so sexy?" he asked.

She smiled another wanton grin. "You think you have all the answers, Warwick, but if we're going to date—how did you put it? Often and maybe other things?—the first thing you should learn is when I try for sexy, you'll know it." She moved closer and spoke, her breath wafting against him. "This old thing is just the warm up. The next thing is, don't say anything you can't back up."

She went to step away back but he put his hand on her waist, stilling her. Lowering his head, he spoke close to her ear.

"And you'll know soon, I don't say things I can't stand behind."

He inhaled, the sweet scent of her hair, the scent of coconut and strawberries filling his senses. He breathed out to clear his head. Katiya moaned softly and shifted.

"You're going to be a handful, Katiya Wright."

She glanced at him, her lips so close to his that if he moved an inch, he'd have his first kiss from her—the first of many.

"You know it. And so much more," she purred.

He laughed. Katiya stepped back and he let her go. She sauntered away only to pause at the top of the stairs, looking over her shoulder.

"Aren't you coming?"

Not yet but hopefully soon. He cleared his throat. "Yes, lead the way, Katiya. For now."

"For always." She glanced down then up his body.

His cock hardened even more. Katiya turned and started down the stairs. He strode over to help her. Warwick had a feeling she was right. He would follow her anywhere. Reaching her before she could get to the bottom of the five steps, he put his hand on her waist and led her down. She stopped short in front of his truck.

"A dark blue 1955 Chevy Cameo Carrier," she whispered.

Surprised, he looked at her. "You know classic trucks."

"More than I ever would need to. Dimitri, my brother, is a classic truck fanatic. He talks about them all the time." She whistled. "If he got a load of this beauty he would be beside himself."

"I know the feeling. I like classic cars and trucks." He chuckled.

Warwick opened the door, helping her in before closing it. As he went around the hood, he could hear her talking about the trucks features through the open window.

"Modern amenities and true to street rodder styles. I bet the engine is made for racing. I can't believe this beige leather interior. A/C unit with custom switches. A Lecarra steering wheel was perched on top of an ididit tilt-steering column. This split bench seat frame has to be custom made."

He opened his door and got in then noticed she was stroking the seat. *It's silly to be jealous of a car seat.* Warwick started the truck.

"Listen to that engine purr. Does the sound system work?" She flipped it on before he could answer. "AM/FM stereo receiver with an iPod hook-up stuffed into the stock '55 Cameo radio. Wow, you went all out for this."

"For someone who only knows what her brother talks about, you seem to know a lot." He pulled onto the road then glanced at briefly her as he drove.

"I got interested in them. So I go to some of the car shows now and then. If you tell anyone I'll deny it." Her sheepish grin was endearing.

"You're secret is safe with me. A show is coming here next month. Maybe you can join me."

"Maybe." She smiled.

"Some of my cars and trucks will be showcased. I'm still trying to decide which ones. Perhaps you can help me pick. Get up close and personal with some of them." He winked.

"Maybe," she said again.

"How does tomorrow sound?" he asked.

"We haven't even gotten through our first date yet and you're already asking me for another? You don't even know if we have anything to talk about or in common," she stated.

He took his gaze away from the road a moment and looked at her. "I'm not concerned about that. So tomorrow. I'll pick you up at, say, eleven."

"You're very confident."

"I know what I want." He shrugged.

"Good to know. Eleven tomorrow then. And be warned—if this date tanks you're still going to be stuck with me at least for tomorrow. I'm still going to come by and check out your classic cars and trucks. I am not passing up that opportunity." Katiya laughed.

He chuckled. "Fair enough. Now find something on the radio for us to listen to."

Katiya made a noise of agreement. Soon the sound of classic rock filled the truck. He relaxed back and continued to drive. About ten minutes later he pulled into the entrance. He paid their fee and drove inside then found a space, making sure they had a good spot. He turned off the vehicle, leant back and glanced at Katiya. A big smile was on her face.

"I love Weatherly. I haven't been to a drive-in movie here in a while." Excitement laced her tone.

He put up his finger and made a mark in the air.

"What was that?" She raised an eyebrow.

"A point in the good date column," he said.

"You are too much." She laughed delightedly.

"So I've been told. You ready for dinner and the movie?" he asked.

"Yes."

He got out and went around, opening her door. Warwick helped her out of the truck and led her to the back that was facing the screen.

"Close your eyes and no peeking."

He waited until she'd closed her eyes then set up the back of the truck. He opened one bag and withdrew the plush blankets, covering the mattress he had put in the back of truck as well as the picnic basket. He wanted her to be comfortable. Next came the various full pillows in the same colours as her office, which he spread all over. Finally he placed the sitting pillow, big enough for two, in the base of the truck by the back windows of the cab. Returning to her side, he took her hand.

"Open them."

Katiya did, then gasped.

"Your theatre seat waits." He gestured with his hand.

"It is lovely. Thank you," Katiya said.

She leaned over to take off her shoes but he stopped her. He lifted her, setting her on the tailgate of the truck before stooping down to take off her sandals. Her toes curled and her legs quivered. Warwick glanced up in time to see Katiya lick her lips. He rose to stand between her parted legs and leaned over her, stopping just before her lips.

"You are a beautiful woman, Katiya. I'm trying everything in my power to be a gentleman and wait to kiss you."

"Ah, to hell with it. I promise to respect you in the morning." She closed the distance between their lips.

Katiya closed her mouth over his. He groaned as her sweet tastes burst over his tongue—coconut and strawberries. She gripped the back of his head, holding him still for her thorough exploration of his mouth. He locked his knees when they went weak and braced his hands on either side of her hips. Katiya's arms came around his head as she held him for her kiss. She suckled his tongue, each lazy pull created a corresponding throb in his cock. Slowly she released him from the kiss. Her slightly swollen, glistening lips caused him to groan again. He rested his forehead against hers and tried to remember how to breathe. Her harsh breaths tickled his lips.

"A handful, Katiya."

"I'm more than that. Now 'feed me, Seymour'." She laughed and smacked him playfully.

"Little Shop of Horrors," he said in delight. "Are you a movie buff?"

"Yep. Love movies and TV."

"Cool. Then you'll like this, as it is classic movie night. Well, you know—what Weatherly considered classics anyway."

"What's playing?"

"*Seven Brides For Seven Brothers.*"

"That is a classic. A great one. So do you like musicals?"

"I love musicals. *Grease* is one of my favourites." He helped her up into the bed of the truck then settled next to her.

"Oh, I love *Grease*. I'm glad lately Hollywood is starting to do more dancing and singing movies. What's your favourite TV show?"

"*NCIS*," he replied.

Katiya stared at him. Warwick looked at her, worried. She was so still.

"Katiya, are you okay?"

She put her hand up then made three marks in the air with her finger.

"What was that for?" he asked amused.

"Three marks for the good date column. One, for the lovely setup here. Two, for your stellar taste in movies. Three, for knowing good TV. Mark Harmon is hot," she said, her eyes twinkling.

"No more ogling Mark Harmon." He growled.

"Don't ask for the impossible." She snorted.

He narrowed his eyes. "Fine. Ogle me as much as you do him," he amended.

Katiya leaned into him with a smoky look in her eyes that made his cock twitch.

"Even more, Warwick," she promised. She kissed him softly then pulled back, resting against the pillow.

"Now where is this mysterious food, Seymour? Unless it's invisible offerings," she teased.

"Warwick and, yep, I am feeding you air pie and wind meat." He chuckled.

"Feed me, Warwick."

"As my lady commands."

With flair, he swept the blankets off the picnic basket. He opened it and started unpacking the finger foods. After he'd finished, he took out the bottle of champagne and poured them each a glass. He offered

Katiya hers. When she reached for the food, he caught her hand.

"Uh uh—let me. What do you want to try first?"

"The strawberries," she said.

He fed her slowly as she motioned to what she wanted. He ran his finger over her lips after each nibble. Katiya moaned, licking his fingers. Each cacophony of sound and swipe of her tongue made his breath catch. He envisioned her making those sounds and using her tongue in much more pleasurable ways. He took a bite right where she had, wishing it was something else even more succulent and sweet. Katiya watched him hungrily and he deliberately swirled his tongue over the final bit of peach then sucked it in.

His slacks threatened to burst under the pressure of his erection. He continued to feed her piece after piece, taking periodic bites for himself from where she had.

"No more—honestly, I can't eat any more." Her deep breaths had her cleavage pressing enticingly against the edge of her sundress.

"Let me just put this away. It's almost time for the movie."

Removing the wet cloths, he first wiped her hands then his. He leant back and pulled her to him and she settled comfortably against his side. The movie started and she shifted, resting her hand against his chest. Warwick pulled a blanket over their legs. She murmured her thanks and snuggled in. Her lush curves fit so right against him.

It's your first date. Control, Warwick. Control.

He tried to relax as the credits rolled up. It was going to be a long night.

* * * *

Katiya attempted to focus on the movie that was almost over but Warwick's warm presence against her was making it impossible. His absent stroking of the bare skin of her back was driving her crazy. She shifted, trying to ease the wetness that soaked her panties. He made a soft sound, not quite a groan or sigh under his breath. His chest rubbed against her aching nipples and she clenched her fist below the blanket. Her other hand was over his heart, and the steady beat that should have been soothing was anything but. The thump seemed to make her pussy throb in time with it.

She inhaled his fresh, clean scent, noting the lack of cologne. He kissed the top of her forehead, the soft brush of his lips making her shiver.

"Cold?" Before she could answer he pulled the blanket tighter over them.

No. I want to straddle you and kiss you senseless. Then strip you down and have my way with you. Out loud she murmured, "Hmmm…thanks."

She kept her attention on the movie screen. The cool, calm and collectedness she was known for was being put to the test. Warwick started stroking her skin again. She bit her lip hard and fought the whimper that was threatening to escape. As the last credits rolled, Katiya blinked, moved away from him and stretched. Warwick sat up and rubbed his hand on her shoulder. She moaned and dropped her head forward, allowing him easier access. He moved her hair out of the way then rubbed a few moments more. He kissed the back of her neck and she shivered as desire washed over her.

"Ready to go get some dessert?" he asked.

"Sure."

He helped her out of the truck and put on her sandals for her. They secured the blankets and pillows in the back of the truck. A few minutes later they were in line with the others leaving the drive-in theatre. Fifteen minutes later, Warwick turned into Capri's. They got out and went over to the window, and when it was their turn, Warwick motioned for her to order.

"Caramel ice cream with almond and pralines on a waffle cone," she stated to the server.

"Coming right up. And you, sir?" the young woman asked.

"Coconut ice cream with pineapples and coconut on a waffle cone," he replied.

They stepped aside and waited for their ice cream to be filled. In moments they had their items. They went over to the tables set up for seating.

Katiya sat at one of the two seat padded bench tables. Warwick sat across from her. She took a bite of her ice cream and she moaned at the first taste of the rich cream and nuts. Warwick groaned, startling her to look up at him. The hunger in his gaze made her gasp. He leaned closer and she blinked, captured by his eyes. He kissed her softly and thoroughly before he leant back then smiled.

"Eat your ice cream while I try to control myself," he whispered.

"You can try," Katiya countered flirtatiously.

Warwick laughed. "A handful."

"Much more." She winked.

He laughed again then started to eat his ice cream. She studied his eyes.

"Dark blue."

"What?" He frowned.

"Your eyes. I knew they were dark but didn't realise they were dark blue."

"My mom called it indigo. It's a family trait. My sibs all have the same eye colour."

She nodded remembering Calix's eyes. They continued to eat their ice cream. After a few moments Warwick cocked his head to the side.

"Do you mind if I ask you a question?"

"I reserve the right to decide if I want to answer or not."

He nodded. "How did you decide to start The Oasis? I've read the official reasons on your centres info, but my gut tells me there is more to the story."

Katiya sat back. His perceptiveness was uncanny. Only her family and a few close friends knew there was more to the official story. She studied him and debated if she should just feed him what she told everyone else. The soft gentle expression on his face made her go with the truth.

"Let's go back to the truck. This is better told in private."

She stood and threw out the rest of her ice cream. He followed her and they went back to the car. After they were inside, she started her story.

"I was twenty-two when I met the man I thought I would spend the rest of my life with. His name was Darren Sharp. We were so idealistic. Even then we were donating time to community centres and had dreams of opening our own centre someday—the two of us. We were together for two wonderful years before"—she took a breath and cleared the lump in her throat—"before it all went to hell. Darren was working in a bad neighbourhood when they held him down and assaulted him." She closed her eyes briefly then opened them. "When he was found we barely recognised him, he had been cut up so bad. Although he denied they had violated him, the test showed they had. His family and I tried to help him. He would not face it. He still loved me and I him. I let it go, knowing he would come to me when he was ready, but things got worse."

She looked off into space, struggling to regain her composure, then spoke in a cool voice.

"He became suspicious of everything. And..." She paused. "It doesn't matter what else happened before that day. We were driving home from his parent's house when Darren got it into his head I was cheating on him. Nothing I could say would get through." The vision of Darren's angry face filled her mind. "He screamed and cursed at me. Suddenly he yanked the wheel and drove us through the barrier on the road. It just snapped. Later, I found out that particular stretch of road barrier should have been fixed by a contractor who worked for the town. We careened down and hit the water below. The airbags deployed and knocked us out. When I came to, we were already underwater. Cars sink fast. Water started to fill it. I was pinned in and couldn't get out. I screamed for Darren. He just laughed and said we would die together."

She paused again. "I thought I was dead. Then the most beautiful sound came. A tap on the glass. I was never so glad to see Mattson McKingley in my life. He broke the glass and got me out. He told me later that he'd been concerned with the way Darren had acted at dinner and he'd followed us. Thank God, Darren's parents had invited Mattson to dinner.

"Mattson returned to get Darren. He came back out dragging his body. The scar on Mattson's cheek is from the glass Darren cut him with before Darren cut his own throat." She shuddered.

"It was a crazy time after that. Trying to recover. Mattson and my family were already close but what happened created a deeper bond between Mattson and I. We both bear scars from Darren. I messed up my leg pretty bad and ended up with a limp." She hugged herself. "Yet I stilled loved him."

Katiya sent up a silent prayer of thanks once again for Mattson McKingley rescuing her. Although the town was named after the McKingleys, the McKingleys and her family had jointly founded the town. The locals held most members of both families in high esteem—not for who they were but for how they cared about the community, the things done to better the town, and their way of helping others. In her opinion it was about being a human being and was nothing special.

Warwick came over and picked her up. He sat and put her in his lap.

"Of course you did." He rocked her.

Katiya leaned against his strength. "And he still loved me. He left me his inheritance he would have collected when he turned twenty-five. He was only a few months shy. It was millions of dollars."

"He's one of *The Sharps*, isn't he? Old money. One of the richest families in McKingley."

"Yes. He was the oldest. I used his money to set up The Oasis. I had some of the money invested and it helps keep funding the centre. Mattson is dynamite at making money multiply. The money pays the salaries of those at the centre. We get donations for our programs and volunteers when we need."

"What about you?"

"The way the centre is set up, every employee must collect a salary. I collect a salary, too, but donate it back to the centre. I have my own money."

He looked at her in question.

"The barrier that broke. My brother Jonathon sued the company who was supposed to fix it. They thought it was a joke. He hadn't been practicing law that long and they thought it would be an easy case to beat. They underestimated him. He fought them and won me a hefty settlement. I kept some to live on and Mattson invested it for me."

"And the rest?"

"I combined it with Darren's fund to open The Oasis, of course." She glanced at him.

"'Of course', she says. Katiya, you are an amazing woman." He lowered his head and kissed her.

She moaned into his mouth. His tongue swept into her mouth, finding all the sensitive spots, and her pussy creamed. The uneasy feeling she'd had that he would view her differently as she'd told him about Darren faded under his sensual mastery. She moved closer to him, twisting in his lap to straddle him. She growled in frustration. With one hand, she fought to free the skirt of her dress from beneath her. Finally tugging it loose, she lifted it out of the way. His hard shaft rested where she was aching. Gasping, she undulated against his erection. Warwick grunted and countered her motion. He gripped her hips, stilling her movements. He released her from his kiss, and she whimpered with frustration.

"Shhh...give me a moment. We can't do this here. Unless we want to give everyone more of a show than we already have." His voice was amused and slightly husky.

Katiya stiffened. She glanced around and groaned at the steamed up front glass. *What was I thinking? Although McKingly is a good-sized town, you still tended to see someone you know if you went to one of the popular local spots. And you know Capri's one of these sorts of places.*

"Don't make me have to arrest you, Katiya and Warwick."

Closing her eyes, she groaned again, resting her head against Warwick's chest. "Please tell me he's not here."

"I wish I could," Warwick said. "Hello, Kai."

"Night, Warwick. Katiya." Kai Carney's voice was a little too cheerful.

Katiya raised her head, glaring at him. He stood by the driver's side door.

"You better not tell Leo."

"Now, Kat—you want me to lie to my boss? I can't do that." Kai put his hand over his badge on his chest.

He blinked his blond lashes exaggeratedly. Katiya knew it was useless to try to stop him. She figured sometime in the next few minutes, Leonardo—her brother and the sheriff—would know about her date with Warwick and that they'd been necking at Capri's. Before the night was done, all the family that still lived in town would know. Those who didn't live there would probably get an email informing them. She estimated everyone in her family would know within a matter of hours—a day at the most. It was the bane of having a large close-knit family. Raising her chin, she slid off Warwick's lap. He shifted to his own seat. Kai leaned in the car window, watching their every move. Warwick started the truck.

"Now don't make me have to look for you at Lovers' Peak." Kai strolled away, his laughter trailing behind him.

"I am so never going to live that down," Katiya said.

"You and me both. Wait until Calix hears about it," Warwick said.

She glanced at him.

"Kai and Calix are close friends." Warwick looked at her then kissed her softly. "All the ribbing I'll get is so worth it."

She cupped his cheek. "Yes it is."

Warwick backed out and drove her home. Half an hour later he walked her to her door. Reaching it, she turned to face him.

"Come in for some tea or coffee?" she offered.

"No," he said firmly.

Katiya blinked at his abruptness. "Why?"

"This is why." He swept her in his arms and kissed her.

She thought his kiss before had been intense, but it was nothing compared to this one. She gripped his shoulders while he stroked his tongue in and out of her mouth. He suckled her tongue then nipped at it. She moaned, locking her knees as his kiss made her weak. Warwick crowded her against the door, his bulky frame warming her. He rubbed against her, moving his leg between her thighs. Katiya gyrated against it, gasping at the delicious friction it created against her aching pussy.

Suddenly he wrenched away. "No, not like this."

She stumbled. He held her up until she could stand on her own. Finally able to, she stepped back, smoothing her dress with shaking hands. Warwick pivoted away from her, his fists clenched. She reached out to him. He jerked away from her touch.

"Don't—my control is tenuous." His voice was tight.

She gulped and stepped back. Warwick turned and pulled her up against his body.

"Eleven tomorrow." He kissed her hard and fast.

He released her and strode away. Dazed, she stared after him. He stopped at the top of the stairs, pausing before going down, and looked back at her.

"Go inside. See you tomorrow." There was a promise in his tone.

She opened the door, flicked on the lights and stepped in. He waited until she was inside then he walked down the stairs and to his truck. The engine roared as he started it and drove away. Katiya stared after his departing truck. She raised a shaking hand to her lips. Warwick had said she was a handful. He was so wrong. He was the one who was going to be a huge complication.

She closed the door, leaned against it and bowed her head. "What am I going to do with you, Warwick Taylor?"

Chapter Three

Warwick stared without aplomb or shame as Katiya moved through the building which held his collection of classic vehicles. Normally the group of impressive trucks and few cars were the centre of his attention. Not today. Every ounce of his attention sucked up by the beautiful and incredibly alluring Katiya. Katiya 'no need for the Miss' Wright.

He'd picked her up this morning in his '55 Chevy Cameo Carrier, and like the previous night, he'd never seen a better adornment for his classic. Her curves were mouthwatering. Now that they were at his place, her attention was taken up by his collection and he had ample time to study the work of art he longed to know on a much more up close and personal level.

Her hair, a shining mass of kinky, dark brown with auburn highlighted curls, floated free around her face. She wore a cut-off halter top, swirled with yellow and cream abstract designs. Body hugging white capris offset the gorgeous hue of her skin and flat slip-on shoes.

His gaze trailed her each step she took, each appreciative caress on a vehicle, each seductive sigh and sway of her hips surged through him, making him stiffer and stiffer until he figured his jeans were about to burst.

"Wow," she said stopping before him, hands in her back pockets. "This is…impressive."

"Yes it is," he replied.

She snorted and rolled her eyes. "I was talking about your vehicles."

"I wasn't," he said, his voice deeper than normal.

"Really?" Her eyes twinkled.

"Really." Playtime was over.

He reached around behind her, cupped the back of her head and drew her close for a kiss. Starting slow, he licked her soft lips, teasing her. When she opened on a sigh, he slipped his tongue in. With the force of hitting a wall, her unique taste sank into him, fanning the already volatile flames within him.

She curled her arms up around his neck, pressing her curves—her all too tempting curves—along his frame. He swore before crushing her to him, his other hand bringing their pelvises as close as possible while wearing clothes. She fit so perfectly against him.

Her tongue dipped and stroked along his. With each second, he was that much closer to taking her right there in the garage. A low growl, one of frustration, poured from him as he ripped his mouth from hers.

Her light hazel eyes, a few shades darker than normal, burned with fevered passion. She loosened her hold from his neck and skimmed along his shoulder with her hand. She slipped her tongue out and dampened her lips. Those damnable, kiss-swollen lips that made him contemplate committing a multitude of sins.

There is one hell of a volcano of passion within her, just waiting to be released.

No words were spoken. For a brief spot in time they remained like that. Close, touching, and silent. Katiya teased the ends of his hair before lifting up on her toes as if to kiss him, only to hesitate a hair's-breadth from his mouth. He heard her deep breaths and flexed his fingers at the base of her spine.

"Warwick," she said on a soft purr.

Wound as tight as he was, he was surprised he didn't explode right then and there. From the top of his head to the soles of his feet all he could feel was 'take her' with each heartbeat. Every inhalation brought the succulent and distracting mixture of coconut and strawberries, a scent that fit her perfectly.

"Katiya."

She touched his lips lightly with her tongue then backed off. He stared at her as she stepped away.

"The first time shouldn't be in a garage, Katiya."

Her eyes raked him from head to toe, burning each inch of skin they touched. The intensity of his feelings for her threw him a bit. Only his wife had created such emotions within him before. With Katiya it was almost more. Warwick's mind flashed to the pain he'd experienced with losing with wife. He frowned, wondering if he could go through this again with someone else. As if sensing his turmoil her expression changed, becoming cool and distant. He shook off his doubt—he wanted this woman—and gave her a slight grin. She smiled but it was a bit stiff. Could she be mad because of his decision to not take her in the garage?

Reaching for her hand, he squeezed it lightly. "I have some lunch waiting for us."

Watching her face, he saw a few questions flicker before vanishing. "Sure."

"Unless you'd like to look at the vehicles some more," he offered.

Her face softened. "Food would be great."

"Food it shall be."

Hand in hand they moved through the extensive collection of shiny vehicles. He held the door for her then followed close, his hand settled on the small of her back. They stepped inside his home and he noticed her glancing around but the only noise was that of their footfalls upon the gleaming marble floors.

He guided her to his sunroom. Three sides were all glass, allowing him a spectacular view of the New Mexican landscape. The spring sun streamed in, glowing off the furniture. On the etched glass table sat their meal. He held her chair and allowed himself a quick indulgence of the intoxicating scent of her hair.

Her eyes were almost unsure when he sat across from her, but the look — whatever it was — vanished so quickly he chalked it up to his imagination.

A smile lifted her amazing lips. "Looks wonderful," she said, removing the cover on her plate and placing the napkin in her lap.

They ate in silence, which was fine with him. He took the opportunity to study her even more. He memorised the curvature of her face. This was no immature girl. Katiya was a woman who was comfortable with herself as a person. That confidence added another layer of sensuality to her.

Another layer too many. I want to know what makes you tick, Katiya. What else besides your centre makes that special sparkle appear in your eyes?

"Something on your mind?" she asked, wiping her mouth.

"A lot," he said, swirling the contents of his drink and refusing to release her gaze.

She leant forward, elbows on the table. "Like?"

"Tell me more about you."

"More about me," she mimicked.

"Yes. Like your family."

There. The twinkle returned to her eyes.

She laid her fork on the plate and ran her tongue over her lips. "There are six of us. Three boys and three girls. Dimitri, who I mentioned being a lunatic for classic trucks, is the eldest. He's an arson investigator. Then there's me. Leonardo—Leo—is next and he's the sheriff. There's also Jonathon—he's next and an attorney. Arissa is the second youngest and is a doctor. The baby of the family is Delicia—Lis. She's an EMS responder."

The love she felt for her family poured across the table.

"Sounds like you have a great family."

She flashed an impish grin. "I like to think so. Although...I may be a bit biased."

He chuckled. "In a good way, though. It seems like your family is all about helping others."

"Yes," she said with a nod. "We were all drawn into that line of work. I suppose we get it from our parents." She sat back and they stared at one another. "What about you?"

"You've met one of my siblings. Calix is younger than me by a few years. And he works with me at Taylor Bytes as do the rest of my siblings." She nodded and he recalled she knew that already. Hell, he was basically babbling.

"Nice."

"Has its moments."

"I understand that. Sometimes being so near to family can be a pain."

They shared a laugh and he cleared his throat before standing. "Can I give you a tour of the rest of the house?"

"I'd like that." She pushed to her feet and met him by the door. "Thank you for lunch."

"My pleasure," he replied honestly, taking advantage of her closeness to brush a kiss along the corner of her mouth.

Warwick kept an eye on her as they toured. He didn't know how much her leg could take before it began to hurt her. At the moment though, all seemed to be well and good. She was mostly quiet, letting him tell her things. He walked beside her, content to just be in her company. It was nice, having her there. To have her here for longer than a single day would be amazing. Eventually, they ended back up in his garage with his collection. It was then he noticed what looked to be a slight strain on her face.

What is wrong? He almost asked if her leg was bothering her but managed to keep it behind clenched teeth. The pinched lines didn't strike him as a physical pain. How he knew that he wasn't entirely sure, but he'd wager something in his house had set her off.

"You have a beautiful home, Warwick."

"Thank you." He strode around her, prior to pausing before her tempting figure. *To hell with it.* "Everything okay?"

"Of course. Except for the fact I have to get going."

Words he hated to hear. He lifted her chin with one hand. Those hazel eyes met his unflinchingly.

"Have supper with me?"

Regret leeched into her gaze. "Sorry, I've got plans for this evening." Her hands settled upon his chest and drew abstract patterns. "But thank you for today."

His other hand cradled her face. "It wasn't nearly long enough." He kissed her lightly, not sure how much control he retained.

Who are your plans with that make your eyes light up like that? Did they light up when you thought of me this morning before you arrived?

He forced his jaw to unclench and gave her a smile, even though he didn't want to let her go. "Let's get you home."

In the truck, she passed the time by staring out of the window while he alternated between watching the road and staring at her. Katiya—in his opinion—was much more pleasurable to observe. Her loose hair blew around her face with the lowered window. He longed to reach out and touch it. Allow it to slide through his fingers.

At her place, he opened the door for her only to box her in against the side of the still-running truck after she got out. His hands on either side of her head, he lowered his face until they were touching foreheads.

"I want to see you tomorrow."

"I'm working all day," she whispered.

He fought a frown. "I know. We're there too. That's not what I meant and you know it."

She drew her lower lip in her mouth briefly and he fought off a groan. He was slammed with the need to lean forward and draw that enticing lip into his own mouth, sucking on it. Then the top one. And then…

He snapped off that line of thought.

I can hardly focus on the conversation. All I see when I look at her is her naked body, beneath, on top of, and near mine. Her sprawled naked on sheets, flushed from making love, and those damn hazel eyes begging for more. Those dark brown tresses with auburn highlights spread across my thighs as those perfectly pouty, full lips slowly engulf my hard cock.

The wave of desire nearly took him to his knees and he swallowed hard, forcing himself to think about something else. Anything that would calm his hardened body down to a point where he could think of Katiya without being half a millisecond from stripping her bare and slamming home until he could sink no farther within her.

"Sorry. I have work to catch up on from my last trip."

That snapped his attention back to her in totality. *She's running.* It didn't make him happy. If she could just give them a chance...

He barely cracked a smile. "Seems like Rhia is one hell of a second in command."

"She is." Flames flickered in her hazel gaze, deepening the hue. "Doesn't mean I should add my work to hers."

The reprimand wasn't subtle. He backed off, not willing to get into an argument over that. *Time for a new tactic.* "Okay. When can you spare some time for me?"

"I—"

He read it in her gaze. "I know what you're doing, Katiya. You're rationalising what's growing between us. And you're scared. I'm not giving up so easily." *Just like I told you that first night, beautiful. I get what I want. And I want you.*

She ducked and scooted around him. He rotated and followed her swaying hips as she headed for the door. She stopped and glanced back at him.

"I'm a lot of things, Warwick Taylor. Scared isn't one of them. What I *am* is busy." The smile was short and tense. "Thank you for today."

Then she was gone.

He chuckled nervously and went to the driver's door. Staring at her place, he sighed.

"You can call it what you want, Katiya. I know what it is."

He drove away and wondered about the change in her demeanour from last night to today. It wasn't glaringly obvious but he'd noticed and picked up on it.

She had still been wonderful company but there had been times when she'd looked…well…uncomfortable at his place.

So many secrets, Katiya. I wonder when you'll let me all the way in.

Katiya sighed and rested against the door. She ran a frustrated hand over her face while she toed off her shoes.

Warwick Taylor.

Just the name alone was enough to send rolling waves of desire through her.

Warwick. Giga. Mr Taylor.

It didn't matter what he was referred to as, her response didn't change. Lust. Hot and fast. Electrifying. Bone rattling with its intensity.

"I shouldn't have gone," she bemoaned, striding to her bathroom where she stripped and stepped into the shower. His collection of trucks had been very impressive. So had his house—his massive, sprawling home with its gated entry. But each second she spent there, the more obvious it became how different their worlds were. Warwick Taylor existed in a world she didn't feel she belonged.

"I can't go through it again," she admitted to the steamy bathroom. "I just...can't."

Despite the number of years since Darren Sharp had been in her life and had passed on to the afterlife, the pain of rejection from his family still burned strong and fresh.

Her pensiveness remained as she stepped naked from the shower stall. She grabbed a large yellow towel and dried off. Once finished, she gathered up her dirty clothes, tossing them in the wicker hamper, and striding to her adjoined bedroom—her sanctuary, done in her favourite colours, like her office.

While she dressed, her mind—that traitorous thing—meandered its way back to rest upon the one and only handsome Warwick Taylor.

He'd worn a pair of khakis and a white polo shirt with loafers. Both items had intensified his muscular physique, daring her to reach out and touch the man beneath. All the attraction came flooding back. Hard. Intense.

"And that kiss," she muttered, as she applied lotion to her legs and feet. "That kiss."

It had robbed her of all common sense and honestly she wouldn't have cared one whit if he *had* taken her against a vintage truck. But he hadn't.

More's the pity, she thought. Her hypersensitive body agreed.

It didn't matter. No matter how much he wanted her. She'd seen the look on his face. Almost like he'd wondered if he'd betrayed someone. She knew he'd lost his wife—maybe he hadn't got over her. She may be horny as hell. She may be attracted like hell to him, but one thing she wouldn't do was be a second to anyone. If he still pined for her then that was fine—not her business, but she wouldn't get involved with him.

"Should have stuck to my no dating rule," she said with a self-deprecating sigh.

There was no denying the sparks between them indicated one fiery joining. She groaned and stomped out to the kitchen. Her body responded to the mere thought of experiencing the thrill of Warwick's hands and touch on her body. Maybe he'd just not wanted to move so fast and it'd had nothing to do with his wife.

Dropping her head to the cool counter, she moaned. "I just need to get laid."

"Wow." Feminine laughter filled the room.

Jerking up, she expelled a sharp breath when she spied her youngest sibling, Delicia, sitting on the other counter. *I didn't even see or hear her.* She muttered a curse.

Bad thing about being in town with one's entire family…they tended to come and go as they pleased.

"Lis, what are you doing here?"

"My big sis complains about needing to get laid and wonders why I'm here? Don't you think I would be the one with questions?"

She glared at her sibling.

Delicia's bone straight, honey-hued hair was gathered in a high ponytail. She wore a silver camisole edged in black and a pair of black shorts. With each kick of her legs, her black high tops swung into Katiya's view. The eyes were a giveaway—the brown orbs told of her exhaustion.

Immediately concern overtook annoyance. "Everything okay, Lis?"

Her sister smiled, it was also tired. "I'm good. Sorry to just drop by but you asked me to drop off some pics for The Oasis. I put them in your living room. Whatever you don't want just set aside and I'll get them later."

She sighed, not for one second believing her claim of being fine and sent her sister a grateful smile. *I totally forgot.* "I'm sorry, Lis. Totally skipped my mind. Thank you."

"Anytime." She slid off the counter. "I have to go, start shift soon."

They hugged briefly and Lis headed to the door. She paused and glanced over her shoulder. "You know, seems to me that Taylor would do great in taking care of that problem you were bemoaning." A devilish twinkle filled her dark eyes, eliminating the exhaustion she had been portraying. "At least, so Leo said based on the reports he received on you two up at Capri's." She waggled her fingers and slipped out. Moments later the rumble of her Jeep could be heard pulling away.

"Did I say how much it *sucks* at times to have your whole family in the same town?"

There was very little hope that her parents hadn't heard about her necking episode. Caught. With fogged windows and everything. Like a pair of randy teens.

"Crap!"

Desperate for something else to occupy her mind, she went to the stack of photos and moved them from the coffee table to the dining room. With one hand she spread them out on the large table.

They were amazing. Lis was an amateur photographer and had dropped off some of the black and white shots she'd taken of places and people around New Mexico. They were all wonderful.

"Bless you, Lis."

She lost track of time as she continued to stream through the large matte photographs. So attuned was she to the items before her that when the doorbell pealed, she jumped. She glanced at her watch and muttered another curse. *I'm late.*

She moved to the door then opened it and smiled warmly at the women standing there. Women she'd gone through school with, a mixture of married and single, they had remained fast friends through the years. Anita, Connie, Bethany and Yurandol.

"Hey! I know I got a bit sidetracked and let time slip away, but why are all you here? Weren't we meeting at the restaurant?"

Yurandol pushed by her into the house, her long braids swaying with each confident step she took. "We picked up pizza, wine coolers, and came here."

Baffled and bemused, she watched in silence as they all paraded in.

"Why here?" she asked again, closing the door on the warm spring night.

"Figured there'd be less prying eyes and eavesdropping ears here when you tell us about you. And about you fogging up the windows at Capri's," Connie said, her hair in its usual spiky style.

"Not to mention who it was with." Bethany chortled, making herself right at home pulling down plates and cups before taking them to the table.

"Warwick Taylor," they all said at once, their voices a collection of dreamy sighs.

She groaned, knowing full well there was no escape. For a moment she wished Lis was there instead. Of all her family, Lis tended to be the least to pry. Sure, she'd tease but she wouldn't be like this group.

"Heffas," she groaned, grabbing a plate and helping herself to some of the piping hot, cheesy pizza. "All ya...heffas."

Anita took a big bite and said without bothering to swallow first, "Maybe, but we're your heffas. Now dish."

How true.

"So...what gives?" Connie asked, removing the top on her wine cooler and taking a healthy swallow.

"We went out and...got a bit carried away."

Laughter exploded around the table. "A bit?" Anita questioned. "Please, you know those impressionable teens that work there will be talking about this for days to come. Usually it's the folks up at Lovers' Peak who get fogged windows and the cops rappin' on them, but...not you. You do it in Capri's parking lot."

"Who cares, Anita?" Bethany interjected. "I want to know how it was. How *he* was. I mean, this happened to our calm and collected Katiya."

Katiya's body pulsed with liquid heat at the mere *thought* of the feel of Warwick's touch upon her. So hot. So passionate. The large evidence of his arousal against her needy core. She shifted on the cushion trying to alleviate the rapidly building pressure between her legs.

It didn't work.

A low whistle cut through her haze of mounting desire. She blinked quickly a few times.

"Damn, girl, was it that good?"

"Must have been, Connie. Look at her, she's flushed. Probably about to mess up her nice chair."

She glared at Yurandol and reached for her drink. The cool sweet liquid ran down her throat, barely tamping her increased core temperature. *I have got to get myself under control.* There was no point in arguing with them. They'd only increase their ribbing. So she settled in, ate her pizza and took it good-naturedly.

After the meal, they chatted about everything. Family. Kids. Work. Nothing was off limits. Each with one of the five choices of ice cream in bowls, they all sat around Lis' photos and helped her decide on some for the walls at The Oasis.

"What's he like?" Connie asked around the spoon in her mouth.

"What's who like?" Katiya countered, even though she had an idea of who Connie meant.

"Kokopelli," she retorted with an eye roll. "Who do you think?"

I knew who you meant. I was hoping I would have been wrong.

"Yeah, is he like a lot of recluses? Hiding out for good reason?" Anita queried.

She shook her head, picked up a photo of the Taos skyline at night and smiled. "No. Not at all. He's very thoughtful." She filled them in on what he'd so graciously done for her centre. "And there is this gentleness about him that…that…" She trailed off.

The women nodded in understanding. She shrugged. "What can I say? He's hot as sin and an amazing kisser."

A chorus of murmurs rose up. Her smile remained until she met Anita's gaze. Those dark brown eyes stared at her, astute and assessing. She lifted her brow in silent question.

"When you two going out again?"

Unsure of how to answer, she put another spoonful of ice cream in her mouth and ate it slowly. The table fell silent as they all waited for her response. One by one she met their gazes. Anita waited, her foot up on the chair, arm resting upon the knee, spinning the spoon through her fingers, her gaze direct and unflinching.

One finely plucked eyebrow rose. "Well?" Anita pried.

She dropped her spoon into the bowl with a clang. "I don't know."

All of her friends frowned. And all she could do was shrug, helpless without any kind of a response.

"Is this because of Darren's family being uptight bastards?" Bethany questioned.

"It's a hard thing to forget," she said by way of admission.

"Bastards!" Yurandol muttered. That comment elicited unanimous agreement from the group of women.

She glanced at them all again—her friends from the days of kindergarten.

Yurandol Blake—single, spitfire, and an attorney for their local field office of the FBI. Dark mocha skin, black braided hair, which fell to the middle of her back, and sparkling brown eyes.

Bethany Donovan—married mother of three, the head librarian at McKingley's main branch. Red hair in soft waves fell to her shoulders offsetting her café-au-lait skin with medium brown eyes.

Anita Poole. Blonde hair, in a pageboy cut. Tanned skin covered her curvaceous figure. She had her doctorate and taught botany at the local college. Single with killer baby blues.

Connie Velázquez was also a married mother, of two this time. She owned a bookstore. Had spiky hair and flawless copper skin. Her jet black eyes always seeing more than one thought she had.

They were the greatest group of friends anyone could ask for.

"Since when do you let the dictates of others make up your decisions for you?" Bethany asked without looking up, instead dishing herself more ice cream.

Good question.

"It's not that simple."

"Sure it is," added Connie. "Either you like him or you don't. You want to spend time with him or you don't. This boils down to you, Kat."

"You're not a teen. You're a grown woman who is capable of knowing her own desires and wants. Do what *you* want." Anita gave her two cents.

A flash of anger sparked at their comments but faded as fast as it had risen. These were her girls, women she trusted to be honest with her. Brutally so, if necessary, like they were being now.

"I know," she replied with a resigned sigh. "I know. But my heart and brain don't necessarily want to forget."

"So you spend the rest of your life alone because of the past?" Yurandol challenged.

Her lip curled. "I'm not the only single one here," she snapped, sending Yurandol a pointed glare.

The attorney was unperturbed. She stared briefly at her perfect nails before sucking on her teeth. "I'm not the one who was caught getting all hot 'n bothered up at Capri's. If you don't want to be with a man who's not only hot enough for you to break your years of no dating but also get a reprimand from the law for fogging up the windows, pick some viable excuse. A man you say is, and I quote, 'hot as sin and an amazing kisser.' Don't lump him into a category. If he's an ass, then fine, but if your only complaint is he's rich—even disgustingly so—that, Katiya Wright, is just stupid."

The others murmured in agreement and she dropped her gaze to her ice cream remnants. Damn that sharp and spot-on lawyer mind. She lifted her head and peered at each woman, seeing determination on all their faces. They wanted her to find happiness and had no problems calling her out on any roadblock she threw in the way. She also knew they'd be first in line to kick the ass of anyone who hurt her. They had her back and she had theirs.

Reaching for the carton of ice cream from the middle of the table, she sighed. "I really wish you wouldn't beat around the bush, Yurandol. Stop holding back and tell me how you really feel," she grumbled good-naturedly.

"Sorry," Yurandol said with a totally blank expression. "I've been trying to be more direct 'n not sugar coat things as often."

Her eyebrows rose at how calmly her friend had managed to spout that malarkey. "Yeah? How's that coming along for you?"

Yurandol flipped her off and burst out laughing. "Well...thanks."

With a harrumph, she dug her spoon into the chocolate ice cream and ate a big bite, forgoing the bowl, before sliding the container across to her friend.

Chapter Four

Warwick watched Katiya surreptitiously from his peripheral vision. She stood with two others, a man and a woman, discussing something. He didn't know what and he wasn't sure he cared. Okay, he knew he didn't care. All that mattered was for the past four days she'd done a bang up job of managing to be too busy for a little one on one time. At least with him. For others, she found time. What little interaction they had, she kept short and professional.

The first day, it had seemed everyone watched them to see if there was going to be a repeat of the happening up at Capri's. But her cool demeanour had nipped that in the bud. Hell, he was feeling frostbite from her.

He didn't fault her, though. She was extremely busy. Every night she stayed well past the time he'd finished for the day. Yes, he knew that because he'd swung by her house hoping for an interaction only to not find her there then later seeing her vehicle by the centre.

Katiya.

He ached for her. There was no other way to put it. He ached. He wanted to hold her, kiss her, strip off that ensemble she wore and make long, slow love to her, memorising every inch and swell of her beautiful body. He longed to sink deep with the heated velvet walls he *knew* would hold him like a dream.

His body throbbed and he muttered a curse. Then stole another glance.

She wore a turquoise belted crossover tunic covering a white shirt. The tunic's belt emphasised her waist and rounded hips — hips made for a man to hold onto as he pounded into her, over and over again until they were both covered in sweat and had no energy to go anywhere. Her pale jeans had turquoise embroidery upon the legs and drew his attention to how much he wanted settle between them. The same hue of blue made up her ballet shoes.

Another round of lust broad-sided him and he barely stopped the groan of need from pushing through his lips. Mouth in a tight line, he tore his gaze from where it lingered over her lush body. *Back to the work at hand.*

"Why don't you just go talk to her instead of standing over here like you don't give a d...crap?"

His head jerked to the side to see his brother standing there. "You should mind your own business."

Calix gave him a grin that did nothing to set him at ease. His brother moved to the other side and blocked his view to where he could no longer see Katiya. "Really?"

A low growl worked its way up from the depths of his chest. "Calix..." he rumbled in warning.

The man must have a death wish. Calix looked at one hand and cracked his neck, not in the remotest way worried about the guillotine hanging over his head. In fact, it was like no warning had been issued. "You've been moody, Giga. You're acting like" — he looked around — "like an ass. If you're going to act like this, go do so at your office. Not here."

He couldn't argue that. It was true. He'd been ready to bite anyone's head off — not a common thing for him. He was a man used to being in control in all aspects of his life. His reaction to not being able to get Katiya alone was unfamiliar and unpleasant. And not doing him any good.

"Right," he said in a monotone timbre. "Anything else or will you be getting back to work *now*?"

His brother's gaze twinkled and he looked behind him. Rhia moved around a corner, a scowl on her face as she averted her eyes from the two of them.

Calix and Rhia?

"What are you up to?" he asked Calix.

"Nothing, brother. Absolutely nothing." He winked and strode off in the direction Rhia had just vanished.

Right. I believe that, just like I believe pigs fly.

Fighting the urge to roll his eyes, he swivelled his head and frowned when he realised Katiya was no longer in sight. Wiping his hands on his jeans, he rotated his shoulders and strode down the hall to her office. The door was closed and he hesitated briefly, hand hovering over the doorknob. He knocked sharply with one knuckle and just about groaned in relief when her sultry voice poured through the wood.

"Come on in."

He pushed through, twisting the lock on the handle before pushing the door closed behind him. As she had been the first day they'd met, Katiya sat on one of the two sofas in her office, her legs stretched out on the cushions. She'd removed her shoes and set them on the floor beside her.

He waited until the decisive click from the door had brought her head up from the stack of papers in her lap. Her eyes widened and she dropped the pencil from her hand.

"Wa...Warwick, what are you doing in here?" she asked, her voice slightly breathless.

Nice to know he still affected her. He leaned against the door and crossed his arms, a slow, sensual smile lifting his lips. He was content now, knowing he had her all to himself.

"You've been avoiding me, Katiya." He rolled the words off his tongue, doing his best to remain in control of his emotions that seemed to go haywire around her.

Her chin snapped up a bit and her eyes narrowed. "I've been working." She picked up the pencil and tapped the stuff before her with the eraser.

"I've noticed."

"Good. Then do you mind?"

He narrowed his gaze on her and shook his head as he slowly pushed away from the door and prowled towards her. "Yes, actually I do. I mind a hell of a lot."

She sighed and put her pencil in the notepad then closed it. "Something you need to get off your chest?"

His eyes raked her form. She couldn't hide her shiver. He didn't stop until he had one hand on the arm of the couch and the other on the back, caging her in. Her nose flared and she swallowed hard, but she didn't back down. She'd pasted one of the most bored expressions he'd seen on her. The closer he got to her, the faster the beat on the side of her neck moved.

"Oh yeah," he growled right before he slammed his mouth over hers.

Katiya remained stiff beneath him for all of a second. Then it was like kissing liquid fire. She melted into him only to explode and meet his passion with a fiery one of her own. Her tongue didn't wait for an invitation. She just thrust it into his mouth, yanking the reins of aggressor from him.

The sound of papers hitting the floor didn't even deter him. He wrapped his arms around her, pressing her close, revelling in the fact she was in his arms again. Her taste, ever addicting, flowed through him straight to the hard rod in his jeans, making it throb with anticipation.

One hand cupped the back of her neck as he readjusted them so she was on his lap on the sofa. Like in the truck, she shot electricity through him as she rubbed along his straining erection. Her panting and whimpers played havoc on his thread of control.

"Katiya," he growled against her plush lips.

She slowly backed away, holding his lower lip in her teeth before releasing it with a pop. Her eyes were smoky with desire and her chest rose and fell enticingly with each rapid breath she took.

"What?" Even her voice was more raspy than normal.

Focus. He had to focus. And *was* he — totally focused upon the full breasts before him, the tunic, which was a gorgeous colour against her skin. Not to mention the way her core was cradled up against him.

"Why have you been avoiding me?"

The heat in her eyes died. He could see it replaced with frustration.

"I know this is difficult for you to understand, Warwick Taylor of Taylor Bytes, but my every moment isn't spent thinking about you. I have a community centre to run. I don't have others to do it for me. This is my baby. My blood, sweat, and tears were poured into making The Oasis. I oversee it all. This...is my life." Her words were clipped and the tone could have rivalled Siberia for warmth.

If not for the flash of heat in her eyes, he would have sworn she meant every bit of that blather about how her every moment wasn't spent thinking about him. It may not be every moment, but he'd bet his fortune it was a hell of a lot more than she wanted him to know.

She began to get off his lap but he grabbed her hips and held her in place. His hips flexed instinctively against her and he was arrogantly pleased when she whimpered and answered with a movement of her own.

Is that how she thinks about me? That I'm all about myself?

"I know, Katiya. Don't go, hear me out."

She relaxed but her eyes were wary. He'd been told how passionate she was about her centre and he'd seen her dedication to it, but until this very moment, he never realised how much of herself she actually gave. It wasn't something she did during the day, turned it off at night and went home. That was the difference between them. He had his business, too, but he had a board who could — and did — make decisions, leaving him to do what he wanted. Katiya had her hands in every single aspect of this centre, ensuring it ran smoothly and giving it her all, every second of every day.

How to say what he wanted to get across? Be blunt.

"I want you, Katiya."

Those stunning eyes darkened and she pulled part of her bottom lip in her mouth.

Jeez, she's going to kill me. I'm ready to explode inside my pants. Okay, I need to focus. Get it out. Tell her what you have to say.

"I—"

He placed two fingers over her mouth and shook his head. "Let me finish. I know you feel it. I've been watching you like a starving man for the past four days, waiting...no, expecting you to come to me. You didn't. And yes, when I came in here, I'm sure it was about me. But that's not what I want. I want it to be about us—*us*, Katiya."

She stiffened and he flashed back to the memory of her at his house. How her body seemed to be stiffer than before. Something else to think about and figure out.

"I don't want to be caught necking in my truck." He shrugged easily. "Well, the necking part would be fun." Her smile was tentative but there. "I want more. Dates, meeting family"—he winked—"sleepovers. Lots of them."

He could feel her tremble even though her expression never changed. Moving his fingers from her lips, he trailed them over her cheekbone and along her chin before sliding down her neck and along the edge of her tunic.

"I want to hold you all night. Fall asleep with you in my arms and wake that very same way." He stared at his fingers as he travelled them farther down towards the belt. "I want to make love to you, Katiya. Strip off all these damn clothes you wear and see your body, which has haunted my dreams since the day I met you. Learn every curve, memorise each inch, taste your skin."

She whimpered and he raked his gaze back up to her eyes. Her lips were shiny and he longed to take them again.

"See me tonight, Katiya." He put it all out there on the table for her. "Make some time for us to be together, without the distraction of work or anything else that may pop up while we're here."

Her tongue sneaked out and dampened her lips again, making him want to growl with primal desire.

"I'm here late," she said, her voice barely residing above a whisper.

"Don't care."

"I won't be home until around nine."

"Want me to bring dinner?" he asked, refusing to give in to any of her lame excuses. If he had to wait until midnight to see her, then that's exactly what he'd do. Whatever it took.

He could see her weighing it in her head. When she nodded, he expelled a breath he'd not even realised he'd been holding. Relief flooded him.

"Okay."

Sinking his hands into her soft hair, he drew her close and dragged his tongue along the seam of her lips before delving inside her waiting mouth. She sighed and kissed him back. While all the heat and fire was still there, this kiss was slower, more tantalising. It had a deeper intensity and meaning behind it.

He massaged the back of her head while their tongues duelled. He was so hard he could have split rocks with his cock. The scent of her, coconut and strawberries, flowed around him and he longed to know how she tasted. Everywhere.

A beeping sound drew them apart. Her eyes were unfocused and passion filled as she pulled away from him. She blinked a few times and gave him a final kiss before climbing off his lap and moving to her desk. She didn't walk—she flowed with this innate grace he'd never seen so natural for a woman before.

"Yes?" she asked lifting the receiver.

He readjusted his shaft in his pants and crouched to the floor to gather up her dropped papers. Pushing to his feet, he noticed she sat on the edge of her desk, watching him. Almost a thoughtful look.

"Time to get back to work?"

"Yes," she said and he was positive he picked up on some regret in her tone.

He strode towards her, loving how her gaze trailed over him, full of appreciation, before meeting his eyes again. He handed her the pile of papers and was blessed with a soft smile.

"I'll see you tonight then, Katiya," he murmured, skimming her cheek with his knuckles.

"Tonight."

One final kiss then he walked to the door, unlocked it, and walked out, closing it softly behind him. His body was already tense in expectation of what it would be like to be with her. There was no doubt what was going to happen. And he was beyond ready.

* * * *

"Kat. Kat!"

Katiya looked up from the clipboard and tried desperately to remember what they were talking about. Her sister, Delicia stood before her, dressed in her work uniform.

What the crap were we talking about?

Her mind was on tonight. Warwick at her house. And what that would lead to. She had something this man was more than capable of soothing. All that muscle would be hers, at least for the night. Those sexy dimples, she could finally lick. She'd analyse it later. Right now there were matters involving The Oasis to tend to.

Like whatever thing my sister is going on about. Crap, if I could just recall what we were discussing.

"What, Lis?"

"Rhia said you changed the room for the CPR class but she didn't know which one you wanted us in."

Glancing behind her sister, she noticed a group of fifteen people waiting. *Shit.* "Sorry." She flipped through the pages on her clipboard. "Use two-oh-five."

Her sister eyed her up and down but thankfully didn't say a word about her space cadet behaviour. "Okay."

Lis walked away, her partner, Thom, falling into step with her, and the rest of the group who'd signed up for the CPR certification class following behind. There wasn't any time to dwell on that, however, because soon after, Rhia came up to her and they got to work on setting up more classes and finding the people who would come in and teach them.

By eight that night, everyone had gone home except for her. She sat in her office and finished up some paperwork. With a groan, she stretched her neck and shoulders before taking a deep breath. Eight-thirty. She was hungry and tired.

Things were coming along swimmingly. The new systems were a godsend. Not to mention how Warwick had left some of his people to teach classes and more. An ugly thought raced to the forefront. Was he so sure they would sleep together because of his donation?

"Don't think that way, Kat," she reprimanded herself. "Things were donated before you met him. Besides, I'm sure he has more than enough willing women to sleep with him."

That thought soured her. Shaking it off, she logged off her computer and began straightening up her desk. Finally ready, she headed for the door. The phone rang right before she got there and she paused. With a firm shake of her head, she left and headed to the front, knowing whoever it was could leave a message and she would deal with it the next time she came into her office. Right now, she had something more important to tend to. Warwick waited for her. Setting the alarm and locking the door, she headed for her car.

The closer she got to home, the more nervous she felt. Butterflies gathered in the pit of her belly and all seemed to flap harder when she pulled into her drive and parked next to the car where he waited for her.

Warwick.

He'd driven a Mercedes-Benz SL-Class Roadster and got out when she stopped her vehicle beside his. The light from her porch framed his physique. And just like that she was wet and could hardly focus on anything but what his touch allowed her to feel. How intense, how heady, how damn addicting he was.

"Good lord," she muttered, turning off the engine and climbing out. She couldn't help it. He just looked...divine.

He wore jeans, as he had today when he'd cornered her in her office. But instead of a T-shirt, he wore a long-sleeved crewneck shirt—her guess, to ward off the chill of the spring night. In one hand he had a bag that she assumed held their meal. Her stomach growled at the thought of food. Her pussy pulsed at the thought of *after*.

Swallowing hard, she locked her car and met him at the base of the steps.

"Hello, beautiful," he murmured, before brushing their lips together in a gentle kiss.

She almost dropped her keys. "H...hello." *This man has entirely too much magnetism for my own good.*

"Hungry?" he asked.

"Starved," she admitted, and she was. Today had been so busy all she'd grabbed was an apple from the kitchen.

"Me too."

Those two words were delivered on silken velvet along with erotic decadent promise. Somehow she didn't think he spoke of food. Another wave of heat slammed into her and her vision flickered. *I have got to keep it together.* Somehow she made it up to the door and unlocked it.

"Come on in," she said, stepping through and flipping on the living room light while turning off the one which illuminated her porch.

He was right on her heels, taking up a lot of her air. She sat her purse down on the small mosaic table by the door and sighed. Her deep breath brought to her nose the evocative scent of Warwick. It was totally unfair for a man to smell so desirable. So fresh, pure and masculine. The notes teased her nose and made her want him even more.

She swallowed hard and silently led the way to the kitchen. He unpacked the bag while she gathered plates and silverware then set the table.

"How was the rest of your day?" he asked, glancing up from the bag.

"Busy. Good, though. We've got a few more new classes that we'll be starting."

"Great." He dished up the rice pilaf and chicken before splitting up the steamed vegetables.

She filled the glasses with ice water and sat down across from him. "How about with you?" *My goodness, this is like we're a married couple talking about our day.* And that didn't scare her like she thought it might.

"Also busy. But time seemed to take forever to pass by."

His indigo eyes smouldered as they held hers. So intense and heated was his stare that her fork wobbled in her unsteady hand. Unsure of how to respond, she ate a bite of the chicken and chewed slowly.

A masculine and knowing smile lifted his lips, showcasing those sexy dimples. He saluted her with his fork and dug into his own meal. The talk was polite as they ate. Unfortunately for her, it did nothing to cool down her craving for this man. The way he took food off the fork, the up and down bobbing of his Adam's apple when he swallowed. How his mouth formed words when he spoke. All it did was increase her desire for him until it was almost unbearable.

He got up and approached with two containers. "I didn't know what you liked as far as dessert so you have two options. Chess pie and lemon cake."

She smiled. "Lemon cake." Her eyes met his. "One of my favourites."

Warwick popped the top on the plastic container and set it before her. She licked her lips in anticipation. Three layers of lemon cake with creamy lemon frosting. One of her weaknesses.

"This looks divine," she said on a half moan.

The sound of a chair sliding across her floor pulled her attention from the confection. Warwick had settled himself right beside her. He lifted her fork, cut into the cake and held it to her lips.

"Open." His command was a whispered thread of passion.

She did. The cake had been done to perfection and seemed to melt in her mouth. *Oh my goodness.* His eyes watched her the whole time and she could see the desire in their depths. Another bite, and another—he continued to feed her until she shook her head at the offer. She couldn't possibly eat another bite. Warwick finished off the final piece on the utensil.

He placed the fork down and kissed her. Covered her lips with his until she opened for his questing tongue. He took his time and explored her mouth, allowing his taste combined with the lemon cake to flood her.

Lord help me.

Her hands settled upon his shoulders, drawing him in closer. His touch intoxicated. Her nipples pressed tightly against the material of her bra. With a possessive growl he yanked her from her chair and settled her across his lap. Tightening his hold on her hair, he plundered her mouth, taking what he wanted. Her submission. Which she gave. Willingly. From her mouth he progressed down along her chin, across her exposed neck to her shoulder, where he nipped. A spear of electricity shot through her at that. She hung her head back, exposing herself to him, offering herself to him.

"Warwick," she panted, her nails digging through his shirt. She rubbed her lower body continually along his shaft.

He cupped her ass and got to his feet. "Bedroom?"

"Down the hall, second door on the—" He swept her off her feet and held her against his powerful chest. Her body felt so right in his arms. Once in the bedroom, the light on, he placed her on her feet and kissed her again, pressed her back against the door and made love to her mouth with his kisses.

She wanted him naked. Wanted him to be deep inside her. Wanted her nails digging into the flesh on his back as he pounded into her while she cried to the room. He gripped the bottom of her tunic, ripped his mouth off hers and lifted the fabric over her head leaving her clad in a ribbed white tank top. The tunic dropped forgotten to the floor.

Dear merciful heavens, I'm going to become a puddle if he keeps looking at me like that.

He reached for the button on her jeans and she took a sharp breath when he undid it, the hiss of the zipper the only sound in the room other than their breathing. When he tugged them down, she almost stopped him but the need pooled deep within her stayed her hand. Once they reached her feet, she stepped out of them, kicked them to the side. Her shoes followed soon after.

A grumble raced out of him. He took the hem of her tank top and slowly drew it up over her head.

"Beautiful," he whispered.

She stood against the wall wearing a white bra and panties. He stared hungrily at her, like a wolf watching a yearling. It increased the liquid heat coursing through her veins, the craving for him amplified one hundred fold.

His hands shadowed her silhouette from head to toe. He trailed his fingers up the outsides of her legs, moving towards her waist. His touch burned her to the core. Her legs trembled as she tried to remain upright.

Along the outsides of her bra, he dragged his touch over the full globes. Her nipples hardened even more, crying out for his touch without the satin of the bra between them.

"Look at you," he breathed. "All swells and curves. Perfection. You have a body the gods made for loving, Katiya Wright."

She felt like it.

One finger slid a white bra strap down over one shoulder. She held her breath. Finally the cup dropped from her breast, exposing the puckered nipple.

Touch me.

His thumb swiped the tip and shot spikes of electricity through her. "Warwick," she whimpered.

"Katiya." His voice low and silvery with seduction.

She screamed when he drew the diamond hard point into his mouth. He sucked hard and dragged his teeth across the hypersensitive nub. Her legs quavered and the arm he snaked around her midsection was the only reason she didn't collapse to the carpeted floor.

Stars flickered before her eyes. She grabbed his hair, pressing him tight to her, needing more. Desperate for more. He released the hooks and worked the bra off, all the while continuing to suck on her nipple. The other nipple ached and when he rolled it between forefinger and thumb, squeezing hard enough to make her gasp at the pain, she purred in pleasure. Then he switched mouth and hand, inciting moans from her as he continued to torment, tease, and pleasure both breasts.

She didn't know how much more she could take.

"Warwick," she panted. Her lids were heavy with want and she pressed her fingers into the back of his skull urging him on.

"I could spend all day on these luscious breasts. But I have to explore more."

He kissed down her belly, delving his tongue into her belly button, eliciting a gasp from her.

"Who knew you liked to wear thongs, Katiya? Beneath all that poise and calm lingers this sexy vixen." His hands palmed the globes of her ass and she wriggled in response to his touch. Warm breath poured along her skin. Goosebumps exploded all over her.

"So sexy," he muttered. He licked at her core, not bothering to remove the thong.

"Shit!" she hissed, her hips bucked hard against his mouth.

His tongue snaked up and down the soaked material, making it wetter. "You taste like heaven," he uttered against her clit, the words vibrating through her.

She grabbed his hair and held his mouth closer.

"What do you want, Katiya?" he asked, his tongue skimming along the edges of her thong.

"You," she sputtered.

He slowly—agonisingly so—peeled off her wet thong, his breath warm on her pussy. When his tongue slid up the cleft she screamed to the heavens. Before she knew it, she ground against him, an orgasm washing over her.

His mouth toyed with her stiff clit, his tongue circled around it time and time again. She couldn't formulate a word. He spread her thighs and slipped a finger up in her. Then another.

"Oh...oh...Warwick!" She shuddered as the orgasm rippled over her.

He added another finger and stroked deep within her. His tongue continued to torment her. Then he switched and she squealed again as she exploded around his thrusting tongue.

She yanked on his hair and ground against his face, totally consumed by passion. With her heart pounding, limbs quaking, he rose up before she could regain her faculties and kissed her.

He delved his tongue deep into her mouth, relentless and with single-minded purpose. Her senses ran haywire as she tasted herself on him.

"Katiya," he moaned against her lips, hips bucking. She rubbed against him, the material of his jeans adding delicious friction to her needy slit.

"Warwick!" She released his hair and tugged up his shirt. "Off," she commanded.

He complied and a hiss of appreciation escaped as she finally got to see his naked chest. Warwick was a work of art. All ridges and planes, his body didn't look like it belonged on a man who'd made his fortune by computers. She trailed her fingers down his pectorals and over the ridges of his abdominals.

He sucked in a sharp breath. She moved up his haired chest and down again to the button of his jeans. She hesitated and Warwick took over, quickly shucking them. Her mouth watered as she took in the large ridge confined by the white boxer briefs.

Her pussy gushed and pulsed. She stared hungrily as he removed the final article of clothing. Her tongue flicked along her lower lip and she bit off a moan.

His cock jutted out from a nest of dark hair. The head shone with drops of pre-cum. She wanted to drop to her knees and take him into her mouth.

"Bed," he growled.

She backed into the bed and watched him pull a condom from his pants pocket.

"Let me," she murmured, plucking it from his hand and ripping the foil.

She reached for his shaft—warm and hard, it rested in her hand. She smeared the pearly drops then rolled the condom over his length. Warwick laid her back on the bed, pressing little kisses along her collarbone. She melted from the inside out. His finger skimmed over the scar on her leg before it brushed her pussy.

"Ohh," she moaned, arching with need into his hand.

"Patience."

Was he kidding? She felt more than capable of going up in flames right now.

"Now," she demanded.

His eyes were so dark they appeared black. No humour in his expression.

"Yes."

The one word should have relieved her but instead it made her want him more.

He removed his hand and settled between her thighs. She held her breath as he sank deep within her.

Oh my God!

He filled her, stretched muscles that hadn't been used in a very long time. Heat spiralled out from within, threatening to consume her. It was too much. It wasn't enough.

"Warwick."

He didn't make her ask just began to move. Out and in, he began a steady rhythm. Slow at first then with increased speed. Her mind whirled. All synapses fired, fast and hard, with the onslaught of feelings. Skin tingled. Her heart pounded out of control. All her focus and energy honed in on the man delivering such an amazing experience to her. She undulated beneath him, encouraging more, faster and deeper strokes.

His handsome face sat carved in a mask of concentration. Sweat beaded along his brow.

"Uh, uh, uh…" Her grunts punctuated each of his thrusts.

His hands were by her ears. Hers were curved around his powerful biceps.

"Stop acting like I'll break," she demanded, tightening her inner muscles. Gentle and slow was all good and well but right then, she wanted hard and fast. "Fuck me, Warwick."

Chapter Five

How he'd managed not to erupt by then was anyone's guess. Warwick had been on the verge since he'd kissed her at supper. Everything since…had only solidified the rod in his jeans. She tasted better than anyone had a right to. When her thick cream had flowed into his mouth, he thought he'd died and gone to heaven.

He was wrong.

Slipping between her firm thighs and into her wet pussy had been heaven. Her tight, wet pussy had literally robbed him of speech. Warmed velvet. It had been like coming home. Katiya had taken him all the way in.

But to hear her demand to be fucked boiled his blood. He picked up his pace and reached down with one hand to lift her uninjured leg up so her knee draped over his shoulder.

"Ohh yeah," she said on a rumble of pleasure.

He couldn't agree more.

He ploughed into her slit faster, the angle allowing for deeper penetration. His balls tingled and he could feel the pain of her nails digging into his skin. It egged him on.

He withdrew until just the head remained and when her eyes—angry eyes—snapped up to his gaze, he slammed home.

"Ahhh!" she cried, her body clenching around him as she found orgasmic bliss.

"Fuck!"

To feel her shatter like that around him was too much to bear. He powered into her, hard, fast, and relentless. She matched his moves, her head tossing back and forth on the bed, her cries filling the air. Her flushed face, parted lips—all added to his total experience. And he lost it. Her pure passion— uncoaxed, uncajoled, totally honest—did him in. The tendons in his neck tightened as he erupted with a low roar.

"Katiya!"

Limbs shaky, he lowered his body and placed her leg back on the mattress. Katiya looked delectable, all flushed and rumpled. With a tender kiss, he withdrew from her warm haven and disposed of the condom. Returning to the bed, he saw her lying on one side, staring at him. A slow grin turned up the corners of her mouth.

Her blatant and appreciative stare made him smile. It also made him begin to harden again. Katiya crooked a finger at him and he did as she bade eagerly.

"We're not even close to being done," he said reaching for more protection and tossing them on the bedside table before joining her again on the messed up bedspread.

* * * *

It wasn't until early in the morning that the two lovers had exhausted themselves and lay intertwined beneath nothing more than a cotton sheet.

He stirred and reached for the woman who'd rocked his world all through the night. She wasn't there. Bleary eyed, he sat up and checked her bedside clock. A quarter to six. He'd barely been asleep for three hours.

Where was she?

The bedroom door was closed. He got up, turning on a light. Locating his jeans, he tugged them on before heading to the door. Once out of her room he noticed there was a light on in the living room and he padded in that direction. At the table, Katiya stood, one leg on the seat of the chair, as she studied something before her.

She was fully dressed with her hair up in some twist. A yellow T-shirt, a pair of medium brown pants, and white tennis shoes rounded out her attire.

"Morning," he said.

She jumped slightly before looking over her shoulder at him. A smile crossed her features, melting away the look of seriousness it had had moments before.

"Morning."

He moved to stand beside her and brushed his lips along the curve of her neck. The desire to remove the pins in her hair so it flowed down around her filled him. He loved how it felt trailing over his skin. She trembled and he kissed her again. She whimpered. Once more until she turned in his arms and kissed him. Her tongue led the way, searching his out and dancing with it. When the kiss ended, he was more than ready to clear the table off with one swoop and take her right there.

"That's a proper way to greet someone in the morning."

Her eyes twinkled. "Is that so? Do you greet all your employees that way? Men and women?"

He popped her on the ass and she laughed. Her voice pealed through the room, banishing any nervousness he'd had about how she may react once they woke.

She faced the table again. Pressing against her back, he stared over her head at the things on the table. Photographs. Black and white ones.

"What's this?"

She gestured with one hand while the other caressed the arm he slid around her middle. "Photos my sister took. She dropped them off so I could put some up at the centre."

He whistled low. "She's good. Which sister?"

"Youngest."

"Ahh, Lis...the EMS responder."

She looked at him over her shoulder, her eyes warmed with gratitude he'd actually listened to her when she'd told him. "That's her."

"So are you still deciding?"

"No. These are the ones I picked. Now I'm just trying to figure out how I want them to go in the halls."

"She should sell her work. These are incredible."

Katiya chuckled. "No, Lis hates the limelight. She is an observer."

He decided he would like to meet this sister. He wanted to meet her whole family. "I'd love to meet her."

"She was at The Oasis yesterday."

He frowned and stared hard at a shot of a coyote standing on a mesa. "She was?"

"Yes. I'm not surprised you didn't see her, though. She stopped by to teach a CPR certification class. They finish up today."

"Speaking of today"—he nibbled along her earlobe—"why are you already up and dressed? We didn't go to sleep until around three. It's the weekend, can't you go in late?"

Katiya sank back into his touch and he breathed in the soothing smell of her hair. "I know but I have to be there by six-thirty today. One weekend a month we do a free breakfast. This is the weekend."

He was continually surprised by the lengths this woman would go to help others. "What can I do to help?"

"We can always use servers and dishwashers."

Dishwashers? "Cooks?"

"Yes, some of those, too. We start getting ready at six-thirty and are ready to begin serving between seven-thirty and eight. The fire department, police, and other groups help with the food. So if you really want to come along, your help would be appreciated."

What he really wanted was to strip her of her clothes and take her back to her bedroom and start all over learning about her body again…and when he finished, do it again. But the chance to be with her proved to be too great a temptation.

"I'll be there." He kissed her again. "Any chance we can be late?"

Her warm chuckle made him smile. "Sorry. Doesn't look good when the boss is late."

"You look good no matter what."

"Flattery will get you everywhere…except back in my bed. I have to get going." She turned in his arms and ran her hands up his bare chest. "But thank you for last night."

"Thank you," he revised, pressing a light kiss to the tip of her cute nose. "If I go now, I'll be there sooner."

Neither moved. They stared at one another, her fingers tangled in the ends of his hair, desire overflowing in her eyes. His hands rested on the swell of her hips, fingers moving in idyllic circles.

"I really have to go," she murmured, pressing closer to him.

"Yeah."

Almost another minute passed before she moved out of his grasp. "Go get your clothes so we can go."

"I'd really rather remove you from yours and go from there."

Her eyes grew molten as they heated with passion. She shook her head and stepped back again. "No. Clothing."

He sighed in disappointment but hurried back to the room and finished donning his clothes. She was by the door when he returned. Preceding her out, he waited for her to lock the door and head to her car. At the driver's door, he pressed her against the side of her car and kissed her until she sank into him, counting on him to hold her upright.

The dark didn't allow him to see much more than her outline. "I'll see you soon, Katiya."

"Yes." Her response not much more than a whisper, quiet sigh.

He didn't want to climb in his car and leave her, even though it was only for a short time. He wanted to scoop her up and take her back inside, closing out the outside world. As it was, there were other things that took priority. Her centre being one of them. So he climbed in his car and used the powerful engine to get him home as quickly as possible. Once he'd showered and changed, the same fire engine red car took him back to the parking lot of The Oasis. The lights were on and numerous cars and trucks were in the lot.

He climbed out, eager to see Katiya again, even though it hadn't been much more than an hour since he'd departed her presence. It was with a light step he headed for the front door, more than ready to enjoy a new experience with his ever adorable Katiya Wright.

Yes. My Katiya Wright.

* * * *

Katiya took a deep breath before pulling open the glass door to Taylor Bytes. It had been two and a half weeks since she and Warwick had first made love. They continued to see one another even if she was hesitant to give him more of her heart. But damn, if he didn't have this way of sinking past all her defences.

So what's the problem? Is it really fair to fault a man because he has more money than Midas?

She sighed. That was the eternal question. And one she'd yet to come up with an honest answer to.

The man was amazing, truly he was. He'd been pressing her about going with him to the auto show. In fact, he still continued to ask her for her opinion on which vehicles to take. As it was, she hadn't said one way or the other.

She shook her head at her actions as she stepped across the tile floor, her slight heels making noise with each footfall. At the front desk she waited until the woman looked up from where she sat busy, typing on the computer. Her fingers had been flying across the keys, the clacking a testament to her skill as a typist. Blonde hair sat coiled up on her head in an elegant yet professional twist.

"Welcome to Taylor Bytes," she said with a friendly smile. "How may I help you today?"

"I'm here to see Mr Taylor. I don't an appointment but I was hoping he could make some time to see me."

The woman never batted so much as an eyelash at that statement. "Of course, Ms Wright. Take the elevator to your right to the top floor. His personal assistant will let you know when he can see you."

"Thank you." She gave a slight smile that was returned before the blonde's attention moved back to her task at hand. *Okay, she didn't even ask my name but she knew it, not only that but she is sending me up to his office floor.* She wasn't entirely sure what to make of it.

Heading off to the right, she moved slowly, taking in the décor of Taylor Bytes. It screamed professional. The decorations were nice but given she'd had insight on the man beneath the multi-billionaire, it didn't seem to fit him. This was…sterile, almost clinical.

She had pressed the button for the elevator when two men walked from around the corner. Her gaze ran over them both. Power suits and nothing but business. Their brows were furrowed and they were deep in discussion, one that it wouldn't take a genius to see they weren't happy about. Still they were very handsome. On their heels were a few more men. All of those in that group looked at her.

"I don't care," one man snapped from the first group that hadn't even looked in her direction. "Get it done or there will be hell to pay." His voice was low and dangerous.

All the men mumbled a response only to fall silent again while the man continued on. His deep voice carried the bark of authority.

Under their assessing gazes, she felt herself begin to wonder what the hell she was doing there. *Maybe it wasn't the best thing for me to stop by.* The doors to the elevator slid open in peaceful silence and she stepped in, grateful for them shielding her from the stares.

The ride to the top floor was swift and she took a fortifying breath before exiting the car. This floor was much more hospitable. Plush burgundy carpet blended seamlessly with the wall accents. Plants sat by large windows, enjoying the New Mexican sun.

A shorter older lady approached from behind a large desk. "Ms Wright, please come and sit down. Mr Taylor will be ready to see you in a few minutes. Can I get you anything? Coffee? Tea? Water?"

She smiled. "No, thank you, I'm fine."

"Very well. Have a seat, dear. If you change your mind, let me know."

"Yes, ma'am. Thank you."

The woman went back to her desk and she sought out the cream leather couch. The time passed as she worked on a few things she'd brought with her.

"Sherry, get the lawyers on the phone. I want Zach personally. Patch him through when you get him. Tell him I don't want to wait either."

The voice, deep and sharp, penetrated her zone. She jerked her head up to see the man from before, one of the two who hadn't looked at her, striding across the burgundy carpet. His dark suit fit him like a dream. She stared, uncertain of what she looked at. Then it hit her. It was Warwick. She'd not even recognised him before. The suit, the attitude, all of it made her not pick up on who he was.

"Right away, sir. Ms Wright is here to see you."

His head snapped towards her and his entire countenance softened. It was like watching a magic trick—the arrogant powerful man melted away, leaving her faced with the Warwick who had done things to her body that no man had ever done before. His indigo eyes heated as he adjusted course and headed directly for her.

"Katiya," he said on a decadent rumble.

"I'm sorry for just—"

"Don't apologise for coming to see me. Come in to the office." He offered his arm like a gentleman all the while his eyes had stripped and laid her bare.

Belly tense, she took his arm and moved with him. His coiled and roped muscles moved effortlessly beneath her hand. That was familiar, even if the suit wasn't. The second the door had closed behind them, she was in his arms, his mouth slanted over hers, tongue sweeping through hers. She curled as close as possible to his hard body.

Just when she thought she couldn't stand anymore, he ended the kiss. Now his eyes burned with fervour and intense hunger. He brushed a knuckle along one cheek. "What do I owe this delightful and most pleasurable distraction?"

She blushed even as she stepped away from him. He was so different while in these walls that she'd not even recognised him. How was that possible? Her first impression of the men had been they were less than pleased with whatever they had been discussing. There had been nothing, *nothing,* about the tall man in the dark suit to indicate it was Warwick. There definitely hadn't been any easy-going attitude or carefree and frequent smiles.

"Katiya?" he asked, capturing her chin in his hand and angling her head so he could see into her eyes.

Blinking rapidly, she cleared her throat. "Sorry. I...umm..." She trailed off, not really knowing how to tell him she'd just wanted to see him where he worked.

It was as if he knew. His expression softened and he drew her in close. "I wanted to see you too. I've missed you these past few days."

Hooking her arms around his back, she nodded against the material of his suit coat. It wasn't black as she'd first thought, instead a dark blue and made of wool. A beautiful fabric, rich in a navy hue, it had a bold cognac stripe that only added to the lean musculature of his body. Under the single breasted, two-button suit coat he wore a white shirt with a tie the same colour as the stripes on the shirt.

Bottom line—the man was a walking ad for sex.

He smelt even better than he looked. They'd barely seen one another recently. He no longer came to The Oasis to volunteer but some of his men still did. Calix was one who appeared there more often than not, but honestly, she wondered if it wasn't to harass Rhia. She didn't know what had transpired, or was transpiring, between them but there sure were sparks.

"Missed you too." She pulled back and stared up at him from under lowered lids. "How come the woman at the front knew who I was before I even said anything?"

That heart-stopping smile he had showcasing his sexy dimples appeared. "I told them if you ever stopped by you were to be sent up straight away to my office."

That gesture warmed her more than she cared to admit. "Everything okay?"

He wasn't quick enough to shutter his gaze. "Fine," he finally said.

The fact he had lied to her didn't sit well with her even though it truly was none of her business. She arched an eyebrow and sniffed. "Oh, okay. Didn't seem that way when I saw you walking across the lobby earlier."

Surprise filtered into his amazing indigo eyes. "You saw me downstairs?"

Extracting herself from his hold, she walked around the burgundy, walnut, and sable hued office. Unlike the outer room where his assistant worked, this place had more of a personal touch to it, a few plants and even a few framed photos on the walls.

She paused before the walnut leather sofa with the accent pillows to match the rest of the colour scheme and sank down upon it. Plucking at the leg of her pants, she took a sharp breath and looked at him.

"Yes. I have to be honest, though, Warwick. I didn't even recognise it was you until you walked into your office up here."

He shrugged out of his suit coat and hung it on a hook before striding over to where she sat, loosening his tie as he approached. Her mouth dried up faster than water in the desert. The man just looked too damn good. Edible even. His hair was drawn back in a tight queue.

Warwick lowered his large frame down on the leather beside her and immediately breathing became more difficult. "Do I look that much different in a suit, beautiful?" he asked, stretching an arm along the back and slowly removing the hand-carved ox bone hair sticks with agates that held up her hair in its bun.

All she could feel was the thudding of her heart and the insistent beat of her pussy. Swallowing hard, she shuddered when her hair fell free and he began playing with it.

"Ye...yes. You're like a different person."

"Explain," he ordered in a low tone, never easing the torture he proceeded to give her scalp.

She worried her lower lip before taking a deep breath and jumping in. "I've never seen you at work, so I guess it's just…just that I'm used to seeing smiles on your face as opposed to the scowl."

It was easy to see him mull over her words. Finally he lifted his shoulders laconically and tugged on her hair. "Business can be ugly at times." That was how he put it—succinctly. She knew he was done discussing it.

"Well, I don't want to take up any more of your time than necessary, but I came to invite you to supper."

He trailed his other hand up her bare arm, her resting upon his shoulder as he stared at her. "You, Katiya Wright, are an incredibly sexy woman."

She flushed. "Focus, Warwick. Are you available for supper?"

"Yes. What can I bring?"

Condoms.

Her heart sank and heat rushed up her face when his expression turned arrogant and she realised she'd said that out loud.

Crap, crap, crap! Damn my inability to keep my mouth shut.

"I've got that covered. What about anything for the meal?" He winked. "Unless you're on the menu."

Mustering up as much haughtiness as she could, she sniffed indignantly. "Nope. I'm leaving in the morning and wanted to see you before I left."

All humour fled faster that a roadrunner flying across the desert. His indigo eyes hardened and narrowed. "Where are you going?"

The sentence dripped with possession and she bristled. "It's work related."

His fingers tightened in her hair. "Katiya…"

"You don't own me, Warwick. I'm heading out of town on a business trip. I know your show is this weekend and I have plans to be back for that."

His muttered response couldn't be deciphered but she got the gist of it. Licking her lips, she crawled the rest of the distance separating them and settled herself across his lap. With slow and deliberate movements, she began to pull out his shirt and loosen his belt.

His darkly intense eyes held hers as she lowered the zipper on his slacks. He lifted, pressing closer to her core, which hovered over his ever-present erection. She dragged the zipper farther down and soon had his cock freed. Her light touch trailed up and down the rigid shaft. She couldn't help it. He was magnificent.

"Don't tease me, beautiful."

She scooted back so she knelt on the floor before him and took him in her mouth. He added a second hand to her hair and she let him set the pace he wanted. This was not about her, even though she craved him deep within her. She wanted to do this for him.

"Shit!" he hissed, thrusting harder and faster.

Closing her eyes, she relaxed her throat and took him all the way in, not stopping until he unloaded his release into her mouth.

* * * *

Katiya disembarked from the plane, wincing at the soreness in her leg. Flights were never easy for her. But they were important. She'd not officially told the truth to her family about her trip. It hadn't been entirely about business. While some had been, she had spent most of her time in Minnesota with a doctor—a friend of her sister, Arissa—who specialised in muscular issues due to trauma. She had been having more pain in her leg than she'd had in a long time and had wanted to get it looked at.

The only problem with being in a town in which all your family lived was that they all would have known before she even got out of the appointment. She had done some digging to locate Arissa's friend, Sarah. She had finally found her and had given her a call

The woman was an absolute peach. Had told her to come on in and she'd clear a day to spend with her. She knew her secret was safe and until she had answers to give to her family, she didn't want them to worry.

Or pester me.

The warm weather was a welcome from the frigid temperatures she'd experienced in Minnesota. They'd had a late spring snow and, needless to say, she was more than pleased to be back home.

She grinned at the sight of her brother, Jonathan, waiting for her beside his Benz. He took her luggage and threw it in the trunk while she got settled in the passenger seat.

"How did it go?" he asked, starting the powerful engine.

For a moment she wondered if he knew about the doctor, but there was no lingering concern, just honest curiosity.

"Good, good. Melken Products has agreed to send us some of their self-defence dummies along with bags and other items."

"You're awesome, sis," he complimented her as he drove.

"Thanks."

"Almost done?"

"I think so. I hope it will slow a bit once all the programs are outfitted and I can just call for donations and stuff instead of taking trips."

"You know there are martial arts places here in town, right?"

She laughed. "Yes I know that. But I prefer to go direct to the manufacturer. Face to face is a bit more personal than someone calling and asking. Now that we have a rapport, it can be handled over the phone in the future."

"I know."

They finished the ride chatting about this and that. When Jonathan pulled into her driveway she smiled. It was always nice to come home.

He carried her bags to the door, gave her a perfunctory kiss on the cheek and headed off. She shook her head. Knowing him, he had a case that needed his attention.

She showered and changed into khakis and a white T-shirt. Once her hair was up and her makeup on, she headed to her car and drove out to the address Warwick had given her for the show. It was about an hour away and she spent the time thinking about how much she'd missed him even though she'd been gone for only four days.

"Just goes to show how much of an impact he's had on my life," she said as she continued up the road.

When she started seeing signs for the show her belly began to flip. In her head, she counted down to the time she'd be able to see him again. Her body responded, letting her know it was totally unimpressed with how she'd handled bringing herself release as opposed to Warwick's magical touch.

She parked in a crowded lot then got out, locking her car before following the stream of people. Young, old, woman, or man—it didn't matter. They had all turned out for the event.

She paid for a catalogue and checked the map of where people were located. Once she'd found his name, she made a beeline for him. Walking behind an elderly couple, as soon as she was close enough to him, her skin began to burn as it did around him. His laughter filled the air. The couple seemed to vanish and just like that she was face to face with the man in her dreams.

Warwick Taylor.

He stood talking to some other folks but when his gaze landed on her, his mouth snapped shut like a steel trap. His eyes flared hot and passionate as they moved up and down her body. He muttered a word to the group standing there and crossed to where she stood, immobile.

This was the man she'd missed. Jeans and a T-shirt. All she cared about was him being back within her reach. He reached out with one hand and cupped her cheek. She couldn't have stopped the burrow into his palm any more than she could have stopped her heart that second.

"Hello, beautiful," he murmured so only she could hear.

"Hi."

The desire to kiss her overflowed his indigo gaze but all he did was give her another private little smile and drop his hand. She missed his touch immediately.

"I'm glad you're here. How was your trip?" His voice normal and could be heard by everyone now.

"It was good, thank you."

While she understood why he didn't kiss her, part of her wished he would have, damn the consequences. *Okay, more than just a part of me wishes he would have.*

She gave herself a sharp mental reprimand—this was neither the time nor the place to dwell on that. She truly was excited to see the show and discover which of his impressive collection he'd brought.

Warwick turned and waved her closer. "Come see my vehicles, Katiya."

She moved to his side, wondering if she would be cast by the papers as his girlfriend, paramour, or just a friend. His smile remained relaxed and at the ready. There was nothing that denoted there was something serious—heck, anything at all other than friendship—between them. Swallowing her uncertain feelings, she shoved her hands in her pockets and said, "Show me what you brought."

Chapter Six

It took everything in Warwick not to ravish Katiya as he wanted to. Only the idea of bringing too much attention to her stopped him. He kept his personal life very private. There was a reason he was able to keep his face out of the media. He gave them nothing sensational to report about him. He glanced at Katiya as she walked beside him. The white shirt hugged her ample breasts while the khaki shorts she wore stopped just above her knees leaving the expanse of her legs visible. It all created an edible view he wanted to eat up.

Warwick put his hands into the pocket of his jeans. If he touched her again he'd give the media more than scandal. He stood back as Katiya circled the trucks he had brought to the show. She moved with a sensuous grace around the side of the truck out of view.

"Ow...shit," Katiya hissed.

Warwick headed around the truck at a run. He spotted Katiya leaning against the side of the truck gripping her leg. Strain clenched her face and there were tears in her light hazel eyes. Warwick lifted her up into his arms. Katiya moaned, not letting go her hold on her appendage.

"Katiya, what can I do?"

"My...leg... Take me...home. Call...Lis," she gritted.

"Warwick, is she okay?" Calix asked, coming around from the rear of the truck.

"I'm taking Katiya to the hospital. Take care of things here." He was glad Calix had decided to come with him.

"You got it. Let me know if I can do anything," Calix said.

He nodded, striding away, Katiya against his torso. Katiya whimpered, turning her face into his chest. Each sound ripped through him. He skirted around the onlookers blocking his way. There were a lot of people at the auto show. He heard them talking as they realised it was Katiya he was carrying. Warwick didn't slow heading outside and to his truck. Gently he put her on the back seat of the cab before closing the door and dashing to the driver's door. He was on his way in moments.

"Take me home." Her voice was strained.

"We're going to the hospital."

"No. They can't do anything for me. It was the travelling and then walking on the leg. It's seizing on me. Call Lis. She can check me out. Please don't argue. Call Lis." Katiya moaned.

The desperation in her voice made him not say anything further. He drove her home. He planned on calling not only Lis but also his own private doctor to make a house call. The tyres squealed as he roared into the driveway. He worked the clutch and slammed it into gear as he killed the engine. As quickly as possible he headed to the passenger side and gently lifted her out. . The sound of screeching tyres reached him. Turning with her in his arms, Warwick spotted the green Jeep he knew was Delicia's. She hopped out, put a bag handle across her body and ran to them.

"I got calls from what seems like everyone who was at the auto show. What happened?" Delicia demanded.

Warwick strode towards the house as he replied, "I don't know. She said it was the travelling and then walking around at the show."

"Really? She travels all the time. Let me get the door, and you take her directly to bed. I'll check her over." Delicia rushed ahead and opened the door for them.

Warwick was surprised that she had keys.

"I have them in case of emergency," Delicia answered his unspoken question.

Warwick took Katiya back to the bedroom. Delicia went around him and pulled back the covers on the bed. He put Katiya down. She still gripped her leg, moaning. Warwick stood by helplessly as Delicia tried to examine Katiya.

"Come on, Kat, let me see," Delicia said firmly.

"It hurts, Lis!" she cried.

"Is it supposed to hurt like this?" he asked.

He'd been so careful not to push by asking her too much about her leg. Katiya came across as being without pain. He sometimes didn't know she was overdoing it until she showed strain. He usually subtly made it so they ended up sitting down. Yet today she had seemed fine one moment and then in agony the next.

"No. I've never seen it this bad," Delicia admitted.

He frowned not liking her response. "I'm going to call my doctor."

He didn't wait for a reply, leaving the room to make the call. Warwick placed the call in the hall. He closed the phone once he knew the Doc was on his way. The sound of the front door opening drew his attention and he headed down the hall. Spotting Katiya's brothers, he moved out of the way as they walked rapidly past him. Warwick went into the living room and stared out the bay windows. Another car pulled up. Not the one he was looking for. A woman he didn't recognise got out. She walked rapidly up the drive. He went towards the door.

The woman opened the door and walked in like she was familiar with the house. Her heavily lashed pale grey eyes studied him. Sienna skin flowed over sharp cheeks—a rounded chin and full lips complemented those captivating eyes. Two curls framed her face but the rest of her hair, dark brown with streaks of gold was pinned on the top of her head with similar hair sticks with coloured tips as Katiya's had been the day before she'd left for her mysterious trip. The stones on the tips in her case were golden, which matched the power suit she wore.

"Where is Katiya?" There was the bite of command in her tone.

He recognised it well. It was the one he used in his business dealings.

"Who ar—"

"Iona? When did you get back?" Yurandol ran up the stairs from the street.

"I just arrived and heard about Katiya. What the hell happened?" Iona replied.

Warwick recognised the name. The woman was Iona McKingley. He hadn't met her yet as she'd been out of town.

"I don't know. I just heard she collapsed," Yurandol said.

"Well, let's go see," Iona said.

The other three women who arrived with Yurandol were Katiya's friends, whom he had already met. They nodded then looked at him expectantly.

"She's in her bedroom with her brothers and Lis."

The women passed him heading for the bedroom. Warwick glanced out the open door relived to see the doctor's familiar Tahoe pull up. The whipcord thin man got out bearing his bag and strode towards Warwick. Once he was closer, Warwick studied those calm ice-blue eyes behind the rounded frames of his glasses.

"Warwick, where is my patient?" Lansing Malone, his personal physician and close friend, asked.

"This way." Warwick led him to the bedroom.

Lansing quickly ordered everyone except Warwick and Lis out. Katiya was stretched out but shaking. Warwick sat on the bed next to her. She burrowed her face against his side, gripping his leg. Warwick stroked her sweat-soaked hair. In some distant part of his mind he heard Lis and Lansing discussing Katiya's leg, but he couldn't focus on anything but Katiya. He soft whimpers tore at him.

"Stop talking and just do something," Warwick snapped.

"If you can't be calm then you need to leave," Lansing said.

"Fu—"

"Warwick, it's okay." Katiya stroked his leg.

He looked at her in disbelief. "You're the one in pain and you're trying to comfort me?"

"It'll be okay. Can you go check and make sure everyone is not worrying too much?" Katiya asked.

Warwick asked suspiciously, "Are you trying to get rid of me?"

"No, just give you something to do so you can stop fretting so much."

Warwick shook his head. "Not possible. I'm staying here until we see what is wrong. As soon as these two can act like medical professionals." He glared at Lis and Lansing.

"They will if someone will stop being such a bear and grumbling at them. Now go," Katiya ordered.

Warwick hesitated.

"Please." Her voice was hoarse.

Warwick kissed her forehead then reluctantly stood. "I'll be right outside if you need me."

"Thanks."

"Do something." He gave the Lansing and Lis another glare.

They ignored him. He left. In the living room, he went back to staring out of the window. He ignored everyone else. Witnessing Katiya in pain had him realising he cared more for her than he had initially believed.

"Warwick." Lansing's voice caught his attention.

Warwick strode to him and they exited out to the hall. Lis touched his shoulder and continued into the living room. He could hear the murmur of her voice but was more focused on Lansing.

"She's fine. I gave her a muscle relaxant for the leg," Lansing said.

Warwick breathed out then said, "So she was right— it was too much between the travelling and the walking around the auto show."

"I've told you all I can." Lansing's face had a closed expression.

"What? I'm the one who brought you here," Warwick said.

"And she's my patient. Not you. She's a good woman for you, Warwick. See you soon." Lansing patted him on the shoulder, walked to the door and left.

Warwick frowned after him. He went into the living room and cornered Lis.

"What's wrong with Katiya?" Warwick demanded.

"Exactly what Lasing told you," she answered immediately.

The response was too pat and yet said nothing. Suspicion filled him. Warwick opened his mouth to question her then glanced around, realising they were not alone. Rethinking, he said nothing further. He made an about-face and went back to the living room door.

"You can see yourselves out. Katiya isn't up for visitors. Call tomorrow and I'll let you know if she is up to seeing you." He went down the hall.

"Did he just kick us out?" Dimitri demanded.

"Seems as if he did." Leo chuckled.

"Who the hell does he think he is?" Dimitri asked.

"Her man." Female voices answered.

"Come on, big bro, you can take it up with him another day. Katiya needs rest," Jonathon said languidly.

Warwick went into the bedroom and to Katiya's bedside. He sat next to her, pushing her hair away from her face. She was sleeping. A noise made him glance up. Iona leaned against the doorjamb.

"Why are you still here?" he whispered, not wanting to wake Katiya.

"Checking on Kat for myself. Besides, I don't take orders from anyone." She strolled into the room and sat on the bed on the other side of Katiya.

Iona raised her feet, taking off her high-heeled sandals, then rested her back against the headboard. Her look dared him to make her leave. Knowing an argument would wake Katiya, he left her alone.

"Did the others leave?"

"Yep. But you should think of locking up. And getting Kat something to drink. She'll be thirsty when she wakes. Bring me some iced tea while you're at it," Iona said.

She crossed her legs and smiled at him. Warwick stared at her. He stroked the side of Katiya's face then stood before leaving the room.

Katiya listened as Iona spoke. She was surprised when the bed dipped as Warwick left.

"You can stop feigning sleep. He's gone. Now explain this bullshit you told Lis to feed us." Iona poked her shoulder.

"Don't be a nag," Katiya said tiredly.

"Then tell me what is wrong with your leg," Iona said.

"I don't know." Katiya opened her eyes and looked at her friend.

Iona studied her. She slid down, her arms coming around her. Katiya gulped, not wanting to cry. One moment she'd been standing then the next an excruciating, crippling pain had gripped her leg. The tests Sarah had run wouldn't be back for at least another week and a half. Sarah had done so many tests and had even taken a little piece of the scar tissue from her leg.

"What can I do?" Iona drew her attention.

"Don't push about this. I want everyone to think it is just the plane ride and over-exertion."

"Kat, wh—"

She cut her off. "Please Iona. I can't say anything. Not yet. Just let it go."

"I will for now. But you better explain soon," Iona growled.

"I will," Katiya promised.

They waited in silence. At the sound of steps, Katiya glanced at the door.

"How are you doing?" Warwick asked.

"I'm fine. Just need to know my limitations," Katiya said.

Iona snorted.

She ignored the noise. Warwick put a glass of water on her bedside, holding the other one over her.

"Put it there. I'm too comfortable." Iona gestured to the bedside table.

Katiya looked at her sharply. Iona winked. Warwick clomped around the bed to the other side. She heard the clink of the glass as he put it down. Then he came back into view.

"As you can see Katiya is fine. Now leave," Warwick said.

"I'm not going anywhere except to sleep. It was a long flight," Iona yawned.

"Then find your own bed. Katiya needs rest." Warwick gritted his teeth.

"Then shut up so she sleep," Iona said cheerfully.

"Help me move over, Warwick. You can lie next to me. Move over, Iona," Katiya said.

Warwick frowned then helped shift her. Iona moved away from her back a little.

"Lay down." Katiya patted next to her.

"She could just leave." Warwick glared over at Iona.

"She's not going anywhere. So you might as well lie down. I'm tired," Katiya said.

Warwick lay down stiffly. Katiya snuggled against him. He put his arms around her.

"I don't think I'm going to like Iona much," he whispered.

"She grows on you." Katiya patted his forearm.

"Like a friendly old puppy." Iona laughed.

"Stop eavesdropping." Katiya slapped back at her.

"I'm right next to you. I'd have to be deaf not to hear," Iona said.

Warwick was silent for a moment. "What's going on with your leg, Katiya?"

"Nothing," she replied quickly.

Guilt at lying to him filled her. But it was for his own good. He didn't need to worry about her. Warwick was stiff again. She stroked along his chest.

"I'm okay. I'll get some rest then I'll be fine," Katiya said.

Warwick didn't say anything but he relaxed. The sound of the door opening made her look up and smile.

"Kat. I came as soon as I heard... Well, hell, you must be better. Can I sleep with you too?" Mattson McKingley asked.

"I'm not sleeping with anyone else," Warwick roared.

"Mattson is kidding, Warwick." Katiya laughed.

"How'd he get in? I locked up," Warwick grumbled.

"He probably picked the locks," Katiya murmured sleepily.

"He broke into your house?" Warwick said.

"That's Mattson. The spare room is made up, Mattson. We'll talk in the morning."

"Why doesn't he go home and take his sister with him?" Warwick griped.

"Because until I can speak with Katiya and know she is really okay I'm not going anywhere. I'll see you in the morning, Kat," Mattson said cheerfully.

The bedroom door slammed behind him.

"There is no doubt they are related," Warwick said dryly.

"Yep. That's my bro. Figured he would be by and I don't like sharing a bed with him. He is a cover hog," Iona said.

Katiya was actually relieved that Iona and Mattson were here. If it had been her brothers, they would have prodded more. At least Iona being here would make Mattson leave it alone for now. In the morning she would use their presence to distract Warwick from asking too many probing questions. It would give her time to garner her defences to keep the truth from him.

What is going on with my leg? She prayed Sarah would be able to give her an answer, and soon. Katiya let sleep overtake her.

* * * *

"Are you ready to go home?"

"It's not necessary for you to keep picking me up. I'm fine. The leg hasn't given me problems." Katiya turned towards Warwick.

Yet. The thought faded as she spotted Warwick. She moaned. His pale grey with darker grey stripe suit fit him perfectly, showing all the wonderful lines of his sexy body.

"I know. I like coming to get you. So, you ready?" Warwick kissed her gently.

Katiya thoughts scattered as she leaned against his frame. Warwick ended the kiss. She tried to recall his question.

When it came to her she cleared her throat before answering, "Yes. Just let me get my bag."

She pulled away and got her bag. Warwick took it from her and escorted her out. He patiently waited as she checked to make sure everyone had what they needed for the night. Assured they were set, she headed out with Warwick. He helped her in his truck then got in pulling out and into traffic. Katiya stared out the side window.

A month had passed since the incident with her leg. Since then, Warwick had insisted on driving her to and from work. Her guilt over lying and continuing to hide the truth had let her agree to him playing chauffeur. She still hadn't heard anything conclusive from Sarah. The tissue from the leg was fine but the unexplained weakness and pain wasn't going away. Sarah and Lansing were consulting together to figure it out. She'd been sneaking to Lansing for appointments. Keeping it from her family was a feat in itself. She'd hidden it from Warwick so far but it was getting harder.

Something at work had him distracted. He hadn't shared what was going on. Most nights he went home with her, she took a shower while he cooked then they ate. After dinner he locked himself in her office, which she had told him he could use. Most of her incidences of pain and weakness happened later at night just before bed. Many nights she didn't even know when he came to bed. She'd sleep 'till morning unless he woke her, making fierce love to her.

Katiya, once she was sure Warwick was in the office, stood and gripped her leg, straightening then limping down the hall. She held the wall as her leg became weak. Barely making it to the bed, she cursed, lying down. She didn't even think of taking the pain pills Lansing had prescribed. She didn't want to get hooked on them. Katiya lay stiffly, willing the pain away.

She didn't know when she'd fallen asleep, but she awoke violently aroused.

Katiya moaned and shifted. She stiffened preparing for the pain in her leg. Thankfully, unlike usual, it didn't come. He slid his hands along her body, setting off need deep within her.

"Katiya." Warwick moaned.

She widened her legs. His fingers rubbed against her slit then he opened her and flicked a finger over her clit. She shivered at the sensation. Warwick played with her then plunged his fingers into her needy pussy. In and out he moved with his fingers. Katiya gripped his shoulders, moaning, rocking against them. He withdrew and his body blanketed her. In one movement of his hips, he filled her.

"Warwick." Katiya slid her hands down and clenched her fingers on his ass.

She pulled him into her. Warwick stroked urgently, his harsh breaths feathering her face. Undulating her hips, she moaned as he took her, demanding all she had to give. Katiya's pulse raced and her heart pounded in time with his taking.

"Come for me." Warwick's decadent whisper filled the air.

Katiya moaned and quivered as she came. Warwick followed her, grunting harshly. He rolled, taking her with him and holding her close. Katiya listened to his racing heart as sleep claimed her once again.

The ringing phone jerked her out of her sleep. Blearily, Katiya reached for it. Pushing her hair out of her face she said, "Hello."

"Kat, sorry. I wanted to catch you before you went to work. I didn't mean to wake you," Sarah said.

Katiya sat up, glancing at the time. It was almost seven. She had overslept. She heard the shower running.

"Umm...that's okay. I need to be up anyway."

"Since I know you've been waiting to find out. I'm not going to beat around the bush. We've figured out what is wrong with your leg," Sarah said.

Katiya heart raced and she tightened her fingers over the phone.

"From what you've told Lasing and myself, you get this weakness and pain at night. With that and the last set of tests, it is not as you feared. The muscles are not deteriorating. They are basically locking up due to not enough exercise and too much sitting. The reason it is bothering you so much more now than before is, basically, that you need to increase the exercises you do for the leg. Lansing is setting up an appointment with a physical therapist for you. And before you protest about the time, the therapist will come to you at The Oasis to work with you. Lansing mentioned the man knew of The Oasis and said the facilities you have there are actually perfect for what you need."

Katiya wasn't sure if she heard her right. "My leg is fine."

"Yes it is. Follow what the therapist says and the pain will get better and the weakness will dissipate. Lansing will go into more details about everything," Sarah said.

"Thank you, Sarah," Katiya said.

"No problem. Take care of your leg. I'll speak with you soon. Bye."

"Bye," Katiya said and hung up.

"Who was that so early?" Warwick asked coming out from the bathroom.

Katiya stood and rushed to him. "My leg is fine. That was Sarah—Arissa's friend from Minnesota. I was so worried when I was in pain, I went to see her. Then the incident at the auto show scared the heck out of me. She and Lansing have been trying to find out what was wrong. I thought it was my muscles deteriorating but come to find out, it is not. I'm fine. Oh, Warwick. I'm fine." She hugged him.

"Good for you." His voice was cold.

Katiya stepped back, frowning. He was fully dressed already for work. His face was aloof and eyes cold.

"Warwick—"

He cut her off. "You knew before your trip something was wrong. And when you came back and collapsed. Yet you said nothing to me."

"I didn't tell anyone. I didn't want you all to worry," she cried.

"No. You didn't want your family to worry. Me, you wanted to keep out. I've been accepting the crumbs you've deemed to give me. Why won't you let me in?" Warwick questioned in a clipped tone.

Katiya heart pounded. "I have—"

He interrupted again. "You have not. I'm not the Sharps, Katiya. Money and supposed social classes don't concern me. I want you. Katiya, Want you to see me as just Warwick the man. Not Warwick, a man with money who could hurt you."

"I haven't been seeing you as that," Katiya defended.

"You have. You've kept me at a distance. Hiding that you were worried about your legs clearly shows that," he said.

"Like you share with me. You haven't once told me what is bothering you about your business," she lashed out.

"Have you asked?" he countered.

"No, bu—"

He overrode her words. "I asked you numerous times about your leg because I care to know. You never once asked about what was going on with me and my business. Never cared to know more than you deemed appropriate to the boundaries you set. Do you even care about me?"

"I do," she whispered.

"You have a strange way of showing it, Katiya." He closed his eyes then opened them.

She gasped at the pain in them.

"I've already barely made it through one loss of a woman I gave my whole heart to. I'm not willing to go through that again with someone who isn't in it with me with their whole heart…their very souls. Can you give me that, Katiya?"

She opened her mouth then closed it. Warwick took a shallow breath then he slipped on what she thought of as 'the cold stranger'. The businessman she had seen when she visited his office stared back at her dispassionately. He turned on his heel and left. Katiya stood rooted to where he had left her. The sound of the front door closing was very final. Her legs gave out. She rocked back and forth. Tears burned her eyes.

"I can't be hurt like that again. If I give my heart to him he will rip out my soul. I can't," she rationalised.

She let the silence surround her.

"Why couldn't you say the words to him? You lost him. He already has all that I am. Oh God, I've lost him. Oh God. Noooo..." Her voice echoed in the silent room.

Hugging herself, she lowered her head, weeping at her loss.

Chapter Seven

Warwick held the steering wheel in a death grip. Mechanically he drove home. Once there, he got out, moving stiffly to his front door and with a steady hand he opened it and stepped inside. Closing it with a thud he started to shake then dropped to his knees, shifting and pressing his back against the door. Resting his head against the wood, his eyes burned.

"Stupid, stupid. You let yourself care too much again." He pounded his head back on the door in time with each word.

He braced his elbows on his raised knees and gripped his hair. His heart was ripped out again. He, better than most, knew one could survive without. It would not be living but he could survive. First he had to rebuild the walls around him. The ones that he had opened up to Katiya.

Why are you giving up so easy?

He laughed bitterly. Easy? Nothing between them had been easy. Yes, they were so compatible sexually, but never once did she let it get emotional. He had felt it after their first date, but done nothing, thinking she would come to trust him eventually. All the times together when he had thought they had been getting close, she'd became shuttered, trying to distance herself from him. There was only so much he could give. Katiya had made her choice. Now he had to accept it and find a way to move on. He sat in the silence, not moving. After some time he stood. He couldn't deal with this here.

He moved purposefully through the house and to his bedroom. Quickly he packed a duffel and changed his clothing. Heading out, he bypassed his classic cars and went to his black Avalanche. Once he was on his way he pressed the Bluetooth. As it rang he took a breath, drawing up the business persona.

"Hey, Warwick. You're late. Drag yourself away from Katiya and get to work, slacker," Calix said.

He heard the work going on around Calix, which meant he was on the speakerphone.

"Going out of town for a few," he said.

"What? Now that we've gotten all the paperwork completed and have the go-ahead, you're going out of town? We're swamped with the new project."

"You can handle it... I need some time." Warwick hoped he didn't hear the pain in his voice.

It was harder than he'd thought to keep it bottled, especially with Calix, who knew him so well.

"Are you okay, Warwick?" Calix's tone was sharp.

"I'm fine, just a little burnt. Been burning the candle on both ends." He forced a chuckle.

"You sound off," Calix said suspiciously.

"I'm—"

"Calix, we need you now," a voice said from Calix's end of the call.

"I'm coming... Gotta go."

"I'm turning off my cell. I'll check my messages daily so if any problems, leave me a message," Warwick said.

"Okay. Where are you going and for how long?" Calix sounded distracted.

He didn't want to tell him but knew that in case of an emergency, either on his side or Calix's, someone should know where he was. At least with Calix busy he wouldn't come looking for him.

"To the cabin. Maybe two weeks. If longer I'll let you know," he said.

"Okay. I can't believe you got Katiya to go away from the centre for two weeks," Calix commented.

Pain filled him. The sounds over the phone continued.

"Warwick?" Calix was back to sounding suspicious.

He cursed himself for not saying anything.

"Calix," the voice called again.

"Christ, I'm coming. Gotta go. Give Katiya a kiss for me." Calix hung up.

Warwick disconnected. He was grateful for the interruption. He hadn't thought he would be able to form the lie. Calix would find out soon enough that he was alone. He focused on driving.

In a little over three hours he spotted the beauty that was Kanderus Canyon. It was high in the Bernus Mountains, which was more towards the outskirts of McKingley. Various homes spotted throughout the mountain. Some people lived there all the time and others, like himself, used the mountains as a getaway place. Warwick didn't turn into the lane that lead to his usual getaway. Instead, he continued on another twenty minutes before he made the tight turn into the smaller area of Kellita Peak.

It had been years since he'd felt the need to come here. He drove down the small road and when the cabin came into view, memories of the last time he was here filled him. He'd bought this place after his wife had died. Calix had thought he was crazy. It'd been rundown and overrun. He'd known what he wanted it for—to purge the pain. He'd rebuilt every piece of the cabin by himself. The manual labour had soothed him. Once it was done, the valley around his little cabin had given him space and time he needed to mourn. Parking in front of the porch, he then got out, grabbing his bag. He threw it on the porch, barely breaking stride.

Pushing his hands in the pockets of his light jacket, he strode around the house and to the pond. It was the main reason he had bought the place. There was something about sitting next to the pond—which he had dubbed Reflective—that made his thoughts clearer. His other cabin, which was larger, had a lake. That one he used at happier times. This place was more for reflection. He sat on the bank with his hands behind him. The feeling of not being alone came to him. Warwick didn't look up—he already knew it was his neighbour and friend.

"Haven't seen you come here in a few years. Hoped I wouldn't again," Hawk Blackthorn said in his deep timbre.

"Needed it."

Hawk was silent then spoke again, "You could have called me as you usually do."

Hawk was the one who he could speak to without filters. He'd been there when he'd first moved in to the cabin. Hawk, who at the time had been a stranger, had just come to see the crazy man who had bought the cabin next to his. Warwick hadn't known what to make of him. There were a few miles between their places, no matter if you took the easy or hard way. Hawk had come every day and watched him almost work himself to death. He was the one who had forced him to eat in order to keep going. Had thrown him into the pond a few times to bring him to his senses. The one thing he'd appreciated and still did about Hawk was that he didn't ask questions. The silence. He didn't even wonder how Hawk had known he was here. Hawk seemed to have an innate sense that he was here when he arrived.

Over the years, these trips had become rarer and rarer. Hawk even seemed to sense when he needed to talk and had called him when he needed it most. For Hawk, who wasn't much for talking and chatter, it said a lot about their friendship. Warwick did the same for Hawk. They seemed to sense things about each other.

"I'll go get you some groceries. You need to eat." Hawk stood.

He didn't reply. Hawk left as silently as he had come. Warwick studied the pond, letting the stillness seep into him. The bright sun seemed to mock his pain. A harsh sound bubbled out of his throat. Tears flowed down his face and he shook. Staring at the pond, he let the mourning for what was not to be, begin.

* * * *

"Katiya, how was you and Warwick's trip?" Calix asked.

What trip? Katiya faced Calix as he strode towards her.

"I thought Warwick said you all were staying for a few more weeks. Must have been mistaken. The cabin is beautiful, isn't it?" Calix stopped in front of her.

Katiya opened her mouth to respond.

"Hold on a sec. I need to speak with someone." Calix strode past her.

Katiya watched his progress. Even from where she stood, she saw Rhianna stiffen then turn and go around the corner. Calix followed her.

Katiya frowned. When she hadn't seen Calix for two weeks, she'd assumed Warwick had mentioned what had happened between them. Others from Taylor Bytes still came to help out with the classes, but not Calix, as he had been prone to do. It seemed as if Warwick hadn't told Calix and he was at some cabin.

Where is this cabin?

Katiya continued to her office. So far she'd been able to avoid direct questions about Warwick. She'd just let everyone draw the assumption that he was busy at work. Entering her office, Katiya paused, staring at the man who leaned against the wall just inside the door.

"You look really good for someone who is dead."

"What are you doing in my office?" Katiya heart pounded and she backed up.

"Watching a dead woman walk. At least that's what it seems like with Warwick at the cabin. I thought better of you, Katiya Wright." The man's tone was chastising.

Katiya stiffened. "Who the hell are you?"

"And to think I was thinking of coming down off my ridge to your wedding." The stranger scowled at her.

Katiya edged towards the door, keeping an eye on what was obviously an unhinged person. The man was even bigger and taller than Warwick. From his sun-kissed skin along with his sharply defined cheeks, narrow nose and mouth capped off by his inky black braided hair, she knew he was Native American. An image tickled at the back of her memory. Katiya stopped moving.

"The man from the picture in Warwick's house. You're his friend, Hawk," Katiya said.

"He has a picture of me? I'll have to take care of that." Hawk scowled.

"What are you doing here?" Katiya demanded.

"Something I never do. Interfering. Do you want Warwick?" Hawk demanded.

Very much. She wouldn't say that to him, though. Instead she said, "Why is it your business?"

"It's not. But you have five minutes once I find Calix to say 'hi' to decide. Then I'm out of here. I'll take you to him. But if you decide whatever stupidly came between you is more important, then stay here. You can try to get back with him when he comes back but by then he'll be stubborn and convinced he is better off without you."

Katiya flinched at his words. Hawk raked her with a dispassionate look then strolled around her and out her office door. Katiya wrapped her arms around herself. A second later she ran to her desk and grabbed her bag. She flew out her office then slowed as she spotted Hawk a little ways away talking with Calix. She moved towards them at a more dignified pace.

"Did you come back with Warwick and Katiya? I'm shocked Warwick got you off the ridge and into town. Aren't you under a deadline?" Calix asked.

"God, you always talk too much. Silence is a good thing." Hawk grunted.

"You need to come off the ridge and be more sociable," Calix retorted.

Hawk didn't respond. He glanced at Katiya then nodded, walking away. She went to follow him. Calix touched her arm stilling her.

"What is going on?" Calix looked sombre.

It was startling—she'd never seen him anyway but joking.

"Thirty seconds," Hawk rumbled in his deep voice.

Katiya glared at Hawk as he continued on, not breaking stride.

"I've got to go." Katiya pulled away.

She hurried behind Hawk as he went out the side door. Hawk paused by a forest green F-450 King Ranch with a crew cab.

"Before we leave you have to agree to my rule."

"What rule?" Katiya gritted out.

"Golden Rule. No talking."

She snorted. "That's not going to be a problem since right now I don't even want to go anywhere with you. I don't know why Warwick is even friends with you. You r—"

Hawk cut her off. "You don't need to go anywhere with me. Suit yourself."

He walked to the driver's side and got in then started the truck with a roar of the engine. Katiya stood, shocked he was leaving. She went to the door, trying the handle and found it locked, so she pounded on the window. Hawk didn't spare her a glance but the locks clicked. Katiya climbed into the truck, putting her bag on the seat next to her. She glanced out the window and as Hawk drove she studied the passing landscape.

Be calm, Katiya. He is taking you to Warwick.

Nervousness filled Katiya at the thought of seeing him. She had no clue what she would say.

What happens if he refuses you?

She rubbed over her heart at the thought then Katiya pushed the idea away. In the over four-hour drive she didn't say a word. When they bypassed the Bernus Mountains, she had an idea of where they were going. A few minutes later, the smaller area of Kellita Peak came into view. She was familiar with the area because her brother Leo had a cabin up there. Leo used it often when he could get time off and she'd been there with him once or twice. The area was a little too wild and remote for her tastes. Hawk made a turn into a bumpy access road. In a few more minutes, they parked in front of a small cabin.

She exited the vehicle and stood in front of it. Hawk came and stood next to her.

"I know this area."

"And you are talking. No talking."

"We're not in the truck," Katiya pointed out.

"Semantics." Hawk walked away from the cabin.

Katiya followed. The area was a little bumpy. Hawk slowed and put his hand under hers leading her. Katiya was startled at his gesture.

"No use you breaking your neck after I brought you here. You need better shoes. Stop." He growled.

Katiya did. She gasped as he bent and picked up her foot. She wobbled. He held her steady and plucked off her shoe then the other before she realised it. Hawk stood in an effortless motion and pitched her shoes into the trees. Katiya gaped then poked his chest with her finger.

"Hey, those were my favourite sandals."

"Useless pieces of crap," Hawk grunted.

He lifted her in his arms. Unconsciously she gripped him. Then she stiffened and fought to get away.

"If you drop, I'm leaving your ass on the ground," Hawk warned.

"Put me down."

"You can't walk on the ground in your bare feet."

"I wouldn't be if you hadn't thrown away my shoes." She bared her teeth.

"Hush. No talking." Hawk carried her.

Katiya held in her frustration. He set her down, turning her to face the water. A man sat staring out at the pond.

"Warwick." Katiya took a step forward.

He stood abruptly, turning to her. "What are you doing here?"

"Hawk brought me," she stated.

His face was so cold. Warwick glanced over her shoulder then back at her.

"He can take you back." Warwick strode past her.

Katiya flinched. She hugged herself, staring at the pond but not really seeing it. Her eyes narrowed and she stiffened.

"Hell no." She turned, setting off after him.

She stumbled on the uneven ground.

Hawk caught her and lifted her up against his large chest.

"Son of a bitch. This is what you get for doing something good. Carting people around," Hawk grumbled.

"Tha—"

"Shut the hell up," Hawk said.

Katiya didn't say anything else as Hawk carried her back to the cabin. He stomped up the stairs and put her down on the porch then turned to leave.

"Thank you, Hawk," Katiya said.

He snorted. "Please don't mention it."

Katiya stared at the closed door of the cabin.

"You will do, Katiya. If you get married, I will come to town for your wedding."

Katiya glanced at him, surprised he was still there. "Okay," she said cautiously.

"Go along that path through those trees to get to my place if he doesn't come around. It is an easier way for your leg." He got in his truck and left.

Katiya stiffened her shoulders, turned and knocked on the door. It was wrenched open.

"You better follow Hawk," Warwick said coldly.

"I'm not going anywhere. Don't pull this cold crap on me, acting all sub-human. I won't be with a man like that. I want my Warwick back." Katiya pushed at his chest with each word.

Warwick stepped back into the cabin. She followed him, ranting.

"Yes, I was stupid, but you're being a bigger ass than I was. Acting all weird and shit. Fuck that. You're mine and I'm not letting you go, damn it. I won't let you go." Katiya stopped, breathing hard, her palm flat on his chest.

He gripped her wrists. "Say the words, Katiya." Warwick's voice was intense.

Katiya raised her head, locking eyes with indigo. "I love you, Warwick. Love you with my heart and soul. I want you in my life now and forever."

She disentangled herself from him then stepped back. Katiya went down on one knee.

"Marry me, Warwick Taylor. Be my husband, partner and, above all, my solace when I need." Katiya blinked, tears filling her eyes.

Warwick went on his knees before her, cupping her cheeks. "I love you, Katiya. So very much. I will always be there for you. Use my shoulders to offer you any comfort you need." His voice trembled. "And I know I have the same in you. I love you, Katiya Wright, and will gladly marry you."

He pulled her face to his, kissing her, and her lids closed over her eyes. Her tears mingled with their kiss as Warwick embraced her. Shivering, she held him close while Warwick slowly released her lips. Her lids fluttered open and she spied his devilish indigo gaze.

"Where is my ring?"

"What?" Katiya said.

"My ring. When you ask a man to marry you, there should be a ring."

"I didn't come with one. But promise to get you one when we get back to town." Katiya laughed.

"Good. But make it special. This is the first time someone asked me to marry them." Warwick winked.

"And the last since we're going to be together forever," Katiya stated.

"That doesn't sound like long enough." Warwick said.

She rested against him, grateful to be back in his arms.

"We need to get a move on so we can go to the other cabin," Warwick encouraged.

"Why?" Katiya protested. "We can stay here."

"This is where I come to deal with bad things, and that is not what we have." Warwick said quietly.

Katiya studied him then suggested, "Let's make some good memories here. Get rid of the bad."

Warwick was silent then he nodded. "Okay."

"I can't wait to marry you. Plan our wedding," Katiya said.

"I'm planning the wedding. You asked me. I'm going to be part of everything. It'll take me at least two years to plan a good one."

"You can't be serious. You're planning the wedding? Two years? Why do we have to wait so long?" Katiya looked at him in disbelief.

"I want everything to be right. And I, as the askee, get to plan, and the asker gets to help. I'll accept your help," Warwick said.

"Ummm...usually the bride, which would be me, gets to plan a wedding?"

"We'll buck tradition. Hmmm...I need to find out about fabrics. And the food. Venues."

Katiya listened in horror as he went on and on about the wedding.

"What does Hawk do for a living?" she asked to distract him.

"Oh. He kills people. And is paid every well to do it," Warwick said cheerfully.

"What? I took a four hour drive with a murderer?" Katiya got chills.

Warwick laughed then tweaked her nose. "No. He's a writer. He writes murder mysteries."

"Oh. Would I have read him?"

"I've seen you and your friends going ga-ga over his books."

"Really. Who is he?" she asked suspiciously.

"HG Black."

Katiya gawked. It was their favourite author. She smacked Warwick in the chest.

"You just said he killed people to tease me."

"Yep." His eyes twinkled.

"I'm glad he isn't a criminal since he'll be coming to the wedding."

"He is?"

"He said he would if we got married."

"I'll be... He hates crowds. He must like you."

"That's his way of liking? I'd hate to see what he does when he hates someone. After meeting him, I don't ever want to hear any more comments about Iona."

"Hawk is a good man," Warwick insisted.

"Hmmm...maybe I should introduce him to Iona. She loves his books and maybe they can find other things in common." Katiya wiggled her eyebrows.

"I wouldn't wish Iona on anyone. Hawk likes quiet and Iona is talkative. Promise me you won't match-make. Don't do it," he warned.

Katiya didn't respond, instead running her hand inside his open collar against his skin. Warwick groaned. She shifted on his lap, straddling him.

"Were you teasing about the planning of the wedding too?" she asked hopefully.

"That too, but I will take part in everything. I want to experience it all with you. And for our lives together," Warwick said huskily.

"Me too. You're the right man for me. The one I needed. Now let's make some memories."

"Damn right I'm the right man for you. Memories coming up." Warwick shifted, lowering her against the floor, blanketing her body.

Moaning, Katiya gripped his ass, pulling him against her. Warwick was not only the right man, he was the only one she needed. He was the Wright move to make.

THE BEST THING YET

Dedication

To the readers who have supported me and embraced this series. Thanks very much. To my mom whose guidance has made me who I am. To my big sis who is my inspiration.
— *McKenna Jeffries*

Thanks to all the readers, y'all's support is so appreciated. To my husband, who never fails to encourage me, and to those who serve this country, risking their lives for all of us!
— *Aliyah Burke*

Chapter One

Chicago

Arissa Wright peeled off her bloody gloves and gown, barely slowing to throw them in the trash. With a practiced move, she sidestepped a nurse and pushed through the swinging door. Her smile was tight and strained as she headed to the doctors' lounge. It was a sucky day. *No, it's a shitty day!*

As the door shut behind her, a sigh of combined relief and frustration poured from her lips. She rotated her shoulders trying to work out the kinks. Heading for the well-worn couch, she stopped at her locker for her coat and purse then Arissa sat down with a groan. It had been a day for losses.

She'd lost her boyfriend. Not her fault, he'd claimed he wanted someone who was more feminine. She'd lost her car. Again, not her fault. That had been boosted and the cops were pretty sure she wouldn't get it back. And just now, she'd lost her patient. While she blamed herself for that as well, deep down, Arissa knew it wasn't her fault.

"You okay?"

Arissa looked up to see her good friend and co-worker, Jackson Carlyle, looking down at her. His blue eyes were filled with concern.

"Just one of those days."

"I know how that goes. But at least you're leaving to go on vacation now." Jackson arched an eyebrow. "Right, Arissa?"

She bit her lower lip and leant back against the couch. "I don't know."

"Don't tell me you aren't going. You've been looking forward to this for the longest time. Besides, it's the Caribbean. How can you not go and get away from all this cold and snow?"

Arissa smiled at him. He was right—she had been looking forward to this for a long time. And even though Deyon, a friend from her hometown of McKingley, New Mexico, and Sarah, her good friend from college, had both had to back out at the last moment, it was no reason for her not to go. A cruise could just be what the doctor ordered.

"I'm going, I'm going," she said with a smile. "It would be nice to see some sunshine and be able to inhale without being worried my lungs will freeze."

"I'm sure you'll have a wonderful time. Now go on, get outta here before anything else comes in." He pulled her to her feet, helped her into her thick coat then pushed her in the direction of the door.

"Thanks, Jackson," she murmured as she readjusted her purse.

"Anytime, sweets."

He squeezed her shoulder as they left the room together. Arissa watched him walk away, his green scrubs flattering his muscular body as he replaced the stethoscope around his neck. Jackson never looked back. Not that she'd expected him to.

Zipping up her coat, Arissa moved towards the sliding doors then stepped out into the frigid night. A chill racked her body as she headed for the 'L'. This was going to be a cold wait. Glancing up, she stepped to the side as an ambulance with flashing lights pulled into the entrance.

She hesitated for a moment as co-workers ran out to meet it. Times like this she was reluctant to leave, but they were just as well trained as she was. Arissa Wright loved her job as an ER doctor. She took another careful breath before she turned away and plodded through the slush and cold to get to the platform and wait for her ride home. There was packing to do and a cruise to get ready for.

* * * *

Somewhere in the Caribbean

Arissa smiled as she lounged on a padded chaise. In one hand she held an iced tea with lemon and in the other was a romance book, *Rarities Incorporated*, a compilation of three stories in one. And an awesome read. *This is the life.* A fourteen day cruise was the best thing she could have taken. Even though this was only day two, Arissa found herself totally relaxed.

A shadow fell over her and she glanced up. What met her stare made her heart leap up into her throat. *Damnation, he's fine.* The man before her was in incredible shape. She scanned up his form as her doctor's brain categorised what she saw.

Six feet two inches of well-muscled, Caucasian male. He had tanned skin, blue-grey eyes, an amazing white smile and blondish-brown hair cropped close to his head. His dark blue shirt hugged his chest in a way that made her envision herself removing it. The sleeves were tight against his upper arms like they struggled to contain the muscles. Gaze travelling lower, she took in the white shorts and the strong legs emerging from them.

And again, damn!

Putting her book down upon her upper thigh, she arched an eyebrow. "Can I help you?" Arissa fought back the urge to shift on the cushion as his look seared her.

He nodded towards the seat beside her before asking, "Is that seat taken?"

She followed his stare. "Nope. Help yourself."

"Thanks." His voice was deep and sensual, dragging along her skin almost like he was touching her. Her belly clenched and she smiled as she picked up her book and stared down at the words on the page.

"Deiter Schneider," he said in a low tone.

Can I say German? Turning her head to the right, Arissa found him watching her. One side of his bow-shaped mouth was tipped slightly up. Licking her lips, she placed her bookmark between the pages and shut it before setting it beside her.

"Arissa Wright."

He held out his hand and when she placed hers in it, instead of shaking it, he brought it to his lips and pressed a kiss upon the back of it. "A pleasure to meet you, Arissa Wright."

She shuddered at the intimate timbre of his voice. It was a tone that made her think of long nights and endless sexual exploits.

Despite having only recently broken up, Arissa had not been intimate with her ex for a long while. Their hours had been polar opposites and when they had been off at the same time, she'd been exhausted. Her hospital had lost three doctors over the past four months so longer hours had been implemented. Part of her felt bad for leaving them even shorter staffed, but honestly, with the warm sun beating down on her and this gorgeous man beside her, dwelling on what was behind in Chicago faded quickly.

"What brings you here?" he asked, still holding her gaze.

"Some friends and I had this planned for a while."

He frowned slightly. "Guy type friends or a girl types?"

"The same persuasion as myself." The grin returned and she found herself chuckling slightly.

"So," he drawled, "where are they?"

"Both freezing their ass off." Drawing the straw back to settle between her lips Arissa took a healthy swallow of the rapidly dwindling liquid refreshment.

"So they didn't come with you? Who would turn this down to freeze their asses off?" He winked before stretching out in the chair and sliding his sunglasses over his eyes.

"Beats me," she responded as she faced forward again.

Silence drifted between them as the noise from the ship flowed around them. Arissa didn't mind, this man didn't make her feel uncomfortable, well, not in a scary sort of way. Just in an increasingly sexual one. She lowered her lids as the warm tropical air flowed over her. She barely moved when her glass was taken from her hand, and a slight sound told her it had been placed on the small table.

"Can I get you a drink, sir?" a soft voice questioned.

"Yes, please. And another tea for the lady, please. In fact, make it two teas. Unsweetened and with lemon."

Arissa fought back her smile. He must have tasted her drink to know it was unsweetened. Cracking her eyes, she watched as the woman walked away. With a sigh and a small wiggle, she settled back into her comfortable position and focused on relaxing. A deep breath brought the smell of the sea to her nose, but along with it came something else. Something masculine and enticing. Something that made her shiver despite the warmth of the day. Turning her head, Arissa peered through lowered lids to stare at the man beside her. As if he knew she was checking him out, he tilted his head and even though he wore sunglasses, she felt his eyes bore into her.

Deiter unhurriedly ran his gaze along the languid form of the woman beside him. Arissa Wright. She had a body to die for, curves that made him want to get down on his knees and give thanks to the Almighty. Her skin was dark brown and flawless, and her pixie-style haircut was reddish-gold in colour. When he'd stared into her light brown eyes, they'd been filled with intelligence and more than a smattering of humour. And yet, beneath that there lingered the tell-tale signs of one who'd seen too much.

He had been on his way to a pool when his gaze had landed upon her. Deiter had almost tripped over his feet. Never had a mere glance struck him more than it had when he'd first seen her. Her peach tank top complemented her sheer sarong, which had patterns of blue and white swirls. The way her dark smooth legs peeked out made his body shift into overdrive. A quick glance at her feet showed him her nails dressed by a French manicure, which matched her fingernails.

Her voice was something old singers had — velvety and slightly smoky. It grabbed him down low and stroked all the way up, setting him aflame. Even when his body had been semi under control, he hadn't wanted to move on. There were lots of attractive women on this ship but none had turned his head until now. Every inch of her was luscious. He wanted to spirit her away to a secluded area and peel away what little clothes she wore and…

Deiter looked away from Arissa to see the cocktail server had returned with their drinks.

"Thank you," he said with a slight smile as she placed them down and removed Arissa's nearly empty glass.

"You're welcome." Without any further comment, she slipped away.

He put his attention back on Arissa. Long curved eyelashes rested against satiny smooth skin. At least, it appeared like satin to him. Deiter longed to reach out and trace his finger along her full lips. Then taste them, over and over again. Another wave of longing flowed through him.

Sitting up, he reached for his drink and took a sip. A grimace crossed his face. It had tasted much better when he'd drunk it from her glass.

"Why'd you order tea if you don't like it?" Her question reached him.

Deiter was struck by the amusement in her eyes. He turned his body towards her and leant back again, smiling.

"Yours tasted different. Better."

She grinned up at him as stirred the drink with her straw. "You didn't squeeze the lemon."

His eyebrow arched. "Excuse me?"

Her smile grew as she shook her head in amusement and pointed a finger at the tall glass. "The lemon. I squeeze mine into the tea and mix it up."

Deiter did as she'd recommended and the next taste was more similar to the way hers had tasted. "Oh, way better. Thank you."

"No prob."

His cock jerked in his jeans as her mouth curled around the red straw. *Damn. If I could just feel those lips curled around my...* Abruptly he stopped that thought. No need to behave like a caveman. This trip was *not* about meaningless sex. *Are you sure?* His libido taunted. *Who said it would be meaningless with her? Have you looked at her? I mean...hello!* Grinding his back teeth, Deiter strove for control.

"Tell me about you, Arissa. From where do you hail and what do you do?"

Arissa moved the drink away from her overly tempting mouth just as a beeping noise reached him. She grabbed her bag and glanced at the watch attached to the wide strap.

"I'd love to but I have a massage scheduled." She slipped on her sandals and put her book in the bag. "I'm sorry."

When she stood, he bit back a groan of approval. *God damn!* Deiter stood as well, reaching out to stop her briefly.

"Dinner?"

He observed the gamut of emotions flashing over her face.

"What time do you eat?"

"Name the time and place," he offered.

She did and Deiter stood still for a moment after she walked away, just staring at her retreating form.

When he could no longer see her, he left the deck and went to a gym on the ship. A good workout would help pass the time and burn off some of the extra energy Arissa had created within him. After his workout at the gym, his body was sore as he let himself into his room to shower and change, but sore in a good way.

The dark beauty of Arissa Wright was with him as he stood under the pounding spray of the showerhead. Fisting his erection, he debated on finishing up with only cold water. Once, twice he pumped his hand before he swore. *Verdammt!* He wanted relief but damn it all, he wanted it *with* Arissa, not by his own hand. Resting his head on the wall, he reached out and turned the hot water knob, shutting it off. A low hiss escaped as cold pellets pounded onto his skin.

Deiter finished quickly and dried off before dressing for his date. With a whistle on his lips and a spring in his step, he headed towards his destination. While he was pleased with her dinner choice, part of him wished she'd suggested a more formal atmosphere.

It was a thought that quickly vanished as his searching gaze found her. All earlier notions of remaining in control disappeared like water in the desert. Arissa's open-backed silver shirt accentuated her breasts and was combined with low rise jeans. She wore heels, he knew for she was taller than she had been earlier. Deiter tried to calm himself, not wanting his blood to rush to one area.

His heart stuttered when her light brown gaze landed upon him and a smile graced her features.

"Evening," she said easily when he stopped beside her.

A low whistle escaped him as he allowed his eyes to move blatantly over her. "Good evening. You look...amazing," he told her as he leaned in and pressed a kiss to her cheek.

Her gaze drifted to the ground briefly before she met his eyes again. "Thank you. Ready to eat?"

Something primal roared to life inside him. "More than you could know. Let's go."

She began walking towards a table. For a brief second he admired her view again, but when he noticed other men doing the same thing, he stepped up beside her and settled his hand on the small of her back. Spikes of power raced through him at the feel of her warm skin against his palm. When he held her chair for her, Deiter couldn't help but allow himself to inhale deeply. She smelt crisp and clean, nothing but her own natural scent. And he loved it.

Sitting across from her he watched as she fixed her tea. No sweetener, just lemon. He had ordered a shake to go with his burger and fries. While they waited for their food to arrive, he waited for her to stop playing with her tea and look at him.

"Now, tell me about you, Arissa Wright."

She continued to stir her tea but she nodded. "I live in Chicago, have for"—she frowned and a cute furrow appeared between her eyebrows—"for nine years now. Damn, didn't realise it had been that long. Yes, for nine years."

He smiled. "What do you do in Chicago?"

"I work in an emergency room."

That was impressive. He stared at her for a moment then one side of his mouth lifted. "So this is a well-deserved vacation."

"Oh yeah. Long overdue." She smiled as their waiter placed their food down. "Thank you," she said, prior to returning her attention to him. "And you? What do you do?"

"I'm a translator. Work for the government mostly, but on occasion I teach at colleges or give guest lectures."

"Interesting. What language?"

"German."

"Was it hard to learn?"

"No. I grew up speaking German. And also English, but mostly German."

"Oh, I see."

"My mother is a linguist so it was understood we would speak the language of our home country as well as the one we now lived in."

"So you weren't born in America?"

"Nope. Düsseldorf. But we moved here when I was young and Mom insisted I learn English as well."

He watched her as she ate some fries, even that was done sensually. Dinner was light-hearted and fun. Afterwards, they took a stroll along one of the decks, allowing the night air to cool the heat growing between them. They didn't hold hands, just kept pace with one another, the conversation still flowing easily between them.

Deiter escorted her to her door. She had a suite on an upper deck. After unlocking it, he placed his hands on either side of her head and stared deep into her brown eyes. It may have seemed too soon to some but in that instant, Deiter knew he was gazing into the eyes of his soul mate. There was no explanation, just a gut feeling. He didn't hear any angels sing. Hell, he hadn't even kissed her yet. But still, just like he understood in order to survive he had to take his next breath, he knew.

Those guileless eyes stared back at him. Lowering his head, he skimmed his thumb along her cheek. Heat flared up in her stare and she blinked once before she licked her lips.

"Thank you for dinner, Deiter."

"My pleasure, Arissa. Can I see you tomorrow?"

One side of her mouth curved up. "I'd like that. Meet for breakfast?"

I'd rather share it in the room with you, but I'll take what I can get. "I'll be here nice and early."

"Good night."

Leaning in, Deiter brushed his lips against her face and allowed himself a final inhalation of her clean scent. "Until the morning." With his fingers, he touched her nose followed by her lips, then span around and strode off before he carried her inside the room and had his way with her.

Chapter Two

Arissa smiled and raised her glass in a silent toast to the man who winked at her from the pool. A low moan rose in her throat as he lifted himself out of the water and moved towards her. The Caribbean sun kissed his skin and the water droplets ran down his body in ways she envied. Not an ounce of fat sat upon him, it was all hardened muscle and mouth-watering physique.

For the past week, all waking moments had been in the company of Deiter Schneider. A wonderful week. Days lounging in the sun and evenings had been spent watching the sunset over the water. Then they had tended to curl up on a chaise together and share kisses, which as the days had passed, had become more and more intense. She'd not slept with him but in her dreams she'd done that and more. Arissa craved him in ways she'd never wanted her ex. Unfortunately, Deiter was a gentleman. Well, not unfortunately, but sometimes a woman wanted more, didn't want a man who kissed her goodnight at the door and left her there.

"Sure you're not coming in the water?" he questioned as he reached her side and grabbed a towel off the lounge beside her.

Holding up her book, Arissa shook her head. "Oh no. I'm good here. Reading, you know, it's good to do."

Towelling off, Deiter leant down and kissed her lightly. "Another romance. Learning anything?" He rose up and ran the terry cloth down his powerful arms.

Skimming her gaze up his chest to his eyes, she smirked. "Oh...the things this book is teaching me. The *Kama Sutra* has nothing on it. This author knows how to write some *steamy* scenes."

His nostrils flared and a muscle ticked in his jaw. A single droplet of water ran down his temple as he lowered his face back to hers. His eyes were dark and swirled with barely constrained desire. "You are one hell of a temptress, Arissa Wright. Teasing me like this. Perhaps there should be a test, I am a teacher after all." He winked and that single action sent shivers of longing through her.

"I suppose I could go for a lesson" — she paused — "or two."

"Be careful I don't carry you off right now." Promise laced his tone.

Arissa wrinkled her nose. "Sorry. Time for my Tae-Bo class." She stood, allowing her body to slide along his wet one. "Enjoy the rest of your swim. See you later." Lifting her bag, she walked away with an added swish to her hips, knowing full well he was watching.

* * * *

As she walked from the gym to her suite, there was a smile on her face. She felt good and from all indications, tonight would be the night she got to see the part of Deiter she hadn't been allowed to see yet. Moisture flooded her pussy at the thought of having the chance to experience the tall, strong German.

"Man," she muttered as she rounded the corner. "I'm bad off."

"Anything I can help with?" Someone with a deep voice questioned.

Jerking her head up in surprise, a gasp escaped her as the image of the man she'd just been thinking about filled her sight. Deiter Schneider. He stood there, leaning against the door to her room, looking more gorgeous than sin. Everyone said that Lucifer had been the most attractive of angels before he had fallen, and she'd bet anything that Deiter could give him a run for his money.

His legs were hooked at the ankle allowing his jeans to pull tight against his rock-hard thighs. Deiter wore a dark blue sleeveless T-shirt and his well-defined arms were also crossed. She licked her lips and swallowed, trying to get moisture into her extra-dry mouth. His blue-grey eyes were full of mischief and longing as he held her gaze.

"Arissa?"

"It's not time for supper yet, is it?" she asked reaching for her key card and swiping it. The door unlocked but still Deiter didn't move, except to place his hand on the handle and keep it cracked open. With no response forthcoming, she glanced up at him only to find his gaze had lost all joviality and now simmered with heat.

"Invite me in," he murmured.

She slid past him and, once in her room, rested her head against the edge of the door and held his stare. Slowly and with extreme attention to detail Arissa scanned him from the floor up. He still waited for her, his eyes straightforwardly direct. And molten hot.

"Come in?" she questioned on a soft breath.

His gaze dropped and did a slow perusal of her own form before he stepped towards her. Arissa held her ground as he closed the distance between them, squeezing past the door. Without taking his eyes off her, Deiter pushed the door shut with his foot as he cupped the side of her face. A shudder overtook her as he placed his other hand on her skin before lowering his face to hers.

A moan slipped out as his lips covered hers. Arissa dropped her bag and latched onto his arms, digging her fingers into his skin. Deiter teased the outline of her mouth with his tongue. Gently he traced her lips, prior to sliding along the seam, seeking entrance. She opened beneath his questing tongue.

Flames erupted deep within her belly as he delved into her mouth. Stroking, sliding and coaxing her tongue out to play, Deiter explored her. The taste of him, which was already embedded in her mind, flared to life as his leisurely search continued. Her toes began to curl against the flat of her sandals. She whimpered as his calloused touch moved down her neck, over her shoulders, and across the plane of her back where his hands drew her in closer.

Arissa wanted to scream in frustration as his kiss ended. He moved back so he could stare into her eyes.

"Make sure this is what you want, Arissa. I'm not going to want to stop if we take it much further."

Dropping her hands from his arms, Arissa then settled them upon his hips only to pull him in closer.

She bit her lower lip as the ridge of his erection brushed against her. Flexing against him, she smiled at the groan which slid past his lips.

"This is what I want, Deiter. So long as you have protection."

He leaned in close again. "I do. After meeting you, I purchased some." He shrugged. "I was hopeful and ever since the day I met you on the deck, all I think about is you and the way you feel in my arms. The scent and silkiness of your skin and the press of your lips against mine."

Her belly clenched with longing and she rubbed against him. "Please, Deiter. Make the ache go away."

He swept her up in his arms. "That could take a lifetime."

She closed her eyes and enjoyed the tight comforting feel of his arms around her as he escorted her to the queen-sized bed. When he laid her across the mattress she lifted her lids. His face was inches from hers and he kissed her again. Heat spiralled up from the base of her spine and spread throughout her body.

No words passed between them as he undressed her with care. Only when she lay naked before him did he speak.

"Holy shit, you're beautiful," he muttered on a low groan.

She felt it. His gaze branded her as it moved up and down her body. Arissa mewled in the back of her throat as he lowered his head to one breast and drew the nipple into the warmth of his mouth. Her back arched, pressing him closer. Shots of electricity rocketed through her as he suckled on her, his teeth and tongue tormenting the turgid peak until she thrashed upon the bed. He moved to the other one and gave it the same treatment, showing her no quarter.

Arissa shivered as a need for completion poured over her. Writhing on the bed, she held the back of his head tighter against her. "Please," she murmured. "Deiter, please." She tugged at the neck of his shirt with her free hand.

He understood and it didn't take long before he stood before her naked. She licked her lips in want as her focus zeroed in on his groin. His large, thick erection jutted out from a nest of brown hair, a drop of pre-cum on the mushroom head. Her pussy clenched as her breathing increased. She longed to taste him, pull him into her mouth like he was a sucker and enjoy everything he had to offer. A ripping sound dragged her attention away from his cock to his hands, where he was removing a condom from its wrapper.

"Let me," she said.

He handed her the latex. A low hiss escaped him as she wrapped one hand around him. Shoving down the urge to taste him, she swiped her thumb over the tip, smearing the pre-cum, then unfurled the condom down the length. Then she dragged her hands up his chest, nails scoring the skin before she latched her hands behind his neck and pulled him close enough to kiss.

The carefulness turned to urgent need as he swept through her mouth. He grunted as they fell back onto the mattress. His muscular body held her still as he slipped one hand down her side and across her stomach. She thrust up, fire pouring through her veins at that mere caress from him. Her belly tensed and breathing hitched as his touch trailed over her bellybutton and down towards her needy slit. Arissa nipped at his invading tongue as he let one finger drift lightly between her nether lips.

"Deiter," she moaned into his mouth.

In the next second her eyes fluttered as a scream of pleasure ripped from the depths of her chest. He sank two fingers inside her and set off one hell of an orgasm. Arissa grabbed onto his shoulders as he pistoned his wrist back and forth. She rode out the unrelenting waves of ecstasy that poured over her.

Deiter almost blew his load when her tight pussy clamped down on his two fingers. It had been hard enough looking at her and not losing control, this...this was damn near impossible, especially when the hairs of her neatly trimmed core teased him.

"Fuck," he uttered on a groan.

Her muscles gripped hard when he began to withdraw. A moan of frustration reached him.

"Easy, baby. We're just getting started."

With a slight readjustment he settled between her thighs and placed the head of his cock against her wet opening.

"Please," she begged.

Ignoring the primal urge within him, Deiter pushed in slowly. Inch by inch, he filled and stretched her. Even through the condom, he could feel her welcoming heat and he hissed in pleasure. He kissed her as he held still, fully embedded in her, to allow her some time to adjust to his size and permit himself to take better hold over his control.

Just resting there, motionless he could feel the ripple of her internal muscles as they began to milk his cock. Deiter shuddered as his balls tingled and started to tighten in response. He broke the kiss and drew back so he could stare into her eyes as he moved. Her irises were a few shades darker and he could see the need in them.

Back and forth. In and out.

They moved as one, her body reacting to his in perfect tandem. Gazes were locked onto one another and the world shrank to two individuals.

Him and her. Two halves of the same whole.

When she tightened her legs around him, he got the message. Deiter picked up the speed of his thrusts. Arissa kept up easily.

Faster. Deeper. Harder. Her hips undulated against his driving strokes. He noticed her eyes had fallen shut and Arissa had her lower lip anchored between her teeth.

She grunted in time with each forward plunge.

"Shit," he moaned.

"Deiter...I...wants...need..."

Her pants and mewls filled his ears as he dropped his head to hers. Arissa sank her nails into his skin with biting force while the sounds she emitted grew louder and louder. She held him tighter with each stroke he delivered and he knew she was close.

"*Fick mich,*" he uttered in German as she came with a rush.

Her cry was muffled when she pressed her mouth into his shoulder. There was no holding back. Deiter ploughed forward like a wild man as her tight pussy worked him. He powered into her five more times before he could no longer hold back. He gave a loud cry as his cock jerked then erupted. He came so hard his body shook with the intensity.

Their sweaty bodies seemed to melt into one as hearts and breathing began to slow.

"Arissa?" he asked in a gravelly voice, trying to move some of his weight off her.

She tightened her arms around him. "Don't move," she ordered in a whisper. Her voice just as hoarse as his. "I like how you feel on me."

Deiter smiled even as he rolled them to the side. "I don't want to squish you."

Arissa yawned. "I kinda like being squished by you." She snuggled closer. "Thank you."

Deiter pulled completely out of her, removed and disposed of the condom, then cuddled back up to Arissa who had got under the bedding. He held still while she got comfortable against him then wrapped his arms around her and anchored them close. Closing his eyes, he could feel their hearts beating at the same pace and he smiled as his lips teased her temple. With a big sigh, he gave himself over to the quest of Morpheus and followed Arissa Wright into the world of dreams.

* * * *

Later that evening, he was still smiling. Arissa was sitting beside him in the casino at a blackjack table. Almost like they were on a playback loop, he couldn't stop the images or memories of their lovemaking from moving through his mind. Arissa was an explosive yet extremely giving lover. Even in the shower before they'd come here, she'd responded eagerly to his touches.

He watched her take a sip of her drink. She had a Disaronno and cranberry. Deiter couldn't keep his eyes off her, which was affecting his playing skills. Arissa was cleaning up and he wasn't. He got to his feet after he'd lost another hand, moved behind her, and placed a kiss on her neck.

"Be right back," he whispered.

"Okay." A small smile was all she gave him before her attention once again returned to the game.

Deiter walked around, stretching out his legs. He was hungry but wasn't going to say anything for he knew after she was done playing they would grab a bite. And later on, the ship was doing a midnight chocolate buffet. He chuckled as he recalled her excitement when she'd remembered that bit of news.

Deiter went outside and leaned on a railing, watching people below him as they played, visited and more. Most of them seemed oblivious to the magnificent sunset occurring at the moment.

"Blackjack not your thing?" Arrisa questioned from his side.

Looking at her, Deiter was met by a pair of brown eyes he'd become extremely fond of this past week. Not to mention the woman they belonged to.

"How'd you make out?" he asked before kissing her lightly.

Deiter caught her wink in the fading light. "How do you say wonderful in German?"

"*Wunderbar*, I believe would be the word you're looking for." Deiter stared at her mouth when she repeated the word to him. The blood headed south as her full lips moved.

"Hungry?" she questioned.

He nodded, at a loss for words. Her question had brought his eyes from her lips and allowed him another opportunity to stare at her dress. It was cream, with a V-neck that gave him a tantalising hint of her breasts. The gauzy material flowed about her as she moved, the hem halting just above her knees exposing her shapely calves. She wore strappy sandals the same colour as the dress.

It was a very nice article of clothing. A fun one. It flirted and teased as well as made him randy as any man had a right to be.

"Let's go eat," he said on a low growl.

Arissa kissed him and sent him into another tailspin. He wanted her all to himself, didn't want to share her. They walked towards one of the elevators to where they were dining. Arissa leaned against him as the car headed down.

"Remind me to stop by the gift shop. I have to pick up a shot glass."

Tilting his head, he glanced down at her, her gaze was straight ahead. "Shot glass?"

A small chuckle left her. "Yes, for my friend who was supposed to be with me on this trip. She's an avid collector. There is a wall in one room of her house dedicated to the numerous glasses she's collected over the years."

The elevator stopped and they exited.

"Wow, that's interesting. My mom is into collecting the spoons." Deiter paused. "What about you?"

"I don't like clutter so the only thing I have is a lot of plants. Easy to care for and they don't argue about my hours of work. And a few of them flower."

"No pets even?" They halted at the opening of the restaurant before continuing inside.

"Oh God, no. My hours at the hospital wouldn't allow for it. Not and be fair to the animal. By animal I mean a dog, I am *so* not a cat person."

"Gotcha."

They were seated and had given their order to the waiter when he noticed her staring off a bit to her left. Following her line of sight, he frowned as his gaze landed upon a decent looking man in a nice grey suit with green accents. As he stared, the man continually ran his hand over his chest and along his collar as if it had grown too tight. Shaking his head, Deiter looked back at Arissa. Her attention was still on the man at the other table. A low rumble of anger and possessiveness began to rise within him.

"See something you like?" he bit off.

Her head snapped back to him briefly before she turned again. From her profile, he could see the furrow of her brow. *Did she recognise him? Was he an ex? Would she rather be with him?* All kinds of ugly thoughts tore through his head and anger was short on its heels.

"That's not right," Arissa muttered.

"What?"

"Find a crew member and have them call for their medical staff."

Her order was issued in such a business-like tone he did a double-take. "Come again?"

Arissa stared at him. "Get some medical personnel in here. Now."

Deiter watched her push to her feet. A noise and a gasp from other patrons reached him. He stared at the man who'd fallen from his seat to the floor.

"Do it now!" she hollered over her shoulder as she shoved her way through the crowd that had gathered around the fallen man.

Deiter did as she'd commanded then turning back to her, he stared as she performed CPR on the man. Moving closer, her muttered words reached him.

"Come on, man. Don't do this. Stay with us."

She was beside him, pumping on his chest when members of the medical team ran in with a gurney. Arissa barely stopped compressions as they rolled the comatose man onto the stretcher.

"Get moving, he's not breathing!" she yelled as she straddled his waist without a break in her administrations, an act which exposed the firmness of her thighs. And he knew he wasn't the only man in the room who noticed.

Deiter observed as they looked at another uniformed person, as if for permission, before moving quickly to the door and presumably to medical. Craning his neck, he stared after the retreating forms for as long as he could.

After going back to the table, he picked up her purse only to slow when a man in a lieutenant uniform came up to him.

"Was that your wife?"

Not yet. "No. Her name is Arissa Wright."

Calm began to settle over the room although the hum of noise told him they were still talking about what had happened. "Can I go wait for her down there?"

"Of course. I'll take you." He held out his hand. "Lieutenant Donalds."

"Deiter Schneider."

Soon he was standing in an elevator on his way to medical.

Chapter Three

The doors closed behind her and Arissa kept up the count in her head as she continued with CPR. "Bag him," she commanded, assuming she would be obeyed. And she was. The opening of the elevator doors didn't distract her.

"Who's this?" A man's deep masculine voice questioned from behind her.

"She was with him when we got there, and hasn't stopped CPR the entire time." A man pushing the gurney spoke.

"Ma'am, you need to get off him so we can help him." A distinguished elderly man pointed to the floor beside him.

This would be the doctor. Arissa opened her mouth to respond when the man on the gurney heaved up, throwing off the bag over his face. Then he puked. All over her.

Really? Are you fucking serious? She climbed off him and the ship's medical staff closed around him. Arissa waved away a nurse.

"I think he has anaphylaxis," she said reaching for a towel and dabbing at the rancid liquid dripping down her chest.

The older man glanced back at her before looking back at his patient. "Why?"

"Tubes in," someone said.

"Before he collapsed, he was tugging at his collar like it was hard to breathe and rubbing his stomach. He also has what looks like hives." Arissa winced as she smelt herself. "I didn't find a pen in his pockets."

"Give him an epi," the man ordered before glancing back at her. "There's a shower over there, some scrubs you can put on."

One final look and Arissa headed to the shower. Once she was cleaned up, she dressed in green scrubs. As she refastened her shoes she chuckled and shook her head.

"Scrubs and heels. I'm gonna start a new trend."

She stood up straight and pumped some lotion in her hand before rubbing it in. Her dress sat soaking wet and tied in a garbage bag. With a groan, she stepped out of the bathroom then moved through the office. She opened the door to find the salt-and-pepper haired man with his hip resting on a clean countertop watching the door, despite having a folder in his hands.

"You saved his life," he said without preamble as he dropped the file on the countertop. "He's resting comfortably at the moment."

"No, I just got him here. You and your people saved his life. Sorry about giving them orders." Arissa shrugged. "It was inexcusable." She walked to a counter then jumped up on it, hooking her ankles.

"So tell me how you knew that. I'm Doctor Eric Hayden by the way." He reached out his hand.

"I'm an ER doctor. He showed anaphylactic shock to me." Arissa took his hand. "Doctor Arissa Wright."

"Looking for a career change?"

She laughed. "No. I love my job, but thanks. And thanks for not being pissed off."

"Didn't say I wasn't. But I know good talent when I see it."

The door opened and in walked Deiter, who was still oh-so-handsome in his dark blue suit, with a man she didn't recognise. She fought a smile as her gaze picked up on her purse in Deiter's large hand.

"Hey," she said to him. "Sorry about dinner. We can try again after I get changed."

Deiter moved across the room to her side and handed her the purse.

"You okay?" he asked. "Is that man okay?"

She patted his arm. "I was just talking to Dr Hayden about him, he'll be fine." Arissa held up the purse. "Thanks for this."

Doctor Hayden hung up the phone and stared at her. "The captain would like to see you in his office." He crossed his arms and looked at the other uniform in the room. "Can you escort her, Lieutenant Donalds?"

"Of course, Dr. This way please."

Sliding off the counter, Arissa looked up at Deiter, whose face held a mixture of concern and uncertainty. "Guess supper will be a bit later. I'll find you when I'm done and I've changed." Picking up her tied bag, she moved to where Donalds waited. "Nice to meet you, Dr Hayden. Thanks again."

"Thank you for everything," he said with a wave.

Arissa smiled at him before wiggling her fingers in Deiter's direction. Then she followed the lieutenant. The walk to where the captain waited was done in complete silence. Although once they'd been told to enter, the lieutenant offered her a smile. One she assumed was to reassure her.

As the door shut behind her, a man stood from where he'd been sat behind the desk. *Wow, not how I pictured the captain.* She'd imagined a tall, powerful man, not the one she was faced with. The Pillsbury Doughboy was a better description in her mind. He was adorable. The urge to reach out and poke him in the belly filled her.

"Miss Wright," he began. "Or should I say Dr Wright, thank you for coming. I'm Captain Finch. Please, have a seat."

She left her bag by the door, then moved across the floor, sank into one of the upholstered chairs, and crossed her legs. He arched an eyebrow as her strappy platform sandal showed. Arissa smiled and shrugged. "Trying something new."

"Interesting." He sat down in the chair next to her and ran his stubby fingers over his balding head. "I don't have to tell you that what you did could have been potentially dangerous for this ship."

"Let me just say something," Arissa jumped in. "I know there are rules and all of that but I am a doctor, have been for a while now and I will never apologise for doing my job. And a dying man *is* my job." She released a sigh. "Go ahead and yell now, I'm sure I've heard it all before."

Captain Finch looked at her and laughed. "I like you, Dr. A lot."

* * * *

Deiter rose from his seat when Arissa walked into the dining area on the arm of the captain. She had changed from the scrubs she'd been wearing into another dress. This one was full length and hugged her curves like a lover. A beautiful muted green colour with a sweetheart neckline that perfectly accentuated the mocha hue of her smooth skin. As the two of them turned down the stairs, Deiter could see the criss-crossed straps in the back. His gaze travelled down to where her hem gathered to a bit of a train, and he paused to watch the hypnotic sway of her ass.

He swallowed hard, grateful he'd changed into a charcoal two button, side vented, flat front suit that was a bit more formal from his previous one. Along with it he wore a three-button black merino polo as well as a matching belt and ostrich square toe dress shoes. Deiter noticed the way other men's eyes followed her progress down the final few steps and as they made their way to the table. Honestly, he hadn't expected the invitation to dine with the captain at all but he wasn't about to turn it down. His heart skipped a beat when Arissa smiled at him.

Holding her chair for her, Deiter brushed a small kiss against her bare shoulder as she sat down. Retaking his seat next to her, he smiled as she closed her hand around his and squeezed. The late supper was enjoyable and engaging. After dessert, he escorted Arissa around an upper deck.

"Everything go okay with Captain Finch?"

She rested her head against his suit coat. "Yes. He had to talk to me about rules, regulations, et cetera, nothing I've not heard before."

"Okay, you just said you worked in an emergency room but not much more than that. From your quick reaction I'm guessing you're not a janitor."

"No. I'm a doctor."

He stutter-stepped slightly. "A doctor? Why didn't you tell me?"

"Does it matter?"

Did it? "Yes." Arissa tensed and he added, "But not for the reason you may be thinking."

"So explain it to me."

Deiter stopped walking and leaned against a rail, pulling her in-between his spread legs. He placed his hands on the bare skin of her shoulders, trailing his fingers idly along her skin.

"It matters because you didn't think enough of what we have to tell me. The fact you're a doctor as opposed to any other position in emergency medicine doesn't matter. I think it's awesome you are one, but I'm not going to like you more or less because of your job. I fell for you when I saw you stretched out on that lounge wearing that tank top and sarong."

Her head dropped. "I'm sorry."

"Don't apologise. I'm sure you have known people who show interest because of your profession. I'm not like that. You could scrub latrines for all I care. It's you I'm after, Arissa Wright, not your job or perks that may come with it."

She sighed and looped her arms around his neck. "I am sorry I didn't tell you. I guess I'm just private about some things. I don't tell a lot about myself."

Deiter nodded. He'd noticed that about her. She hesitated to talk about herself or family. Arissa was quick, witty and a lot of fun, but forthcoming on personal things she wasn't.

Leaning down so they were nose to nose, he asked, "Got some time before midnight, care to join an old man in his room?"

"An old man? Hmmm, don't know about that. I kinda need one who can keep up with me." Her lips brushed his. "Do you know of anyone?"

"I'm sure I can think of someone," he retorted as he smacked her lightly on the ass.

Arissa rubbed against him. "Wonderful. Then allow me to escort you."

He slid his arm around her and together they headed for his room. Deiter gasped as she sank to the floor before him the second the door closed.

"Arissa," he began, only to hesitate when her fingers left the buttons of his suit coat and reached for the belt on his slacks. "What are you —?"

Deiter fell silent as she slid her fingers into his boxers and wrapped them around his growing erection. She didn't say a word as she freed him. A shudder rocked through him as her hot breath flowed across the sensitive skin of his cock. *Ah hell!*

With a loud thunk, his head hit the door as it dropped back. His eyes closed and his belly tightened as her warm mouth settled over him. Her tongue danced along the rim of the head before she took more and more of him in her mouth. Lights flickered in his mind as she worked his cock. Up and down. Where her mouth didn't touch, her strong hands applied the perfect amount of pressure. When she released one hand, a groan of longing welled up within him. Shortly after, her short nails skimmed across his balls.

"Arissa," he uttered in a gravelled tone.

Her other hand dropped to touch his thigh and her mouth slid all the way over his full length. The tightness of her mouth combined with her teasing touch on his balls nearly drove him out of his mind. Deiter gripped the sides of her head and thrust his hips towards her, driving his cock deeper into her mouth. Glancing down, he almost came at the sight of her kneeling there. Her eyes were closed, her long lashes settled against her skin.

Licking his lips, he tried to slow the speed of his hips and savour the experience a bit longer. Her increased suction and caressing told him that wasn't about to happen. He shivered as her teeth skimmed along his length. Tighter and tighter her hold on him became, and he began to move faster. She gave his balls one final squeeze then put that hand on the back of his thigh. A low roar of pleasure rumbled up from his chest as he continued to drive deep into her willing wetness. He could feel her nails digging through his slacks as he moved.

"Shit!" he shouted as he unloaded deep into her mouth.

Arissa never relented or lessened until he had nothing left to give. With a pop, she released him from her mouth and stood slowly. Her eyes swirled with passion as she held his gaze. Arissa gently put his softening cock back into his boxers and pants. She trailed her fingers up his chest to touch his cheek.

"I need a drink," she murmured before stepping away from him and going towards his refrigerator.

Legs still a bit shaky, Deiter remained against the door for a moment until he felt he could walk without embarrassing himself. He pushed away and headed to where she leaned against the counter drinking a bottle of water. He trapped her there, placing his arms on either side of her. He nuzzled into the side of her neck before he pressed tender kisses there.

"Thank you," he muttered.

Arissa turned in his arms. "I need to go get changed before the buffet." She slipped a hand through his hair. "Meet you down there?"

He turned his head and looked at the blue digital readout on the clock. About an hour until the buffet began. Deiter wanted to be selfish, wanted to keep her to himself. He nodded.

"Okay, sounds like a plan."

She ducked under his arm and walked towards the door. When she began to open it he reached out and wrapped his fingers around her wrist. Her eyes opened wide with surprise.

Deiter stared at her. "Arissa...I...I..."

Her gaze softened but he could read the retreat on her face. "I'll meet you later." After kissing her fingertips, she pressed them to his lips. "Bye." Then she slipped out and closed the door in his face.

"Fuck," he expelled as his head fell forward to rest against the wood.

Every time he closed his eyes, even at night, it was Arissa he saw. He wanted more than a vacation fling with her. Arissa Wright was a woman you married, took home to meet the parents and raised children with. And that's what he wanted. He just didn't know how to broach it with her. The way she'd reacted during that incident in the restaurant, he knew she was damn good at what she did. And was passionate about it.

Shoving his hand through his hair, he went to grab some different clothes and a shower. As he dried off, he chuckled. *Who knew I'd wear so many different outfits in a day?*

Ten minutes before midnight he got off the elevator and strode to where the buffet was going to be. Rounding a corner, he smiled as his gaze landed on Arissa. Her dark shirt and faded jeans looked amazing on her, and he could see bare toes peeking out. The warm breeze moved through her short hair, ruffling the strands.

Like she had a sixth sense, she turned her head towards him and a beautiful smile graced her features. She adjusted her stance so she was propped against the railing, he watched her gaze remain steady upon him as he closed the remainder of the distance between them.

"Ready?" he asked, stopping before her.

"I'm *always* ready for chocolate." She ran her hand down his arm and laced their fingers before tugging on him. "Let's go."

"Worried it's all gonna be gone?" Deiter almost choked with laughter at the 'hell yeah' expression on her face. Holding up his free hand he said, "Okay, okay. I'm right behind you."

The words had barely left him when she turned again and began pulling him towards the door. Glancing up at the star-studded sky, Deiter smiled, thanked God, and gave himself over to the joy Arissa exuded.

He'd never seen so much chocolate in his life. There were landmarks, animals, amazing geometric designs and so much more. And Arissa seemed to be in heaven. She moved nimbly through the increasingly packed room and just when he figured he'd totally lost her, she appeared before him, eyes sparkling with elation. In her hands she held two plates.

"Brought you some things. Wasn't sure what you wanted though. Hope it's all good."

"I'm sure it is. Where do you want to go?"

"Doesn't matter, let's just grab some seats."

For the next few hours, they ate and talked with other people on the ship. It was one of the best times Deiter had had in a long while. Happy and full, they walked together back to his room and climbed into bed where they made love before exhaustion finally took over.

* * * *

In the morning, Deiter was alone when he woke. There was no note, no nothing from her.

"Damn it. Why didn't she wake me?"

She's not your girlfriend, his brain reminded him.

A very sobering thought. After a shower and getting dressed, he headed down to where he and Arissa usually sat. His heart lightened when he saw her on a lounge, only to sink when he noticed she was talking to a man. One who looked familiar.

The man from the restaurant last night.

"Arissa," he said as he strode up.

Arissa laughed at something the man in the next chair had said. When she heard Deiter behind her, she turned and was struck by the fire raging in his eyes. *He's jealous.* The problem was she didn't know if she wanted to think about his reaction to that. Living for the moment had been going along so well. His black shorts with a red stripe down the sides worked great with his white shirt.

"Hey, Deiter." She held her hand out towards him. "I'd like for you to meet Timothy—"

"Tim," the man interjected.

She dipped her head in understanding. "Tim Vastin."

"Nice to meet you," Deiter said reaching around her to offer his hand. "Am I interrupting anything?"

Arissa could hear the hard edge to Deiter's tone. She watched them shake hands before Deiter settled next to her on the lounge. *Didn't even give us a second to answer that question.*

"No," Tim answered. "I was just thanking her for saving my life. And then I learnt we live in the same city and are on the same flight home."

Deiter looked at her and Arissa swallowed at the tic he had in his jaw. "Is that so?" he asked.

"Yes," Arissa answered. "So we've been talking about our familiar watering holes."

"Nice," Deiter answered. He got to his feet. "I'm going to get a drink. Can I get you two anything?"

"I'm good," Tim said.

"Me too, but thanks." Arissa watched as Deiter walked away. Part of her wanted to call him back, but she let him go, putting her attention back on the man across from her.

Unbidden her mind began to compare the two men. Both were tall, but Deiter was much more muscular than Tim. Blond-brown hair compared to jet black. Deiter's lips were much more attractive, he had a firm kissable bow-shaped mouth, not a thin line. Both men had very nice smiles though. And where Deiter was clean-shaven, Tim had a goatee. Even their eyes were different. A stormy blend of blues and greys made up her German's gaze, while Tim's was a vibrant, almost piercing blue. *What makes him mine?*

As she sat across from the good-looking man with the blue eyes, she stared in the direction Deiter had gone off in. She didn't have to look far—he was against a bar beside the pool. Watching her.

She could hear Tim still talking so she smiled at Deiter and put, albeit reluctantly, her attention back on the man chatting. Throughout the conversation she sneaked peeks over to where Deiter still remained.

Near the bar with a drink in his hand. His gaze continually on her.

"He your boyfriend?" Tim questioned.

"Deiter? No. Just a good friend."

"Good."

Her brow furrowed. "Good?" She looked at him and frowned.

Tim stood and leaned over until his mouth was beside her ear. "Yes. That means I have a clear field in pursuing you. Thanks for not letting me die." He pressed a light kiss to her cheek before walking off.

She touched the spot where Tim had kissed her as her eyes drifted back to where Deiter had been. He was gone. Getting to her feet, she craned her neck and tried to find him. Her heart sank when she found his retreating form. There was a stiffness about him she'd not seen before.

With a groan she sank back down on the lounge. *What am I supposed to do now?* Arissa sat there for another hour attempting to read a crime novel. When she realised it wasn't working, she returned it to her navy blue beach tote. After shoving her feet into her flip-flops, she got to her feet and headed for the elevator. Once she'd arrived at the desired floor she went down the hall then knocked on the door of the suite and held her breath as the handle turned. The door swung on silent hinges and left her facing a sombre man.

"Hi," she said calmer than she felt. "Mind if I come in?"

He stepped back so she had enough room to enter. She passed him then turned and watched him lean against the door, crossing powerful arms over his chest. His legs were braced apart and he remained quiet. Blue-grey eyes stared at her from beneath dark blondish-brown lashes.

Chapter Four

At his silence, Arissa rethought even being there.

"You know what, I think this was a mistake." She walked towards him as she spoke.

"What do you mean?" Deiter narrowed his eyes.

"This. All of it." She gestured between them. "There is no place we can really go with this anyway. It's just a vacation fling."

"Is that all you think we are. *A fling?*" Deiter spat out.

He stepped closer to meet her, stilling her forward momentum. Arissa studied the fierceness on his face and in his gaze. She lowered her own, not able to face what she saw there. Deiter's blunt fingers went under her chin, raising her face to his.

"This is more than a *fling*. Are you willing after the cruise is done to give us a chance? We might live in different parts of the country but I want more than a passing booty call. Say you are feeling the same way that I am." His expression was as sure and fierce as his tone.

Arissa pulled away, turning from him. She took a breath. There was no way in such a short time they could have become so close. Talking about going beyond the cruise. Her mind filled with all the moments they'd shared. Raising a shaking hand, she pushed her hair behind her ear. She felt his heat before he pressed against her. Arissa stilled a shudder. Just the feel of his large frame beside her made her lose all sense, yet her gut told her there was more to it than that. Sighing, she gave in to the inevitable. She reached into her tote and found her cardholder and a pen. After taking out a business card, she scribbled on the back then turned in his arms.

"I want there to be more. I'm willing to see if there is. Here is my home phone and email." She pressed the card into his hand.

Deiter closed his fingers around it. With his other hand, he cupped her cheek then kissed her fiercely. Arissa moaned and leaned into him returning the kiss. When he pulled back, a small smile curled his lips.

"You're going to be a handful," Deiter said.

"Definitely." Arissa laughed.

"Handfuls are my speciality." He winked.

"Do tell." Arissa wound her arms around his neck.

"In a moment. Let me get you my info, too." He kissed her gently then disentangled himself from her embrace.

With rapid strides, he went to the table by the bed and leaned over. Arissa followed him, humming at the view of his spectacular ass. She moved her hand along the firm flesh and squeezed. Deiter looked over his shoulder.

"We have time. Give it to me later. For now I want this." Arissa turned him to face her taking the card out of his hand and placing it on the table. She manoeuvred him then pushed him back so Deiter fell onto the bed. He braced on his elbows and watched her. Arissa quickly divested herself of her clothing before she reached for him. She stripped him before straddling him. Deiter gripped her waist to steady her. Leaning down, she licked along his lips. He opened, giving her access and she slid her tongue into his mouth to duel with his. Arissa moaned at his taste. There was just something about it she couldn't place. Letting it go for now, she enjoyed the kiss.

With a moan, she rubbed along his heated naked flesh. Deiter cupped her ass guiding her motions. His hard shaft teased her slit. She released him from the kiss, shifted then sighed as he pressed right to her clit. Rolling her hips she groaned at the delicious friction. Deiter's harsh exhalation joined hers. Arissa moved forward, intent on having him.

"Condom." His raw, husky voice stilled her.

Arissa came to her senses, shocked at what she had been about to do. She had never forgotten something so important. Biting her lip, she pulled away and reached into the bedside table for protection. She put it on him then repositioned herself over him. Deiter squeezed her waist and Arissa met his gaze.

"When we get back to terra-firma we'll both get tested? That way when we come to see each other we can go without them." He leaned up close to her lips. "I want to feel you around me."

Arissa nodded mutely. She shifted and sank down onto his hard erection. Deiter bit back a moan then repositioned his hands to cup her butt. She rocked with him, murmuring. In seconds she was moving urgently against him. Deiter clenched her ass in time with her thrusts. His head thrashed on the bed while he muttered in a language she didn't recognise. He rolled his head back. The muscles of his neck stood out in sharp relief.

She rubbed her nipples as she moved on him. Each downward motion of her hips made his cock rub her inner walls, driving her into frenzy. Plucking at her aching buds, Arissa whimpered as she increased her movements. She moaned, squeezing her throbbing nipples. Deiter murmured as she took him. The base of her belly tightened then pleasure overcame her. Arissa shuddered, coming, then flopped beside him and shivered.

Deiter held her firmly whispering against the side of her face. She couldn't distinguish what he was saying. He rolled them over so she lay under him. Arissa glanced at him, startled as he stroked into her. Her lids fluttered closed as his hard length ploughed deep. With slow, measured thrusts, Deiter plunged into her pussy.

"Look at me," he demanded softly.

Arissa blinked. Deiter smiled tenderly as he continued to move. She moaned. The contrast of him taking her like she was precious to him was her undoing. The motions of their joined bodies seemed to be in time with her pulse. A slow, steady throb, with a skip as he deepened his thrusts. She could feel the difference from their previous couplings—while they all had been intense and heated they'd not included anything except getting off.

This encounter had all that, as well as the emotions of something deeper. Arissa's breath caught as she wondered if they could actually have something more. Being on a cruise in such close quarters had led to an instant connection but what would happen in the real world.

Do you want more with him?

Without hesitation she knew she did. Arissa gripped his shoulders. Deiter's hot skin flexed under her palms. He began again to speak in another language. She held on for the ride.

Deiter moved deeper into Arissa's wetness. He placed his arms beside her head, caging her beneath him. He couldn't stop the words flowing from him in his native tongue. They poured so fast from him he didn't even know what he was saying. Yet he knew it was all the emotions he had been holding back since he'd met this amazing woman. Arissa Wright was all he could ever want and he was not about to let her go. He had planned to broach the subject of after the cruise later, but seeing that man next to her had made him feel something he never had before—jealousy. Arissa coming after him pleased him but her words had made him realise he needed to let his intentions be known. The fact Arissa had accepted his words and gave him her contact information was a gift he would not forget.

He stroked slowly into her. The hitch of her breath made a fierce pleasure fill him. Her loveliness only increased each time he was with her. Seeing her spread out below him, he vowed no other man would have her. Arissa was his. For the rest of the cruise and when they parted, he would show her they were meant to be together. He leaned over and kissed her.

She dug her fingers into his shoulders. The clench of her pussy around his cock drove him on. With a jerking motion of his hips, he revelled in her wetness. Inhaling deep, he took in their combined scent. Arissa's was exotic and captivating. Arissa tightened her legs around him as she came. Groaning, Deiter increased his thrusts. His sac drew tight then his seed pulsed out. Arissa moaned, arching as her second orgasm joined his.

How would it be without condoms? At the thought, he slid his hands behind her head, raising her slightly, and kissed her hungrily. Arissa whimpered and returned his fervour with her own. His thrusts slowed as his release ebbed. Her vibrations squeezed his erection.

Once they had calmed and he'd disposed of the protection, he pulled her to his side, cuddling her. He kissed her forehead. Arissa's hand rested over his chest while her breath feathered the side of his neck. She moved her fingers lazily against his chest. Deiter breathed, enjoying just being with her. Her touch stilled then her breathing deepened. Closing his eyes, he went to sleep.

* * * *

"Come on, I don't want to miss the class," Arissa said.

Deiter let her drag him as she rushed. He stifled a smile. Her enthusiasm was sexy. "I'm not the one who jumped the other after our shower," he pointed out.

Arissa stopped just before the door. "You enjoyed it." She turned to him with an impish grin on her face. She raised her head back and Deiter leant down and kissed her. He deepened it as Arissa gripped his waist.

She withdrew, shaking her head. "Uh, uh. You're not making me miss this class. Come on."

Arissa pulled the door open and motioned him in. Deiter pouted and went. A hand smoothed over his ass. He glanced back at Arissa.

"Later." She winked.

"Definitely," he said.

Arissa laced her fingers with his and pulled him along beside her to an empty table. The room was filled with lots of people, the noise level and excitement could be heard.

"Are you ready to make some yummy creations?" A feminine voice cut through the noise.

Deiter brought his attention to the instructor as she explained what they were going to do. People were focused on her, listening with rapt attention. Deiter glanced at Arissa. She had an intent look on her face. He returned to the instructor and listened.

"Now come on up and take a sheet for what you want to make. Then go back to your table and just go with it and have fun. I'll be coming around to help each of you with what you need," the instructor said.

"Stay here. I know what we're going to make." Arissa headed to the front of the room before he could reply.

His eyes narrowed as he spotted the man from the pool. He tried to remember his name. "Tim," Deiter said softly.

Tim laughed and joked with Arissa, but they were too far away for him to hear. Arissa shook her head then gestured in Deiter's direction. Tim glanced over and smiled thinly. Deiter stifled a smirk as Arissa walked back to their table. He looked away and noted Tim watched her as she walked. Tim met his gaze again and grinned then turned, going back to his table across the room. Deiter pulled Arissa against his side when she reached their table.

"Don't think I didn't see the death glares you were shooting at Tim. He's a nice man. And just for reference, I'm a one-man woman. I don't do the possessive crap." Arissa looked exasperated.

Deiter sighed. "I don't know what is wrong with me. I don't usually act this way." He grinned sheepishly, partially lowering his lids over his eyes.

Arissa snorted. "Don't try that innocent look on me."

"Is it working?" he murmured against the side of her face.

"No." She breathed out.

"How about now?" He kissed the tip of her ear.

Arissa shivered, then said in a husky voice, "Maybe." She cleared her throat. "Stop that. Let's get to work."

She pushed out of his arms and put down the paper she had retrieved. Deiter glanced at the picture then back at the pile of cupcakes, icing and other things on their table. He returned his gaze to Arissa.

"No way are we going to be able to make those cupcakes look like a plate with burger and fries." Deiter shook his head.

"With pickles on the burger and ketchup on fries. Don't worry—it will look like it. Come on, I'll help you," Arissa said cheerfully.

Deiter observed her as she started to put things together. It didn't look like the picture. He read, then started his own.

"Have you done this before?"

"Nope. But I've heard about it from my friend Deyon. She's done it before on another cruise. Sounded like fun. And we had planned to take the class so I could do it too." Arissa shrugged, biting her tongue as she studied her cupcakes.

Deiter resisted kissing her, instead focusing on his own cupcakes. "Deyon?"

"Oh. I think I mentioned her to you when we met. She's one of the friends who is probably freezing her ass off. We planned to go on this cruise together along with another friend but they both had to back out at the last moment." Arissa made a noise, dismantled her cupcake then started over before she spoke again. "Deyon, Sarah and Jackie ganged up on me to make me come on the cruise. It's a shame they couldn't come."

"Why'd they have to gang up on you?" Deiter glanced at the mess he was making then at the instructions. He wasn't very good at this.

"I'm sort of a work-a-holic. They felt the need for me to take a break. Been trying to convince me for a while. Jackie was going to come too, but before we booked it something came up. That's why it was Deyon, Sarah and I. Then just me, since Sarah had an emergency at work and Deyon had to fly out to Milan for a show," Arissa replied.

"A show?" Deiter queried absently. Pursing his lips, he wondered if icing would make the glob look any better. Shrugging, he reached for a tub.

"Yep. Deyon's a designer. A hell of a good one. Some snafu made in scheduling rearranged her showing in Milan. I'm going to rib her about it. Hell, Sarah too. My being here to enjoy this fabulous cruise without them. Especially with a scrumptious man." Arissa pushed against his shoulder playfully.

Deiter put down the tub, cupped the back of her head and kissed her. Arissa made a soft sound then withdrew.

"Are you trying to distract me?" she questioned.

"Is it working?" Deiter asked.

"Not at all," she said straight-faced, then smiled cheekily. "Back to work."

"I don't think I'm any good at this." Deiter glanced at the mess that was no way looking like a burger and fries.

"It's not so bad." Arissa's voice sounded strangled. She was biting her lip.

"No laughing at my pitiful creation." Deiter frowned.

"It's not so bad. We'll put more icing on it," Arissa said.

"I don't think they have enough icing in the world to save this mess."

"Maybe not. But that's okay. It's about the fun. Not beauty." Arissa chuckled.

Deiter studied her plate. It was perfection, looking like a burger and fries. It made him want to eat it.

"You said you haven't done this before." He accused turning to her.

"I haven't. I'm just..." She bit her lip.

"More creative." He helped her out.

"I'll show you how creative later. For now, let's salvage this." Arissa picked up a tub.

Deiter's mind was filled with her creativity. "Do you think we can sneak out a container of icing?" he whispered.

"For what?"

Deiter studied it, then her. He saw the dawning of what he wanted it for on her face. That devilish grin he was coming to know so well curled her lips. She made sure no one was watching before picking up one of the icing containers and putting it in her tote.

"Yellow is my favourite colour. It will look good on you." She patted her bag.

Deiter shifted, trying to relieve the strain on his slacks. He took up another tub.

"I like the taste of strawberries. It'd be delicious against your skin."

Arissa's eyes flared with need then she took the tub. Checked again to make sure no one was looking and put it inside her bag. She cleared her throat.

"Now then. Let's get this done." Arissa picked up a spatula then started working on his mess.

Deiter helped. They laughed and talked as they worked. After some time, they stepped back to view their creation.

"It just looks like we slathered icing to cover up the wreck underneath," Deiter said.

"It does but didn't you have fun doing it?" Her face was alive with mischief.

"I did because it was with you," Deiter murmured.

"Deiter," Arissa moaned.

"Oh this is wonderful. Let's take a picture." The instructor's voice caught his attention.

She was readying a camera. The instructor lowered her gaze to his cupcake and her lips twitched before she looked back at his face.

"And yours is lovely too," she said.

Deiter stifled a snort.

"Actually this is mine and this is his." Arissa took up her creation and gave it to him.

Instinctively, he took it. She picked up his then leaned against his side holding it.

"Arissa, you don't have to do that," he growled.

"Hush," she hissed. "Smile pretty for the nice lady with the camera."

Deiter put her in front of him, so her back was to his chest, and held out the perfect cupcake burger and fries. Arissa put his less than stellar one next to her face and posed as the woman took the picture.

"I'll have it for you in a few moments if you want to wait."

"We'll wait. Can we have two?" Arissa asked.

"Sure. Give me a sec." The woman walked away.

Arissa turned to him and Deiter hugged her.

"You didn't have to lend me yours. I'm proud of my toothache," Deiter said.

"I'm giving it to you but you'll have to share it with me. We can have it later today. We can't eat yours, because if we do with all the icing we'll definitely get a toothache." She laughed.

"That was fun wasn't it? Let me see what you made Arissa," someone else interjected.

Deiter stifled a growl as Tim walked up to them. He was holding what seemed to be a rendition of a cup of coffee with a donut. And, of course, it seemed very real. Tim was turning out to be a pain in the ass. Tim's eyes widened as he spotted what Arissa held. Deiter stifled a grin, wondering what he would say.

"This is mine. I love it," Arissa said cheerfully.

"It's ugly," Tim said abruptly.

"You think so? I thought it was great." Arissa sounded hurt.

Deiter was already familiar with her pulling pranks.

"You're such a liar," Tim said.

"Shoot, you figured me out." Arissa laughed.

Deiter grudgingly admitted Tim hadn't fallen for it. Deiter didn't pay attention as they talked—instead he enjoyed Arissa leaning against his chest, comfortable as she chatted with Tim. He didn't even think she realised how comfortable she was with him already. He wasn't about to tell her.

"Here you go." The instructor came back.

She handed them a picture. Deiter smiled as he viewed it. Arissa had a cheesy grin on her face as she posed with the disaster of a burger and fries. He was behind her holding her perfect rendering, a smug smile on his own face.

"Are you coming to the chocolate carving class tomorrow?" Tim's question caught his attention.

"I will be. Can you come, Deiter?" Arissa asked.

He glanced at Tim with a slight smile on his face. Tim rocked back on his heels, his gaze steady.

"Sure. I'll love that."

"Good. So we'll see you tomorrow then." Arissa put the plate with the cupcake burger on it over the picture then picked it all up.

She balanced it then reached for him. Deiter copied her actions before accepting her hand. She laced her fingers with his and they went to the now open door. Walking down the hall, he took a moment to appreciate the view and was awed by the beauty of the crystal clear water beyond the ship.

"You have a thing for food," Deiter commented as he walked.

"I don't know what you mean by a thing."

"You get really animated when it comes to food activities. First the chocolate party. Making this thing and then tomorrow the chocolate carving class," Deiter said.

"I like various foods. Learning to make new things. It is my way of relaxing. I've been told I'm good at cooking. After this class I'm thinking of taking a pastry class. Well, if I can find the time." Arissa shrugged.

"You should. You're good at it."

"I might. Are you still going to the rappelling wall?"

"Yep. Have you changed your mind about coming with me?" Deiter asked.

"I wish I could. Love doing that sort of thing. But I promised Eric I would come by so we can talk shop."

Deiter nodded. She had already mentioned she and the ship doctor had made plans to meet for lunch at the barbecue place. She'd asked him, but he really wanted to go to the rappelling wall. They still had over a week together before they parted. The thought of that did not sit well with him. He was silent as they walked to her cabin. At her door he waited as she opened it then turned to him.

"We'll meet up later for the dancing lessons," Arissa said.

"Three o'clock. I'll be there. I'm looking forward to it." Deiter kissed her then pulled back.

"Maybe it isn't such a good idea to take a Samba class." Arissa wrinkled her nose.

"No backing out of it. I want to dance with you," Deiter said.

"Are you going to behave?"

"Probably not," he admitted.

"Good." Arissa laughed.

"Here."

"Nope. That is for you. My first gift to you." She kissed him then went into her cabin.

Deiter glanced at the cupcake burger and fries then went towards his own cabin. Making a stop, he got a red cupcake box with clear top covering. It fit the cupcake perfectly, displaying it. Remembering Arissa's favourite colour he got a yellow one for her and requested it be delivered to her stateroom immediately. He whistled as he left. In moments he was in his cabin and changing his clothing. He frowned at the knock on his cabin door. Pulling it open, he scowled. "What the hell are you doing here?"

"Is that anyway to greet a friend?" Lieutenant Commander Tarak Brady smiled.

He might be out of uniform but you could clearly see his military bearing. His inky black hair was closely cropped. His reddish-brown, rugged face looked slightly strained and a slight bead of sweat rolled down the side, and his lips were pulled in a tight line. Thick curly lashes framed icy green eyes that echoed the strain on his face. Deiter missed the smiling friend who he knew was behind this now sombre man.

"Why aren't you still in the hospital?" he asked sharply.

"I'm fine," Tarak snapped.

"You're not. It's only been a month since—"

"Leave it." Tarak's tone held a clear warning.

Deiter frowned but said nothing else.

"We've got to go. Already informed the ship's captain," Tarak said.

"I've already told *them* I've done my last job for the military. My things are already on the way to my new home." Deiter shook his head.

"They know, that's why they sent me," Tarak replied.

Deiter scowled. They knew him too well. Sending Tarak for him might make him more prone to agree to go wherever they wanted him too. Tarak's expression was impeccable.

"We need to go." Tarak said.

"Fuck," Deiter cursed and went to pack.

After emptying his drawers into his duffle, Deiter grabbed the boxed cupcake. He went to the door. Tarak stepped back then swore softly, leaning on his cane heavily. Deiter knew better than to offer to help. He closed his cabin and walked, matching Tarak's stride. He knew Tarak wouldn't tell him what the job was, so instead he asked, "I thought you had decided to leave the Navy?"

"I am. But they asked me to come get you so I did. Once we're done that's it for me."

"You could still serve."

"I'm a SEAL. That's all I ever wanted to be. Can't do that anymore with my lungs and bad leg." His tone was matter-of-fact.

Deiter knew how hard it was for him, although he acted like it wasn't. Even before Tarak's injury, Deiter had decided to not work with the military anymore. He was tired of the travelling and them calling on him whenever they wanted.

"Are you ready to go home? See your family?"

"They were glad that I didn't plan on moving back home and bought my own house." Again, he was matter-of-fact.

Deiter stifled a rude sound. Tarak's relationship with his family was complicated.

"I have other's there that are more family to me than my own. In addition, I'll have you as part of my family too," he said softly.

"You know it, buddy. I'm there for you. I'm glad I took the job in your hometown. You talked about your hometown so often. At least you'll get to show me it yourself," Deiter agreed.

They were silent as they made their way to the waiting chopper. Once on board, Deiter strapped in, donning his headset. As the helicopter rose off the deck, he looked at the ship. A beautiful face flashed across his mind.

"Shit," Deiter hissed.

"What's wrong?" Tarak's voice came through the headset.

"I need to get word to someone on the ship," Deiter said.

"You know that's not possible until after the mission is done."

Deiter clenched his fist. That was the other thing he hated. Not being able to tell those who he cared about, that he was leaving for an unknown about of time. As the ship faded, he hoped Arissa would understand that he had left without telling her.

At least I have her information so I can contact her.

An uneasiness filled him. Deiter picked up his duffel and searched inside. Not finding the card, he leant back against the seat.

"Damn it!"

"I've never heard you swear so much." Tarak sounded amused.

"I left something important on the ship," Deiter replied.

"What?" Tarak asked.

Deiter didn't reply. He'd contact the ship as soon as he got back and find out her info. Then beg her to forgive him for leaving. He glanced at the seat beside him at the container with the gift she had given him.

I'll be seeing you soon, Arissa Wright.

Chapter Five

Arissa paced in front of where the Samba class was getting ready to start. She paused, peering down the hall. Still no Deiter. She tapped her foot then started to pace again.

"Arissa."

She turned to the sound of Tim's voice. He was hurrying towards her, then paused in front of her.

"Has the class started already?"

"No. They will any moment," Arissa said. She glanced behind him searching for Deiter.

"Aren't you going in?" Tim asked.

"I'm waiting for Deiter."

"He can join us when he gets here. Shall we, my fair lady?" Tim said.

She looked at him and saw he was holding out his elbow. Arissa checked back down the gangway then put her hand on him and let him lead her inside.

"Only until Deiter comes."

"Of course." Tim smiled devilishly.

Arissa laughed at his expression. "You are a troublemaker."

"Who *moi*?" He batted his eyes.

"You're a strange man." Arissa chuckled.

"I am. Now let's Samba." Tim struck a pose.

Arissa laughed while keeping an eye out for Deiter. As the class progressed she got caught up in it but at the back of her mind she wondered where Deiter was.

"Okay. That is it for now. Next class is tomorrow at the same time. Good job everyone," the dance instructor said.

"You want to go dancing tonight?" Tim asked.

She walked with him as they left. Once they were away from the others she replied gently, "Tim. You're a good guy but I'm with Deiter."

"I figured from the looks he was giving me. Bring Deiter. Just dancing as friends." Tim shrugged.

"Okay. Where?"

"The upper deck. I heard they have some great Latin music. Say eight o'clock?"

"We'll be there. Later." She hurried away.

She knocked at Deiter's cabin. Not getting an answer she tried the door. Surprisingly, it opened. Entering, Arissa frowned at the empty cabin. Unsure what was going on, she left and went to find someone to ask. Turning the corner, she bumped into someone.

"Sorry."

"Dr Wright, are you okay?" Captain Finch asked.

"I'm fine. Just not watching where I'm going," Arissa said.

"In a rush for something?"

"Not really…" Arissa thought about it then said, "I was in Deiter's cabin. And he wasn't there."

"He is no longer on the ship," the Capitan said.

Arissa frowned. "I'm referring to Deiter Schneider the man who was with me at dinner with you the other night."

"I know who he is, Dr Wright. He's no longer on the ship," the captain said again.

"Where is he?"

"I can't say. Have a good afternoon, Dr Wright," the captain said walking away.

Watching him leave, Arissa wondered what the hell was going on.

"Did he leave anything for me?" Arissa blurted out.

The captain stopped looking back at her "Not that I am aware. Was he supposed too?"

"I guess not." Arissa continued on her way.

"Dr Wright. Check with the steward, maybe he has something," the captain called.

"Thanks, I will." Arissa went to find the steward.

She found the steward, and was told he had nothing for her. She returned to her cabin and flopped on her bed, frowning as she wondered what had happened. Deiter leaving and saying nothing seemed weird. She sat up and lifted the yellow cupcake box he had sent to her room earlier. His messy cupcake was inside. Picking up the picture of them, Arissa stared at them together.

"There has to be some reasonable explanation for this."

Arissa put them down. If there was, she had no idea what it was but would wait to hear from Deiter. It was a good thing she had given him her contact info. She went to the bathroom to take a shower.

* * * *

"It's good to be back home."

Arissa glanced at Tim sitting beside her as the plane taxied down the runway to the terminal. He had switched his seat so they could sit together. Tim had turned out to be lots of fun after Deiter left. He'd refused to let her wallow over Deiter being gone. Tim and she had become inseparable—he was a good friend.

"It is. Don't forget you're coming over next weekend to meet Jackson and to watch the game. You have my info right."

"Yep. Programmed into my Blackberry." He patted his suit pocket.

"I've got yours in my iPhone," she replied.

They were silent as the plane finished docking at the gate. Once done, they got up and joined those departing the plane. After retrieving their luggage they headed to the exit.

"You want to share a cab?" Arissa asked.

"I've got a car picking me up. I'll give you a ride," Tim said.

"Okay."

"I'm at the terminal," Tim said into his phone.

She glanced at Tim. He put away his phone.

"He'll be here in a sec."

Arissa waited beside him silently. A black limo glided in front of them then a driver got out and came to meet them. Arissa blinked at his attire. His coat was opened to show a blue, yellow, orange and green Hawaiian shirt. Yellow slacks complimented the shirt.

"Tim, it is good to have you back," the older man said.

Arissa was surprised at the crisp British accent.

"Jorge. It was a fabulous cruise," Tim replied.

"At least you got to relax, I hope," the man said fondly.

"I did. Seeing as someone stole my Blackberry." Tim laughed.

"And you got another one. What am I going to do with you?" He rolled his eyes.

"Put up with me," Tim teased then turned to her. "Jorge, I want you to meet a very special lady, Arissa Wright. She made my cruise enjoyable."

"Nice to meet you, miss," Jorge said. He smiled at Tim slyly. "Did you find a girlfriend finally?"

"Jorge. She's a friend. Just a friend," Tim said in warning.

"Boy, what have I told you about lost opportunities. Letting this one be only a friend," Jorge said, winking at her.

Arissa laughed. "I can see where Tim gets his incorrigible behaviour."

"Pash. I've been trying to teach him to misbehave but failed miserably. Let me get your bags." Jorge took her bags before she could protest.

"Have a seat in the car." Tim opened the door for her.

Arissa did as he'd bid and slid into the spacious back seat. Tim moved away. She listened absently as he and Jorge talked.

"Give me my Blackberry," Tim said.

"Fine. Here. You know you're still on vacation for a few days," Jorge said.

"I know but I can at least check email," Tim replied.

"If you do, you're going to get back to work," Jorge said.

"I won't."

"I've heard that before."

"Don't make me fire you," Tim said.

"As if you would. No one would put up with you. Now get in the car and let's get the lovely lady home."

Moments later, Tim joined her. Jorge got behind the wheel and had them on their way.

"Do you want something to drink?"

"Nah, I'm good." Arissa watched Tim curiously.

"Go ahead and say it," Tim said.

"You're an architect?" Arissa asked.

"I am. I've done okay for myself." Tim shrugged.

Jorge snorted.

"Nothing from the peanut gallery," Tim said.

Arissa interjected. "This looks more than well for yourself."

"Is it a problem that I have some money?" Tim studied her with his piercing blue gaze.

"Please, like I give a crap," Arissa said.

"I like her. Can we keep her, Tim?" Jorge said as he drove.

"For Christ's Sake she's not a pet, Jorge," Tim said in exasperation.

"I know that but she could be your girlfriend and maybe become you wife. Then we can keep her."

"She's a friend. Why are you trying to marry me off all of a sudden?" Tim demanded.

"I'm not getting any younger. My biological clock is ticking. I want some of your kids to spoil."

"Humph. Probably so they could torment me."

"Exactly. Tick tock, Tim. We need a woman for you. Are you sure, miss, that you won't take him off my hands?" Jorge gave her a puppy dog look in the rear-view mirror.

Arissa laughed. "I'm sure. We're just friends. But I'll keep you as one too, if you like."

"See she wants to keep me. Do you need an all-around guy Friday? I'm a hell of a cook and organisational guru. And a great driver." Jorge was playful.

"But then what would Tim do without you?" Arissa asked in the same tone.

"Work himself to death. The boy needs a keeper or jailer." Jorge gave Tim an evil look.

"One of these days I'm going to fire you," Tim warned.

"Yeah, whatever. I'm so afraid," Jorge said cheerfully.

"Behave so Arissa doesn't think we're lunatics," Tim said.

"If she spent the cruise with you then she already knows you're crazy." Jorge shot back.

"I do." Arissa laughed and Jorge joined in.

"Now the two of you are picking on me." Tim sounded affronted.

"Poor baby." Jorge mocked.

Arissa listened as they baited each other back and forth, laughing. Before she knew it they were at her apartment. Tim escorted her to her door.

"I'm sure Deiter will call now you are home," Tim said gently.

"It doesn't matter."

"You're such a liar. It does and he will." Tim squeezed her shoulder.

"Thanks for hanging with me on the cruise." Arissa stood on her tiptoes and kissed him on the cheek.

"Please, you kept me from jumping ship and swimming back to the mainland to work." Tim grinned.

"From now on, we both have to promise to take some time just for fun. Okay," Arissa said.

"Okay." Tim hugged her.

"Arissa." She glanced at Jackson as he strode off the elevator towards them.

"Hey, Jackie. Jackson Carlyle. This is Timothy Vastin. We met on the cruise."

A rolling, drumming sound interrupted them.

Tim winced and said, "Excuse me a moment." He walked away a few steps. "Jorge, I've told you about messing with the ringtone on my phone." His voice faded as he walked farther down the hall.

"Only you would go on a cruise and come back with Timothy Vastin," Jackson said.

"What does that mean?" Arissa frowned.

"You don't know who he is?" Jackson looked at her in disbelief.

She shook her head and he chuckled. Arissa slugged him in the shoulder. She pushed open her door and went inside. Jackson followed. She put down her bag and turned to face her.

"So who is he?"

"He designed this building and all the brownstones on the block. Not to mention a few other notable structures. And has won a boatload of awards," Jackson said.

"Okay so he's good. But he's just Tim." Arissa shrugged.

"See that is why I love you my friend. Just accepting anyone for who they are. So fill me in on the trip."

"In a sec. Let me check on Tim."

"Okay. I'll grab some drinks," Jackson said going into the kitchen.

Arissa went back out into the hall. Tim, from the sounds of it, was still on the phone with Jorge. Arissa walked up behind him. "Have him park the car and come up. There is a garage across the street."

Tim glanced at her. "I'll be down in a moment." He pressed a button to end the call. "I'd love to but need to get home to get a jump on work."

"Jorge said you were still on vacation."

"He's an interfering pain in my ass." Tim grinned.

"And I'm sure you need it."

"He's already won you over to his side." Tim groaned.

"It was the shirt and pants," Arissa said.

"He loves to be shocking. Confuses people when they hear that British accent and then see his clothing. It's amusing to watch." Tim laughed.

"I bet." She studied Tim then added, "Jackson mentioned you designed this building and a few others. And are some kind of big shot."

"And does it matter to him?"

"Nope but I'm curious why you didn't say something on the cruise."

"It wasn't relevant. And still isn't. Or is it?"

"Are you going to keep asking me that?"

"No need to get growly on me. Come give me a hug and let me get on my way." Tim laughed.

Arissa went over to him and hugged him. Tim embraced her and kissed the top of her forehead.

"See you this weekend." Tim released her.

She followed as he went into her apartment. Tim approached Jackson and put out his hand.

"It was nice meeting you at least briefly. We'll talk more this weekend."

"This weekend?" Jackson said.

"Arissa invited me over to your game day. Hope you don't mind."

"No, that's cool."

They shook hands. Tim came towards her, touching her shoulder as he passed.

"Tell him about Deiter."

Arissa shoved him. "Get out, troublemaker."

Tim laughed as he left. She locked the door behind him then went to join Jackson on the couch. She picked up the beer he had got her then curled her legs under her.

"Who's Deiter?" Jackson asked in a mild tone.

"Nobody."

"Rissa," Jackson said in his calm way.

Arissa sighed, knowing it was useless not to tell him. He'd get it out of her. Or gang up on her with Deyon and Sarah until *they* got it out of her. She filled him in. Jackson listened not interrupting her. Once she was done she leant back and they drank their beers.

"You really like this man." It wasn't a question.

Arissa shrugged.

"He'll call then explain what happened to make him leave. I'll get us another one and you can fill me in on the rest of the cruise," Jackson said.

He stood and went to the kitchen. Arissa picked at the label of her beer. She didn't want to get her hopes up, but she would be willing to listen if Deiter did call. Jackson returned.

"Turn up the heat," Arissa said.

Jackson paused by the thermostat, adjusting it. "This is one thing I will not miss when we move to New Mexico."

"Amen. Just three more months," Arissa agreed.

Jackson finished with the heat then sat where he had been before. He held out a new bottle. She put down the old one and grabbed the new one.

"Are you sure you're ready for the climate change and relocating?" she asked.

"Yes. I've loved all the times we've visited McKingley, your family and Deyon. Deyon telling us about the open positions in McKingley Hospital came at a great time. For us both."

"It did," Arissa said.

The thought of returning to her hometown of McKingley made her happy and apprehensive all at once. She loved the town but hadn't lived there in a long time. She wondered if she could once again get used to the different pace. Arissa shook off the apprehension. She wanted this. Working in Chicago was draining her. It was time to reconnect with her close-knit family. Emails and phone calls only did so much to keep up with their large extended family.

"I think Deyon was more excited than we were when we got the jobs."

"Deyon has an ulterior motive. Having at least two of her three best friends in driving distance to bug made her dance a jig. She insists she will convince Sarah. But Sarah is stubborn and loves Minneapolis. She isn't moving from there anytime soon." Arissa snorted.

"You're right. Deyon recorded her dance of joy and sent it to us. She is nutty." Jackson laughed.

"Yep, she is," Arissa agreed.

"Now tell me about your trip." Jackson prodded.

She filled him in on her vacation. Much later, she closed the door behind him. She retrieved her laptop and booted up. As she waited, she picked up her house phone and dialled voicemail for her messages. She listened to all the messages from her family welcoming her back, waiting to hear that one voice she longed for. As they droned on she skimmed through her emails. All the messages were from the familiar names of her family and friends. Even the spam folder didn't show anything. Clicking off the phone after the last message, she closed her eyes. He hadn't called. She stood and got ready for bed. After cleaning up, she slid between the cotton sheets.

He'll call soon. She went to sleep hoping it was true.

* * * *

McKingley, New Mexico
Three months later

"Is this it?"

Arissa startled, looking out of the window then at Tim. "Yes."

"It is beautiful. I wonder who the architect is?" Tim murmured.

"Iona McKingley."

"Like the town? I want to meet her," Tim demanded.

"Yes like the name of town. And yes, she's in town, you can meet her," Arissa said.

"But no working while you're here," Jackson said.

"You're worse than Jorge. It's not work just admiring the house," Tim grumbled.

"I'll tell Jorge on you," Jackson said.

"Tell me what?" Jorge said.

Arissa motioned to Jorge outside her window. He stepped back. She opened the door and Jorge helped her out of the black Chevy Tahoe LTZ. Arissa bit her lips, stifling a grin. When they had arrived in the warmer climate he had gleefully changed his pants to matching Hawaiian shorts. Today's shirt was red, blue and green.

"Tim is thinking of work already," Arissa said, heading for the sprawling house.

"Christ, Tim. We're helping our friends move to New Mexico. A beautiful place with scenic views. Take in the sights instead of thinking of work," Jorge said.

"Rissa, you're a traitor. You know how he nags," Tim called.

"Yeah, yeah. You need it." Arissa waved her hand over her head not breaking stride.

Jackson was laughing as Jorge continued to bitch. She and Jackson had gratefully accepted their offer to help them move. Between them splitting the drive time they hadn't been too tired. Jorge had insisted that they'd made some stops along the way and act like tourists. Being fond of the older man, they had all agreed and had had a great time. As they'd got closer to McKingley, Arissa had become more anxious to get home than taking in the sights. She stopped just before the house and inhaled deeply. The familiar scents filled her nose.

"Rissa," a melodious voice said.

She smiled and rushed to the woman running towards her out of the house. The woman hugged her tightly. Arissa leaned away, looking up into her face. She studied Deyon De'clare. The familiar teasing grin was on her lush lips and her captivating face enhanced her curly lashed, light grey eyes. As usual, Deyon was dressed stylishly. Her burgundy and pale yellow shirt sloped off one shoulder, highlighting her rich caramel skin.

Arissa released her to take in the rest of her ensemble. She realised that the outfit was actually a pants suit. The shorts matched the top and stopped just above her smooth legs. Stylish red, high-heeled sandals finished the look. Arissa made a twirling motion with her finger. Deyon turned around in a slow model spin, making sure Arissa got a good look. Once facing her again, Deyon struck a pose, lowering her head making her wild kinky hair frame her face enticingly.

"Now strut," Jackson said.

Deyon raised her head then strutted her stuff. Arissa stood back and watched the walk that had made Deyon the most recognised full-figured super model in the world. The walk was graceful, powerful and all out sensual. Deyon had used her talent and success to create a fashion line then a boutique that catered to full-figure women. Deyon's home base was in McKingley, however she travelled for various fashion shows and events. She was in high demand. Deyon reached Jackson then put her hands on her hips and moved from side to side.

"Is that what you meant, Jackie?"

"Exactly, divalicious," Jackson teased.

"I'm so glad you're moving here, studly." Deyon laughed delightedly.

"Me too." They hugged.

"Can we keep her, Tim?" Jorge asked.

Deyon pulled away from Jackson. "You must be Jorge. It is great to put a face to the voice." Deyon hugged Jorge.

She glanced at Tim and cocked her hip. "What, no hug after harassing me so many months?"

"You're the one who was harassing me." Tim laughed then hugged her, lifting her off her feet.

"Oh you're strong. Nice. I have so many great buildings to show you. But no working. Maybe you'll move here too," Deyon said.

Arissa grimaced, recognising the tone. It was the one Deyon had used when she had been working on getting Jackson and her to move here. She walked over to them.

"You might as well give in and move. She is relentless," Arissa said.

"I like the weather here. I'd love it," Jorge said.

"Hush, you. Go unload the truck," Tim said.

"See how he treats me? I should stay here with you and Jackson." Jorge linked his arms with Arissa's.

"You know you'll miss him. And he needs you," she whispered.

"He does," Jorge said.

Arissa went with him to the back of the U-Haul he had been driving. They opened it then Jorge reached for a box.

"Not that one." Tim growled.

He stopped Jorge from taking out a heavy box handing him some cushions instead.

"I can damn well lift a box. I'm not that old!" Jorge roared.

"You won't hurt yourself." Tim's tone was impeccable.

Arissa stifled a laugh. It was the same argument they had when they loaded the truck back in Chicago.

"Don't think I don't know you bought the Tahoe so when we drive back I have lots of space so I won't feel cramped. It wasn't needed, boy. I'm fine."

"And you're going to keep that way. Now go into the house and supervise," Tim said, turning his back on him.

Jorge hit him across the head with the pillows. Tim spun.

"Just fluffing them against your hard head. I'll go check out the house." Jorge smirked and walked away.

Tim sighed. "That stubborn goat will be the death of me."

Arissa pulled down a box and said, "He'll keep you young and on your toes."

"You're not lifting that. Go to the house with Jorge." Tim plucked the box out of her arms.

He passed it to Jackson. Arissa frowned.

"Come on, Rissa. We feeble women folk have been banished to supervise." Deyon beckoned.

Arissa glared at Jackson and Tim as she went to join Deyon, sitting at the table under the shaded porch on the one side of the house. Jorge came from in the house with a tray. He placed it on the table and shared the iced tea. Jorge sat and sipped his tea. They watched as Tim and Jackson sweated and unloaded the truck. They called out directions, ignoring the looks and grumbling.

"They wanted us to direct. I bet you they will be sore later." Arissa snickered.

"Serves them right," Jorge said.

"Nah. They are big, manly men," Deyon said dryly.

They looked at each other and laughed.

Relaxing in the chair Arissa said, "Thanks for letting Jackson and I live here with you."

"No prob, Rissa. It's a lot of house for one person. I rarely let anyone stay in the two apartments on the second floor anymore."

Arissa frowned. That was news to her. As far as she knew, Deyon used the apartments to house the models she flew in for her shows. They stayed in the apartments, which had their own separate entrances just inside the front foyer. The centre door led to the main house where Deyon lived. The other two—one on the right and other on left—led to the second floor apartments. The main floor had beautiful, high vaulted windows with seats built in and lots of space, since that was what Deyon had wanted when she'd had the house built. It wasn't just her living area, it was partially her design studio where she worked on some of her projects. With the ground floor space it made the two apartments over it very spacious and they had some of the same features. The whole house was a visual and physical oasis.

"Why?"

"One of the male models who I'd invited to stay in the apartment thought I wanted him in my bed. Crazy fool broke into my house then got all huffy when I said hell no. He couldn't imagine that I didn't want him," Deyon said.

"No. What did you do?" Arissa asked.

"Showed him my gun. Then when he didn't think I was serious I got out my other gun and tranqued his ass. Then called Leo. He was huffy about my brandishing my weapons, as he put it. He knows I have a permit to carry them. I almost darted his butt too, but resisted seeing as he is your family. Leo took my guns and the knives. Fucker."

Arissa started to laugh.

"You were right to do that, Deyon," Jorge said.

"You know it, Jorge."

Arissa calmed down then asked, "So what did you get to replace them with?"

"The same type of guns and the tranq gun too. But then I saw this sweet pistol crossbow and had to get it. Made sure to tell your grumpy butt brother about my new weapons." Deyon took a sip of her tea.

"What did he say?"

"After lecturing me for what seemed like forever, he called your brothers and cousins and they came over and had a grand old time trying it out. Of course, you know Lis wasn't about to be left out. She rounded up the women and came over. We had a fabulous cook-out and tried out my new weapons."

Arissa shook her head. "It's a good thing your closest neighbour is miles away."

"Hell, when they saw the crowd coming they came over too. They brought the booze."

"Sounds just like I remember." Arissa chuckled.

"I'm glad you are here." Deyon put her hand over hers.

"I am too." Arissa squeezed it.

"We want some steaks cooked on the grill." Jackson sounded out of breath.

"Then I guess you're going to town to get some," Deyon replied.

"You don't have any?" Jackson asked in disbelief.

"Nope, I'm out. Have chicken if you want that."

"After you all working us to death, we want steak," Jackson griped.

"There's the road. Go and get some." Deyon gestured.

"Fine. Come on, Arissa."

"What? Why do I have to go?" Arissa demanded.

"I've been here but I'm not that familiar with the area. And as we already know, even with GPS, Tim could get lost in his own driveway," Jackson said.

"Hey. I don't get lost in my driveway," Tim protested.

"Not recently." Jorge snorted.

"I'm tempted to fire you." Tim glared.

"I'd just stay here. I'm sure these lovely ladies will have some use for me." Jorge chuckled.

"I so would, Jorge," Deyon said.

"No trying to steal my Jorge," Tim snapped playfully.

"Stop your yakking and let's get the steaks so we can eat." Jackson pulled her behind him.

"Jorge and I will work on some side dishes. Call us when you're on your way back so we can fire up the grill," Deyon said.

Tim followed and they all piled into the Tahoe and headed to town. Arissa sat in the passenger side, giving directions. She smiled as they went to the quaint shopping area. Exiting the SUV, they laughed as they went into Lewis Grocery and Marketplace.

"Arissa Wright. I heard you were moving back. Deyon already called with an order." Carl Lewis continued to fill their order.

"Carl, how is your dad and mom?" Arissa smiled at the man who had once been her high school sweetheart.

"They're doing well. Once you've gotten settled we'll be by to see you. You know Mom will want to bring you a Sock it to Me cake." Carl smiled.

"Oh. *Yes*. Tell her to come by and we'll make it together. I still can't get the recipe the way I want it," Arissa admitted.

"I'll let her know to call you. What's your number?"

Arissa rattled off the number Deyon had already had installed for her.

"Good. Here is the order. Where's Jackson?" Carl said.

Arissa looked behind her, realising the men weren't with her.

"They were just here a minute ago. Hold that for me a minute." Arissa walked away.

She peeked down the various aisles of the store. Finally spotting them, Arissa went to them. She looked inside the already rapidly filling cart.

"We're not here to shop. Just to get some steaks."

"Knowing Deyon, she already called in an order. I just want to get a few things for my place. I picked up some of your favourite foods for your apartment too," Jackson said.

She had already seen that. Arissa sighed and moved to the side, following the men as they shopped. After over an hour, they went to the butcher counter. Jackson and Tim placed orders then coerced her into placing one. Once Carl had it all ready they headed to the checkout with two heaping carts of food. Tim started putting things on the belt.

"Hey, that's mine."

"I'm buying everything. It's my housewarming present to both of you and thanks to Deyon for putting us up, Jorge and I, for our visit."

"You don't need to do that," Arissa protested.

"Really, Tim, it's not necessary," Jackson added.

"Hush. It's done. Oh crap, we're going to eat the steaks. Arissa, go and order some more ask them to give you what Deyon usually gets so she can have some for herself." Tim made a shooing motion.

Arissa returned to the counter.

"Back again." Carl teased.

"Yes. Give me what Deyon usually orders."

"Everything?" Carl asked.

"No—"

"Yes, whatever is her standing order," Tim said behind her.

Arissa glared at him. "I thought you were checking out."

"Jackson is unloading the carts. I knew you wouldn't do as I say. Don't let her change the order, Carl."

"Will do, Tim," Carl said.

Arissa rolled her eyes. Tim, as usual, had charmed everyone he met. He and Carl were already buddy-buddy. Tim put his hand around her waist, hugging her against him.

"*Arissa*," someone with a deep voice said.

"*Deiter*?" Shocked, Arissa turned to face the owner of the voice. Cold blue-grey eyes stared at her from beneath dark blondish-brown lashes.

Chapter Six

Deiter's glance dropped to Tim's hand on her waist. Then raised back to her eyes.

"I'll meet you up front," Tim said.

Arissa didn't take her gaze away from his. Deiter crowded her. Instinctively, she stepped back as he came closer. She took a few steps before she realised what she was doing and she stood her ground. Deiter still looked as good as he had when she'd first seen him. His six feet two inches of well-muscled maleness set her pulse racing. His skin was more deeply tanned while those blue-grey eyes seemed to miss nothing. They were locked on her. His blondish-brown hair was slightly longer. The white shirt, which hugged his chest, was open at the column of his neck. A neck she wanted to bury her nose in and just inhale the scent that still haunted her.

He left and never contacted you.

At the thought, Arissa stiffened. Deiter didn't stop. He came to her and took her arm pulling her into one of the aisles. Arissa let him, since she didn't want her business all over McKingley. Given Deiter's familiarity with her, she already knew there would be speculation over who he was. She could do nothing about that, but she wouldn't give any more to fuel the gossip. Once they were out of view of Carl, she jerked away and stepped back from him.

"What are you doing here with *him*?" Deiter asked, his tone clipped.

Arissa stared at him in disbelief. "Is that all you have to say to me?"

"Answer me," Deiter snapped.

Arissa didn't even bother to reply. She turned and walked away. Deiter grabbed her. Not even thinking, she gripped his arm and flipped him. He went down with a loud thump. Arissa put her hand over her mouth. Deiter looked stunned.

She dropped to her knees and said, "Oh my God. Sorry. Are you okay?"

"I'm fine. Answer my question."

Arissa sat back. "You know what, I was going to help you up but now you can get your damn self up."

She went to stand. Deiter reached for her again.

"*Don't touch me,*" she warned.

She could see Deiter weighing the odds about touching her. Arissa stood and left him on the floor. She stopped by Carl, got the order then went to the registers. Absently, she noticed only Jackson was at the counter. The cashier continued ringing out. Arissa wrapped her arms over her chest.

What the hell is Deiter doing in McKingley?

From his prone position, Deiter watched Arissa leave. Seeing her again so suddenly was startling. His first reaction had been joy. He'd been trying to find her in Chicago but had had no luck. Noticing who was with her, all rational thought had fled from his mind.

It seemed as though this *Tim* had wormed his way close to her.

What are they doing in McKingley together? They had looked really familiar. An ache filled his chest. Here he had been thinking what they had was so special, and Arissa had already moved on. Deiter moved to stand.

"You really deserved that."

"Fuck off, Tim," Deiter said.

"Shut up you asswipe. I'm about to help you. Come by for a barbecue here in two hours. Get your explanation for leaving and apology for not getting in touch ready for Arissa," Tim said.

A piece of paper dropped on his chest. Deiter picked it up. It was an address. Footsteps passed him. Deiter glanced at Tim's retreating figure.

"Why are you helping me?"

"That's what friends do. Just like they kill people who hurt their friend again," Tim said.

He'd delivered the threat so subtly it wasn't until he had disappeared from view that Deiter realised what he had said. Tucking the paper in his shirt pocket, Deiter sat.

"You seem to be making friends. How'd the hell did he get the drop on you?" Tarak asked.

Deiter stood before answering, "He didn't. She did."

"Hell, a man knocking you on your ass is bad enough. You let *a woman* get the jump on you?" Tarak's disbelief was clear.

Deiter knew the reasons were not that a woman had, but that anyone had. Tarak had taught him to fight. And fight dirty if he needed to. Tarak was a perfectionist and demanded the best.

"Arissa—"

Tarak interrupted, "*Arissa*. You finally found her?"

"More like she found me." Deiter stared off in the direction she had gone.

"What's she doing in McKingley?" Tarak asked.

"I have no clue. But we'll find out in two hours. We're going to a barbecue," Deiter said.

"We are?"

"Yes. I don't know all the areas of McKingley well enough yet so I need you to drive. Come on, let's get the shopping done so we can get out there," Deiter said.

"Okay," Tarak agreed.

Deiter looked at him sharply. That had been too easy. He'd at least expected some type of resistance. Since they had arrived in McKingley over two months ago, except for getting groceries, Tarak hadn't left the house much.

"What, I want to see this mysterious woman who messed with your head." Tarak shrugged.

"Humph. Nosy is more like it," Deiter said.

Tarak smirked as he pushed their cart. He had done away with the cane. He still, and would always, have a slight limp but it was much better. Deiter followed him, barely paying attention as he shopped. They only had time to drop off their groceries before they were on their way.

"Here's the address." Deiter handed Tarak the paper.

Tarak took it then laughed.

"What? You do know where it is?" Deiter asked.

"Oh, I know where it is."

Tarak had a grin on his face that made him uneasy. Tarak said nothing further as he started to drive. He took a direction Deiter hadn't been before. The sight of the beautiful landscape didn't fill him with awe as it usually did. All his thoughts were on Arissa. Deiter sat straighter as they turned onto a road and a gate came into view. There were pillars, which led into red-clay adobe style walls. Periodically, there were designs in the walls made of stone and glass pieces creating a mosaic. They drove between the pillars and the estate came into view. It was magnificent—there was no other word for it.

The walls had to be enclosing at least a few acres of land surrounding the massive house in the centre. The house was made in the usual adobe style with all the typical New Mexico flare, yet it seemed to be two floors. A little way away from the house, to the right, there was a smaller yet still generous sized house, a scaled down version of the main house. The road they drove on was smooth, hard-packed dirt—leaving that natural feel. Once they were close enough to the house, he noted the path to the door had the same smoothness, but on either side there was a rock garden with pea gravel and small shrubs throughout. It was welcoming and warm.

"You getting out or are we just going to sit here?"

Deiter was startled by Tarak's question, realising that they had parked. He wondered who Arissa and Tim were staying with. He got out and waited for Tarak to join him before they both walked to the door. It opened before they reached it.

The woman standing there was beautiful. She studied him with an intensity that made him wonder what she knew about him. The woman shifted her gaze from his then a wide smile curled full lips.

"Tarak, I was wondering when you would come by."

"Deyon, it's good to see you, sexy," Tarak said with a teasing Deiter hadn't heard in a long time.

Deiter recognised the name as the woman Arissa had mentioned who'd been supposed to come on the cruise with her. He looked at Tarak sharply, since he hadn't known he knew her. Tarak smirked at him then stepped forward, hugging the woman. She laughed delightedly, a musical sound. Tarak's voice clearly came to him.

"Be gentle with my friend. He's a good guy."

"For you I'll give him a chance. At least until Arissa tells me to kick him out. You know your way to the back come on back when he works up the courage," Deyon replied.

She glared at him then sauntered away.

"Why didn't you say you knew where we were going?" Deiter raised an eyebrow.

"It was more fun watching you act all anxious," Tarak said.

"You don't have to say that with such glee." Deiter glared.

"Oh, you haven't seen my glee. I could have told you months ago who Arissa was." Tarak said.

"Why didn't you?" Deiter demanded.

"Because you, Mister Obsessed, didn't in all the times you talked about her. You never once mentioned her full name," Tarak said calmly.

"I did." Deiter frowned.

"You didn't."

Deiter frowned and thought about it. "Fuck. I didn't. Christ."

"Arissa seems to turn you into a potty mouth. She tends to have the effect on people. Hell, most of her family does."

"How do you know so much about her?"

Tarak smiled slowly. "You remember my buddy Leo who came by."

Deiter nodded, remembering the whipcord thin man Tarak had introduced him to. Leo was the sheriff and from what Tarak had said, they'd grown up together. They had got into some major mischief along with the rest of the Leo's family. The other thing that Tarak had mentioned was that Leo's family was well known as they were descendants of the founders of McKingley. Leo's family along with the McKingley's—the family the town was named after—had jointly founded the town. That the families were founders had nothing to do with why the majority of the family were so well respected. The respect was from the fact most of both families were in professions dedicated to helping people. Deiter hadn't stayed long after meeting him since he'd had to finalise some things.

"What about him?"

"He's one of Arissa's older brother's. I'm close to them. They are the family I mentioned that sort of unofficially adopted me. If you had only told me her full name I could have put you in touch with the family." Tarak bit his lip.

"You mean—"

"Yep."

"All this time of trying to find her and her family lives in McKingley? And you know them. Hell, from what you told me I could have asked anyone in town and they could have told me about her," Deiter said in disbelief.

"Yep." Tarak's eyes twinkled.

"Fuck."

"Yep. Potty mouth is what happens when dealing with the crazy Wright clan." Tarak started to laugh.

"Why didn't you just recognise her name when I mentioned it earlier in the store?"

"The same reason it didn't mean anything when you told me a few months ago. There are probably thousands of Arissa's in the world. How was I to know she was the same one I knew? Besides, I didn't even know she was back. Haven't been keeping up with the family emails. Which I know I will be hearing about. Oh well." Tarak shrugged.

Deiter blew out a breath. All the months of searching and the answer had been right in front of him. He smacked Tarak on the shoulder.

"Let's go so I can talk with her."

Tarak said, "One more thing. Be prepared to deal with her family if you do convince her to give you a chance. They are really close-knit. And her brothers and male cousins well they all…have a unique way of looking at things." The glint in his gaze was even more gleeful.

"I'll deal with whatever for Arissa," Deiter vowed.

"I hope you mean that, buddy. And so we are clear. Hurt her and I will skin you, friend or not," Tarak stated.

Deiter didn't doubt his words. Tarak led the way as they passed through a tastefully decorated living room then through a chef's dream of a kitchen to a glass door. They went outside. He locked gazes with light brown eyes.

"What's he doing here?" Arissa said loudly enough to hear.

"I invited him," Tim said lazily.

"You had no right," she said furiously.

"You need to talk and you will after we eat. Now, sit," Tim said in a calm tone.

Deiter didn't like the way he spoke to her. Like they knew each other well. Arissa took a step towards Tim. A tall, large man stepped between them. He placed his hand on her shoulder, pulling her against his chest and spoke in her ear too low for Deiter to hear. Not only did he have to contend with Tim now, but this other man had his hands all over her.

"Fine, Jackie. I'll let it go for now. But Tim, me and you are going to have words about this," Arissa said.

"Anytime, Rissa." Tim smiled and winked.

Arissa scowled then walked over to them. Deiter watched her sure stride. It was all confidence and sensuality. Arissa ignored him as she hugged Tarak, then stepped back.

"Tarak, it's good to see you. I heard you were back. How's the leg and lungs?" Arissa asked.

Deiter waited for the familiar snap and coldness.

"Working on it. Didn't know you were back. Along with that reprobate Jackie boy." Tarak's response was mild.

"It's not my fault you don't check emails or deem to reply." There was a reprimand in her tone then she continued, "I'm going to take a look at your leg. And I'm bringing Jackie. I want you to go by The Oasis and use the pool to work the leg."

"Stop ordering me around." Tarak growled.

"I will when you stop being an ass. Let us help you. We're family." Arissa squeezed his arm.

"Ah, shit. How long do I have before the rest of them descend on me?" Tarak sounded resigned.

"Hell, you're lucky they left you alone for as long as they have." Arissa was sympathetic.

"Leo has been by bugging me. That alone should grant me a reprieve."

Arissa laughed. "It should but it won't. Because of Leo you've had over two months of being closed off. No more. I'll be by to check on you tomorrow," Arissa said.

"God, you are such a pain in the ass."

"Yep. Now let's eat." Arissa linked arms with Tarak and led him away.

Deiter didn't say anything at the slight. He strolled over and sat beside the older man in a Hawaiian shirt.

"You're the bloke who didn't call." The crisp British accent coming from the man in the floral clothing threw him for a moment.

"Yeah."

"You are so screwed," he said.

"Jorge," Tim said sharply.

"What? He is." Jorge harrumphed then stood and went to join Arissa on the other side of the table.

Tim put a plate and a beer in front of Deiter. He looked askance at Tim.

"Better eat to get strength. You're going to need it." Tim walked away.

Deiter observed the others as they chatted, teased and ate. He picked up his fork and ate his food, listening absently at the conversation flowing around him. After he was done he leant back and slowly drank his beer. Darkness descended and lights came on automatically, illuminating the area of the patio. He took in the spaciousness of the area. Just like the house it had lots of space. They only sat on a small part of it. He turned his attention away from everyone and to the view. Letting his mind drift, Deiter relaxed.

"Why are you here, Deiter?" Arissa demanded.

He gave her his attention after glancing around and realising they were alone. Placing his beer down, he stood and held out his hand.

"Walk with me."

Arissa didn't take it. She walked across the cobblestone floor then down the path. Lights were all around the area making it easy to see, showcasing the beauty of the backyard. Various trees ranging from empress, eucalyptus and weeping willows were spread around the area closest to the house. Random areas with a plethora of seating—stone benches to tables and chairs and a low couch shaded by a lean-to—were spread throughout. Arissa stopped under the shadowed area of one of the willow trees. She pressed her back against it.

"Talk, then go."

"I'm not going anywhere," Deiter said.

"You did on the cruise," she lashed out.

"That was unavoidable. I'm sorry I didn't get to say something to you."

"That I wondered about but I figured something really urgent came up."

"It did."

"Fine then, that is that." Arissa nodded abruptly.

"I've been trying to get in touch with you."

"You had my info."

"I didn't. I thought I did but somehow I left it on the ship. And they wouldn't give me any information on you. No matter how much I asked." Deiter frowned.

"I would hope not. But you knew where I was from."

"I did. But do you know how many Arissa Wright's there are in Chicago? Hundreds. Hell, I called them all and still couldn't find you."

"Actually my number is unlisted. But that doesn't matter. I didn't put it together at the time but you're the Deiter that Tarak talks about in his emails and calls. You could have just asked him how to find me." Arissa shrugged.

"Hell, until tonight I didn't know you knew each other."

"How's that?" Arissa didn't seem to believe him.

"I mentioned your first name to Tarak but never your last name. He didn't make the connection you were the same woman from the cruise I was trying to find. I did try to find you, Arissa," Deiter insisted.

"That's probable. Tarak only knew I was going on a cruise but not which one."

Deiter moved closer, his pulse leaping. She seemed to be actually listening.

"But none of it matters. What we had was just a fling on a cruise. I'm over it. We both can go on with our lives." Arissa's tone was cool. Her words weren't what he wanted to hear.

She straightened and went to pass him. Deiter caught her. Arissa went to throw him but this time he countered her and pushed her until her back again rested against the tree. He crowded her, pinning her to the tree. Arissa moaned softly as their bodies touched. Deiter groaned, inhaling her scent. In that second, it was as if his soul settled.

"It was more than a fling. I still want what I said on the cruise. For you to give us a chance at building more," Deiter said huskily. *I want you to be my wife.* Deiter didn't say it out loud, knowing she would need time to come around to his way of thinking.

"What? You expect me to forget not hearing from you for three months? For me to just trust you, to drop at your feet and say yes please take me? If it is then you're delusional. Our time has passed. It is not going to happen." Arissa sounded resigned.

"No, I don't expect any of that. That is not the woman I met on the cruise and I got to know. I want that woman. I will gain back your trust and we can find out if we actually have something. How long are you in McKingley?"

"I live here now. Just moved today. But—"

He interrupted. "Good. We live in the same place. One obstacle out of the way."

"What you live here? I thought you were visiting."

"Didn't Tarak tell you? I live here now. Been staying with him. I have a job as a linguist professor at the university."

Arissa frowned. "I didn't know that, I knew about Tarak's injury and he moved back. But not about you moving here. Then again, I haven't been keeping up with the family going-ons that closely, since work was a mad house and I was getting ready for my move."

"It has to be fate that you and I are living here now. It's a perfect opportunity to work to something more. Give me a chance. Or are you already taken by Tim?" Deiter bit out.

"Don't pull this possessive shit on me. We've already had this conversation." Arissa pushed at his chest.

Deiter didn't move, saying defensively, "Seems like you all are really friendly."

"Emphasis on friendly!" she snapped.

"And Jackie is a man, not a woman, like you led me to believe."

"I never said such a thing."

"You did on the cruise."

"No. I told you the friends coming with me were women. Deyon and Sarah are. Jackie wasn't booked to come with us. If this is going to work, you'll have to get over your jealously. I won't stand for it. I have lots of male friends. Some very touchy feely and I won't censor myself to appease you," Arissa said through gritted teeth.

Fierce joy filled him. "I can accept that. Thanks for giving me a chance." Deiter kissed her hungrily.

Arissa rested against him. He suckled her tongue, cupping her ass. The need to have her rode him. He reined it in reluctantly — he would wait at least for a little while so they could become comfortable again with each other. He withdrew, kissed the side of her mouth then released her.

"I'll be by tomorrow at nine a.m. for our date," Deiter said, then strode away.

"I haven't agreed to a date," Arissa cried out.

"You did, and I'll be here tomorrow morning."

"What the hell kind of date starts at nine a.m.?" Arissa sounded disgruntled.

"Wear comfortable clothing and boots. Pack something dressier for later, we're going to dinner too," Deiter said.

He didn't look back or stop. Arissa was silent. Deiter smiled. He already knew what they had had been real, he just had to convince Arissa. And he would. Of that he was sure. Whistling, he went back to the house.

Arissa sagged against the tree. Deiter's swagger as he walked away infuriated her. The stubborn man thought he could convince her to actually open herself up to him again. No matter his explanation, he had left and not contacted her as he'd promised. And the devastation she'd felt when he hadn't wasn't something she would go through again.

But damn, he can kiss.

She raised her hand to her still tingling lips. In the months of dreaming of him, she had thought she'd remembered everything about him. She was wrong. The softness of his lips and possessiveness in his touch had been more intense than she'd remembered. His herbal scent had been even more intoxicating. That muscular body she knew so well had felt harder than before. He'd made her feel cherished and feminine, wanted and desired.

"Snap out of it, Arissa. He's not good for you," she muttered.

"Seems as if the man knows how to handle you," Deyon said.

Arissa gasped, looking towards her. She scowled as she spotted not only Deyon, but also Tim and Jackson. Tim and Jackson were on either side of Deyon. She was draped against Jackson, and Tim against her.

"Nosy."

"It was a hell of a show too." Deyon fanned herself.

"One I did not want to see," Jackson said.

"Ditto," Tim said.

"How long were you all spying on me?"

"Just in time for that damn hot kiss. Was it as good as it looked?" Deyon asked.

"I don't want to know," Tim and Jackson said together, both looking pained.

"Even better," Arissa said, smiling widely.

The men groaned painfully.

"Go girl." Deyon moved from between them.

She linked her arm with Arissa and led her towards the house. Jackson and Tim followed.

"What are you wearing to your date?"

"I don't have a date."

"Please. You know you are going. I can have two outfits delivered from the boutique. A sporty one and a dinner one. Both geared to bring him to his knees. Well, if that is what you want?" Deyon waved her free hand.

Arissa harrumphed. Deyon was right, she would go. She thought about Deyon's offer. "Okay. But this is only one date."

"Keep telling yourself that, dear." Deyon patted her hand.

Arissa refused to even contemplate more. She'd go out with Deiter, once. Just to show him that it wouldn't work between them. Well. Maybe a few times to be sure. But she would not let herself even consider more with him. No matter how damn sexy he was. Or how he made her want to jump him. Once Deiter saw how wrong they were, they could be friends. After all, with him being friends with Tarak, they would see each other. No need for it to be uncomfortable between them.

A few dates and then you are in the clear. You can do this Arissa. With her mind set on the course of action, Arissa ignored the twinge of regret.

Chapter Seven

Man knows how to be on time. Arissa knew that from the cruise ship, he'd always been spot on. She pressed the button on the security system fitted with a camera to see who was outside to let him in through the outer door. She smoothed her hands down her jeans as she walked down the stairs towards the front door of her apartment. The clock on the wall by the door showed nine on the dot. *Can't ignore it any longer.* Halting before the door in the good-sized foyer, she tugged on her sweatshirt and sighed. The weather had dropped about twenty degrees with the cold front that had moved through late last night.

Quit stalling, she reprimanded herself. One final deep breath, then she swung the door open. Only to promptly lose it. Deiter stood there and, like it had the first time she saw him, her breath left her in a rush.

He wore a steel grey sweatshirt, blue jeans that amplified the strength in his legs, and dark brown hiking boots. Deiter removed his sunglasses and pierced her with his intense blue-grey eyes. Her heart—the traitorous organ—pounded with renewed want.

I did say I could do this, right?

"Morning, beautiful," he said as he leaned close and brushed their lips together.

She cursed him repeatedly as he withdrew before she was ready for him to. "Good morning," she replied.

"Ready?"

She could do this. Reaching to grab her garment bag, which contained her dress for dinner, from where it hung on the coat rack, as well as her purse, she shrugged. "As ready as I'll ever be."

He seemed to stare at her for a few moments, as if assessing her mood, before he gestured her to leave. As she closed the door, ensuring the lock caught, she wasn't at all surprised when he relieved her of her items. In silence, they walked to where he'd parked. He opened the back of an older model silver Dodge Durango. Once her things were stowed, he held her door before making his way to the driver's seat.

"Are you planning on giving me the silent treatment, Arissa?" he queried after they'd been on the road for a while.

"No," she said, avoiding his gaze and glancing around the interior of his vehicle.

"So it's to be one word answers then?"

He seemed so calm she ground her jaw. "Looking for a soliloquy?" she asked.

"I already apologised for how things went on the ship, Arissa," he said.

"I know. I heard you." She gazed out of the window.

"But?" he prompted.

She shrugged. "They're just words."

His angry rumble filled the vehicle. She tore her attention from the passing scenery and stared at him. He had a tic in his jaw and he gripped the wheel so tight his knuckles were white.

"What, Deiter?" She shifted to angle her body to him. "Did you honestly think because you kissed me last night and grabbed my ass things would be okay?"

"No. I expected my words to be believed." She heard a hint of his accent and it made her shiver. Damn accents were an aphrodisiac to her.

"I'm not following."

He turned off onto a narrow dirt road. "You're acting like you want me to crawl through fire for your forgiveness when I had no choice but to go."

She thought about it for a bit as they moved over the bumpy road. Deiter didn't try to fill the silence with chatter. He waited. He was right, she wanted him to suffer as she had. Still, it had hurt to not know for those long months.

"And if you'd had my information?" she posed the question.

He stopped the Durango and faced her. His eyes burned with a feral heat. "*I* would have been the one to help you move."

Shivers of want licked at her like flames. She even ignored his possessiveness. True, she didn't like it on men, but damn if his way didn't make her a bit wet. She dampened her lips and revelled in the way his gaze followed the quick dart of her tongue as his eyes swirled with dark desire.

"Why did you leave?"

Deiter began driving again. His expression sobered. "I can't tell you that, Arissa and I have no wish to lie to you, so please don't ask."

Her brow furrowed. "No wish to?"

He sighed and gave her a quick peek. "I will not lie to you, Arissa, not on anything but this. If you pressure me in this, for an answer, I will have to. And like I said, I've no wish to do so."

She let it go, not wanting to put him in that position. Government work sometimes could get messy. Suddenly she got nervous. She was supposed to be showing him how ill-suited they were for one another, but...that plan wasn't exactly working. Being with him was a lot of fun. He made her comfortable.

"How are you liking McKingley?" she asked, figuring it would be a safe topic.

"Beautiful area, although" — he glanced pointedly at her — "I'm liking it much better now."

So much for a safe topic. A blush ran up her cheeks and she shook her head in silence. Deiter parked before a row of boulders and shut off the engine. He reached for her chin and instigated eye contact.

"Ready?"

Was she? Hell no, not even close. *A way to show him we're not compatible.* "Sure," she lied, climbing out.

At the back of the Durango, he pulled on a pack and settled it on his shoulders. "Let's go."

She struck out after him, grateful he didn't walk too fast. The trail was wide, relatively easy to navigate, and some parts of were shaded by the trees.

Even so, she was winded and feeling lightheaded and nauseous when he stopped. They could see out over the mountains and despite the aches in her body, she enjoyed the view.

"Are you okay?" he asked, shedding his pack and gripping her shoulders in a firm but gentle hold.

She nodded but didn't speak. He guided her to a rock and nudged her down on it. Moments later, he thrust a bottle of water into her hand.

"Drink slowly."

She did and licked her lips when he took it from her. With deep breaths, she hung her head and waited for the symptoms to pass.

His hand stroked along her sweaty cheek. "Sorry," he said, on his haunches in front of her.

"For what?"

He moved his hands to rub the outside of her thighs. "Forgetting you just got back here and aren't acclimated to the thin air."

The feeling of nausea faded as her attention zoomed in on the feel of his hands on her body. They moved in small circles. *Focus!*

"It wouldn't matter," she said.

Up and down he stroked, driving her to distraction. "Why not?"

"I'm not an outdoors girl."

"Not even growing up in this place?"

She gave a bark of laughter and shook her head. "Nope. I don't like the constant fear of poisonous snakes or being out for the damn tarantula migration. Then there's the free-range cattle thing they do out here which really freaks me out. So, no. I'm not a huge fan of outdoors."

The only way to describe the look on his face was amusement. "Didn't you grow up here?"

"Yes. But, I moved my happy ass immediately after high school. Haven't been back since. The last nine years, as you know, I spent in Chicago."

"Where there was gangs, murders, carjacking, et cetera."

She grinned. "Exactly. Much safer." His return smile warmed her. "Lis, the youngest of us all, is the outdoor one. She barely goes home. Hell, I believe she'd live outside if she could."

"But not you."

"Oh God, no. I love my bed too much and let's not forget indoor plumbing and whatnot."

He drew her to her feet and brushed a teasing kiss along her lips. Then they retrieved his pack and continued. This time though, their fingers were interlaced.

"Why did you come with me, then?" he asked as they walked.

"You didn't really give me any choice." Her response held no heat—she'd begun to enjoy herself.

Still, he paused and brought her head up to meet his gaze. "I wouldn't have brought you here, Arissa, had I known. Do you want to go back?"

Good opportunity to make things difficult for him, he'd opened the door for it. Yet, she couldn't do it. *Damn him and his way of getting under my skin!* "No."

His smile made the nausea she'd experienced worth it. *Cripes, I'm becoming such a sap.* For a moment, Deiter appeared almost boyish. Then his gaze turned hot and there was nothing about him that was boyish. Nothing but six foot two inches of hot ass German male.

"Not much more to go."

He gave a little tug on her hand. She fell into step with him and enjoyed the fact they were together. It was unexplainable to her how come she felt so comfortable with a man she'd not even known for two weeks. She didn't count the time they had been apart—she hadn't had the chance to get to know him then. But she'd thought of him. With him thoughts of forever, kids, a minivan and being a soccer mom flashed through her mind.

"Here we are," he said, grabbing her from the direction her thoughts had headed.

Arissa scanned the area and a smile, the first real relaxed one since she'd arrived in McKingley, crossed her face. There was a cliff's edge to the right and a few large trees with twisted trunks, courtesy of the punishing winds that moved through here on occasion. Almost no grass yet the view...well, it astounded her. Snow-capped mountains, gleaming in the sun, made for one hell of a backdrop.

"Wow."

"Yeah, I kinda thought that too."

She watched him stride to a large tree and take off his pack. Before long, he waved her over to sit with him on the blanket he'd spread out.

Deiter watched Arissa situate herself on the old quilt he'd brought up. She looked amazing. Her reddish-gold pixie style hair was longer than before, and he wanted nothing more than to sink his fingers in it. He'd never known hair to be as soft as hers.

She wore an old college sweatshirt and some jeans that were slightly baggy. Her hiking boots looked new. Not that it mattered — he knew what lay beneath those clothes.

Perfection, and his own idea of heaven.

God, he'd missed her. He stretched out and braced himself on his left elbow. "Come here." He removed his sunglasses and watched her approach. She stretched out, her smaller body fitting just so against his. And this way, she was out of the wind.

"Thank you for coming with me," he said.

He took his right hand and began to trace his fingers along her delicate facial features. Touching her was as addictive as any drug, he loved how her light brown eyes watched him.

"Did you have a good move?" he asked.

"Long," she admitted. "But, yes, it was good. Went along smoothly, which is always nice."

He did his best to ignore the fierce jealousy at the knowledge of who had come with her. "Good." He stroked over her full lips and up one cheek. "When do you start work?"

She shifted on the blanket, bringing his attention to everything on her below the neck. Stifling his groan, he focused on her eyes and waited for the answer.

"A week. Figured I should give myself a bit of time before I delve back into it."

"Time zone difference?"

"No, that never bothered me, besides we're just an hour different here. I worked all hours at the ER in Chicago so time zones mean nothing. I get sleep when I can."

She said it so matter-of-fact he almost smiled. Lowering his head, he nuzzled her chin. Her gasp went from her mouth to his groin.

Shit, he was harder than the rocks beneath them. She slid her hand along the back of his head and tangled her fingers in his hair, drawing him to her mouth. He obliged. Lightly, he licked her lower lip and traced the shape of her tempting mouth before covering it fully, slipping his tongue between the seam and sinking into her warm depths.

He caught her groan and answered with a rumble of his own. This was how it should be. Him and her. She smelt as she always did, clean and fresh. No perfumes or scented lotions on her, and it drove him to an even harder state.

He stroked through her warm haven, relearning the taste, which he hadn't got over since the day they'd first kissed. Their tongues duelled and he dragged his along the sides and roof of her mouth. When she sucked on his tongue, he rolled them so he lay on top of her, pressing her into the quilt and ground.

She circled her arms around his neck and she arched into him, her whimpers and moans hitting him low and hard. He manoeuvred one hand up under her sweatshirt and purred when it came in contact with bare skin. She tugged once, sharply, on his hair and he pulled back.

Arissa stared up at him, her eyes overflowing with barely leashed passion. "Now," she demanded in a soft whisper.

It didn't matter they were outside. Nothing did, but that he'd found her and she wanted him. He sat up and removed her boots and pants.

"Christ," he mumbled as he dragged a hand over her panties and found them wet. He took them off and sank two fingers deep inside her while with his other hand he unfastened his own jeans.

"Ahhh!" she screamed as her back bowed, hips thrusting against his driving fingers.

She was so tight, so wet, so hot he didn't think he'd make it. Her cream coated his fingers and, grinding his jaw, he freed himself, hardening further when her eyes landed on his cock.

"Deiter," she begged.

He nudged her legs apart and withdrew his fingers, licked them clean, and used that hand to guide his cock to settle at the entrance of her core. With her taste on his tongue, he placed both hands by her head, plunged forward, and sank fully into her slick pussy.

"Fuck!" he uttered as her heated walls surrounded him.

She latched her legs around him and he began to move. Deep strokes. Hard strokes. Unrelenting strokes. Sweat beaded on his brow and more ran down the back of his neck. He never looked away from her big eyes, which watched him, full of smoky passion. She undulated in time with his thrusts, allowing him deeper penetration.

"Uh, uh, uh," she panted.

He couldn't find the breath for any words himself. When she tightened around him and came with a rush and another cry, he lost it. With a guttural curse in German, he drove hard and fast into her until his roar echoed hers as he released his seed into her.

Arms shaking, he lowered himself carefully to her body, not wanting to crush her. She waited with a kiss, one that chased away that niggling bit of doubt he'd forgotten something and put his mind on one thing only. Pleasing Arissa.

* * * *

A few hours later, sated for the time being, they lay together, now dressed. He used his pack as a pillow and she used him, something that he had no problems with at all. Arissa slept against him and he just held her, moving his fingers idly up and down one arm. He knew she was exhausted — she had just got back to town.

He lay there, eyes watching the clouds floating through the clear blue sky. *Shit! I didn't use a condom.* He wasn't a man who didn't suit up. Protection was as natural for him as breathing. But today, he'd not intended to do what they had just done. Well, not out here anyway. Back in his room, he had plenty beside the bed.

Shifting slightly so he didn't wake her, he stared down at the woman whose head was on his shoulder. Her black lashes rested against her cheek as she continued to sleep, unaware of his racing thoughts. She was a gorgeous woman. How would she look pregnant with his child?

The thought didn't bother him as much as he thought it might. Kids with Arissa seemed right. He glanced down to her belly. Hell, it could be happening even now. He grinned and brushed his lips over her forehead, loving how she snuggled closer.

He berated himself for not telling his friend her last name. If he had known sooner he could have taken the next few days off and spent them with her. In bed. Grabbing the edge of the blanket, he pulled it close around her and with another kiss to her forehead, he too, closed his eyes.

* * * *

They woke a few hours later and, after making love one more time, they righted their clothing and packed everything up. She spoke as they made their way leisurely back to his vehicle.

"Sorry for falling asleep like that."

"No need to apologise. I'm the one who should have realised how tired you'd be from moving."

She slid her arm around his waist for a brief squeeze. "How long are you in McKingley for? I know you said you had a job at the university, but is it a temp one?"

"Looks like it's going to be a permanent job for me," he said, watching her reaction from behind the safety of his sunglasses. Her eyes widened before a slight smile lifted the corners of her lips.

"So we'll run into each other then, especially if you're also friends with Tarak."

He almost stumbled. *Run into each other?* Why did that sound suspiciously like he was being reverted to the same category as Tarak?

"What do you mean?" he asked, amazed his voice wasn't more of a growl.

The look on her face alerted him. She was trying to act like what they'd just shared didn't mean a damn thing. Her arms swung at her sides in time with her steps.

"Just that Tarak does a lot of things with the family, so I'm sure I'll see you as well." A brief pause. "On occasion."

He bit back his growl as they passed a few more hikers on the trail, opting instead to smile and nod at them. Back at his vehicle, he stowed the pack and trapped her between the door and his body.

"Is that what this is to you, Arissa? Something that is done just to scratch an itch?"

Her eyes flashed with warning but he didn't care. He wanted the passion, the emotions which came with her. Not this person who seemed content to have him in the 'friend' category.

"We've not seen each other for months, Deiter," she said, an edge to her voice. "I just got home and need to get settled."

"That your excuse to keep me at arm's length? Job, just moving home?" He lowered his face to hers and rumbled, "Because if it is, Arissa Wright, it's a shitty one and you damn well know it. I told you I wanted more than a fling and we just made love out here—numerous times—without protection." Her eyes widened and he knew she'd not even realised that. "That isn't something you do with a 'fling' partner."

Then he opened the door for her. He tried to calm his raging emotions as he walked around to the other side but damn if it didn't piss him off to hear her throw away what was between them so callously. Surely it meant more to her and she was just ignoring that?

"I need to go check Tarak's leg," she said as they were headed back.

"Fine," he said. They'd stayed up there later than intended with the nap, but in his mind, it had been worth it.

He gave them some privacy once they reached Tarak's house, knowing his friend didn't want him hovering while Arissa checked him out. Then they went to dinner and despite every cell in his body demanding he bring her back to spend the night in his bed, he drove her to her place.

He could see the surprise in her expression but he didn't say anything. Just got out and got her stuff from the back. Then he walked her up the walk to her door.

"Deiter?" she asked.

"Thank you for spending the day with me, Arissa. I had a wonderful time." Leaning close, he brushed a chaste kiss over her lips then backed off before desire overrode his sense. He opened her door and placed her bag inside, before taking his hand and trailing it down the side of her face.

It was hard as hell to leave her there, but he did. Turned on his heels, walked back to his Durango, and drove away. Back at Tarak's, he growled at his friend then headed off to work out, needing to do something to expend this excess energy. Even when he finally made it to bed, all he heard was his heartbeat pounding out *Aris-sa. Aris-sa.*

Chapter Eight

Arissa fumed. Damn him. Damn him. *Damn him!* She'd seen neither hide nor hair of Deiter since their date. But all she could do was remember in vivid detail how it had been to be back in his arms. She started work tomorrow and she felt even more exhausted than she had after the drive out here.

"Hey, you okay?" Tim's voice snapped her from her well of wallowing self-pity.

She breathed deep and nodded. "Yes."

He chuckled. "Liar. Come give me a hug."

Sighing, she did as he said. He and Jorge were heading back to Chicago today and while she was sad to see him go, part of her was ready for things to settle down. She'd been running nonstop since she got back, visiting old friends and seeing family. The only sibling she'd not seen yet was the youngest, Lis. Not that it surprised her. Eventually, she'd just swing by her house and say hi.

This week had been full of fun and laughter. With the exception of not seeing Deiter. She knew everyone had been watching her and they'd asked why he wasn't coming around. She just shrugged. *Makes me miss my place in Chicago. Not so many damn people in my business.* She'd not seen Tarak either, though.

Waving goodbye to Tim and Jorge, she watched until she could no longer see the SUV, then she turned and walked with Jackson back inside to her apartment. Once the heavy door shut, she made her way up the stairs with a sigh, rubbing at her eyes. Barely eight in the morning and she felt like taking a nap.

"Everything okay, sweets?" he asked.

Making her way to a chair, she then flopped down in it. "I'm just beat."

He sat across from her. "Things will be quieter now. It's just us and we've got opposite shifts. With Tim and Jorge gone you don't have to worry about entertaining. Deyon is busy with her upcoming projects so she won't be bugging you on your days off trying to drag you places. You'll catch up on your sleep."

She hoped he was right, although she wasn't entirely sure. "So what are you doing for your last day of freedom?"

"I thought I'd go car shopping. Care to come with?"

"Sure, why not. I could use one as well." She got to her feet and followed him to the door. Hopefully spending time with Jackson would keep her mind off Deiter.

He left you again, her brain taunted. The part of her that felt anger fed on that and grew. The rational part tried to offset it but didn't succeed.

Hissing in disgust, both at herself and Deiter for making her feel like this, she grabbed her purse and locked the door behind them. She waited as Jackson headed up to his own apartment. She was thankful that they each had their own space. The thought of living together would have been out of the question — she liked her own space and so did Jackson. Once he came back down to join her they got in the rental and headed off to a dealership.

* * * *

It was after noon when the two of them drove up to the house, each in their new vehicle. New being a relative term in her case, for she'd purchased a used one. Jackson had bought a new one though, but he'd always been flashier than she had. She smiled at her older model Honda Civic and parked it in the drive. He parked beside her and they went inside then shared a nice lunch in his apartment.

"Are you going to tell me about Deiter and why I've not seen his mug around here for the past week?" Jackson asked as he plunked a big bowl of double chocolate dream ice cream before her.

"Can't you just leave it alone?"

He snorted and took a bite. "I suppose I could, but we both know I won't. So you may as well just get it over with and tell me."

She grunted and glared at him. He held her gaze and she knew she was out of luck. Taking her sweet time, she ate a bite of ice cream and smiled as the chocolate slid down her throat.

"I fucked him."

Jackson stopped with his spoon on the way to his mouth. "Christ, Arissa, give a guy some warning first, would you. I could have choked if I'd had this in my mouth."

"Serves you right for demanding I talk about this," she sassed.

"I figured you two would be sleeping together."

She shook her head. "No. Not like after dinner or anything like that. Outside, on the walk and...get this...no condom. Not any of the times."

This time he dropped his spoon. It missed the bowl and fell with a clang to the countertop. She got up and got a rag to clean it up. He was still shaking his head when she sat back down.

"You didn't... Christ, Arissa, are you telling me you love him?"

"I don't know what I'm saying, Jackson. I'm just telling you what happened."

"You're...well, you know"—he waved his hand—"on some form of protection."

Despite the gravity of what she was about to say, she had to laugh. Here Jackson Carlyle was a doctor and looked positively green about talking about her being on birth control.

"That's the thing, Jackson, I'm not." His eyes widened. "Don't ask, I'll tell you. You know I'd been using the implant but lately it has been making feel off so I decided to have it removed. Then with the move coming up I just figured I'd get on something after I got settled in. I had no intentions of sleeping with anyone." She dropped her head in her hands and moaned.

"So you could be pregnant."

The words hung there heavy and she was unable to ignore them. She ran a hand through her hair and stared at her friend, hoping he could say something to make her feel a bit more confident.

"Did you take the morning after pill?"

Arissa sighed. "No. I can't kill a person because of my carelessness, Jackson. You know that."

"You need to tell him."

"I was afraid you were going to say that."

His gaze grew serious. "I mean it, Arissa. Don't wait. Go tell him now so it's not a surprise if it turns out you are."

"I know, I know. This is *sooo* not the way I expected my homecoming to McKingley to be."

Jackson reached across the island and chucked her under the chin. "You left in a blaze of glory, sweets, makes sense you'd come back the same way."

She ate some more ice cream. Eventually Jackson's laughter grew so great she stopped and looked at him. "Everything okay over there?"

"I'm just trying to imagine you first out hiking then…to actually have sex out there…" He gasped for some air and she arched a brow as she calmly lifted her middle finger. "So not nice," he said around more laughter.

She snapped her teeth at him, ignored his continued laugh, and focused on her ice cream. Once she'd finished, she rinsed out her bowl and made her way to the door. "Good luck, sweets," he hollered down the steps after her.

I'm going to need more than luck to get through this. With a fortifying breath, she grabbed her keys and purse from the table by the door then slipped out of the apartment. With quick steps, she crossed the area then out the front door of the house. The bright afternoon sun made her squint and search for her sunglasses.

The ride to Tarak's didn't take all that long and she parked along the street and sat in the hot car for a few moments, trying to make sense of how she was going to do this. *Get moving you wuss!* Her brain chided.

She breathed deep and got out. Moving up the walk, she reached out to press the doorbell. A few moments later, Tarak opened the door.

"Hey," she said.

"He's not here," Tarak said by way of a greeting.

"Where is he?"

"Where he's been all week. On campus teaching."

Of course. Why wouldn't he have been working? Just because she wasn't didn't mean the world stopped for everyone else.

"When's he coming home?"

Tarak shrugged. "I rarely hear him come in before nine at night. Then he's gone again before six in the morning."

"Where's his office?"

Tarak raised an eyebrow and she crossed her arms and did the same. "Why?" he asked.

"Is it any of your business?" she snapped, a bit put out by the fact he was protecting Deiter.

"Yes. I warned him about hurting you, but he's my friend and I don't want him hurt either." Tarak's words were straightforward and she knew he meant them.

"He's the one who left me on the cruise without so much as a word, I'm the one here trying to talk to him."

"I'm the reason he left, Arissa. He wasn't allowed to get in touch with you. And he'll never be able to tell you what he did after he left." Tarak shifted his weight. "He wanted to tell you, I wouldn't let him. You need to let that go."

She stared at him in disbelief. "What do you mean, you wouldn't let him?"

Tarak barely blinked. "Orders are orders." He reached into his back pocket and pulled out a card.

Handing it to her, he said, "Take care you don't hurt him."

Then the door shut in her face.

Standing before his door, she blinked a few times before she looked down at the paper in her hand. It had Deiter's name and numbers on it, along with his office building and number.

After pivoting around, she headed back to her car and drove to the university. She was lucky to find a spot and rolled her eyes at the continual lack of decent parking at a college. Smoothing down her skirt, she shouldered her purse and struck off towards the language building.

Walking across the campus brought back memories of her own time in college. She'd not gone here but there was something fun about being back on this one. With a smile on her face, she wove through the student body and made her way up to his office.

"I'd like to see Mr Schneider please," she said to the receptionist.

The blonde-haired woman looked up at her and gave her a smile. "I'm sorry, he's not in right now. You can wait here for him, if you'd like. He should be back in about fifteen minutes."

"Thank you." She walked away and took a seat along the wall. With each passing second, her nerves got worse. Again, he was on almost to the second of the time. Fifteen minutes passed when she noticed his blond-brown hair coming down the hall.

"Hi, Carly," he said as he stopped by the desk.

"Afternoon, Deiter. How was class?"

An easy shrug had the woman grinning and Arissa seething. Who the hell was this woman to flirt with him?

"Oh, these are for you, and you have a visitor."

He took the messages from her and glanced over his shoulder. Arissa knew he'd not been expecting her — his eyes grew wide before he regained control. "Arissa," he said with a smile. "Didn't expect to see you here, come on back. Thanks, Carly." He flashed Carly a smile and strode away leaving her to follow.

Biting back her rising ire, she walked behind him and waited for him to open his door. She could see the looks he got from the women who walked around there and it fanned the flames of her anger.

"I'm surprised to see you here," he said, putting his stuff down on his desk after he shut the door, then gestured her to a seat.

"Apparently," she snapped. "I didn't mean to ruin your flirting hour."

He turned towards her and leaned against his desk. Arms crossed, he arched an eyebrow and looked at her intently.

Deiter hid his smug smile. "Jealousy, Arissa? How weird considering you told me you didn't put up with it."

Her glower deepened. "Really? That woman was basically all over you, if not for me and the desk she was sat behind I'm sure she would have been."

"So what?" He looked at his fingernails. "She's a friend. She can touch me if she wants." A shrug. "Besides, I've known her longer than you've known Tim. I've known Carly for years."

He knew his words hit home. The easy thing would have been to tell her that Carly was just like that with everyone. But he didn't. He wanted her jealous. Wanted her to feel what he did every time another man touched her.

She looked delectable. A peach and blue shirt showed off her incredible breasts and flat stomach. A white skirt with a handkerchief hem allowed him to ogle her legs. She had low heels on and he could see her toes were painted a pale peach colour and her fingernails were the matching blue of her shirt.

She took several deep breaths as if in an attempt to calm herself. "I didn't come here to argue with you, Deiter. I have to tell you something."

The seriousness of her tone grabbed his full attention. "So talk."

He watched her sit and fidget with the hem of her skirt. Shrugging out of his suit coat, he took the chair next to her then gently lifted her chin so she would meet his gaze. A good plan but a failed one, nonetheless. Her eyes were scrunched shut.

"Look at me, Arissa," he ordered. He dropped his fingers from her face.

She did and the uncertainty in her brown eyes concerned him. "Umm, I'm not entirely sure how to say this." Arissa took a big breath and blew it out between pursed lips. "I'm not on any kind of birth control."

Deiter stared at her for a moment, the words running over and over in his head. Bam! It hit him. "So you're telling me when we made love out there..."

Another big sigh. "There was no protection. At all. Period. And I didn't take a day after pill."

Hope flickered in his chest. She could be pregnant. And she didn't use the final precaution to prevent pregnancy. "It's too soon to know, right?"

Her nod told him of her concern. "I don't expect—"

"Stop right there, Arissa!" he interrupted. "If you are we'll deal with it together. You said you didn't know now. There is no reason to make any decisions."

She met his gaze and he bolted from the seat to scoop her up in his arms. Tightening his hold on her when she struggled, he sat them down in his previous seat. "I'm at fault here too, Arissa. I didn't even think about a condom. I had them at home for later that evening but I'd had no plans of anything but hiking out there."

Sniffles reached him and he tucked her head under his chin. For the time being, he had her in his arms. It didn't matter to him why she'd come to him, just that she had.

"I didn't care either," she whispered after they'd sat there in silence for a while. "All I wanted was you."

This time, he didn't even try to stop the grin. She smacked him on the shoulder and he jumped. "What?"

"I felt the smug smile," she sassed without looking up.

"Did you now?"

She burrowed closer. "I've missed you this past week."

His lips hovered over her temple he then brushed light kisses along her skin. "I missed you too, Arissa. My schedule is just so hectic right now."

"I had planned on showing you how wrong we are for one another."

"I know I saw it on your face. Why are you fighting this so much? Why are you fighting the idea of *us*?"

"I don't know. You scare me, Deiter. Everything you stand for."

"Everything I stand for? Should I be insulted here?"

She shifted in his arms, bringing her ass across the increasing erection in his pants. "No. I'm talking about what you represent to me when I look at you."

Staring down into her eyes, he stroked along her cheek. "Like kids and a house?"

"I've been dreaming about being a soccer mom." She hit him again when he smiled. "It's not funny. I had a damn minivan and everything."

"I'll have you know I excelled at your soccer, and I happen to think our children will be stars at it."

She rolled her eyes at him and climbed off his lap to pace around the office. When his phone rang, he bent over the desk to grab it. Carly. After a quick conversation with her, he hung up and found Arissa scowling at him.

"What?"

With a shake of her head, she ground her jaw, and looked away. He pushed up from his seat and stalked to her. When her back hit the wall and she could go no farther, he braced his arms on either side of her.

"Look at me, Arissa," he murmured.

Eyes shooting brown sparks met his. "What?"

"What are you so angry about?"

"Nothing."

He nibbled along the shell of her ear, taking the time to tug gently on the lobe. "Are you sure?" Another nip. "Because from where I'm standing it sounds like you're jealous."

"So what if I am?"

He captured her jaw in two fingers. "Nothing. Just that you know you have nothing to worry about. Carly is a friend, like I told you before." He kissed her fast and hard until she sank against him. "I'd love to stay and explore this with you, Arissa, but I have to get to my next class."

Deiter felt her sigh as much as he heard it. He rubbed his hands up her bare arms. "Are you free tomorrow?"

She shook her head. "No, I start work tomorrow and am not sure when I'll be done." She worried her lower lip for a bit. "Two days after tomorrow?"

He thought over his schedule and shook his head. "Nope." A grumble of discontent filled him and he wanted to say the hell with all of it. Pushing away from her, he went to his desk and bent over his computer. Moments later, the printer spat out a sheet. "This is my schedule. If you have some time on yours, I want it."

Arissa glanced at it and nodded but her eyes told a different story. Again forcing eye contact, he raised an eyebrow and waited for her to explain.

"This is why my last boyfriend broke it off with me. He wanted someone who was around more and...and why are you smiling?"

"You basically said I was your boyfriend."

"I did not."

"Yes, you did. It was implied." He grinned at her and she huffed but couldn't hide the sparkle that replaced the sadness in her gaze.

"You...truly are incorrigible."

"I know. That's what my mother says." A quick brush of his lips along hers. "Your last boyfriend was not worth spit, so forget about him. I know our schedules are different but we'll make it work, Arissa. I'm in this but I can't go it alone. Give *us* a real chance."

For an answer, she wound her arms around his neck and kissed him. Pressed her all-too-tempting body against his and thrust her tongue deep into his mouth. Harder than steel in mere moments, Deiter had her backed up to the wall as he slipped one hand under her skirt. He growled low in his throat when she ended the kiss and stopped his inquisitive hand.

"Sorry, professor. You have a class to get to."

He swore in both English and German. Arissa laughed as she swiped her thumb along his lower lip.

"Let's go," he said. Stepping away from her, he put his coat back on and grabbed his briefcase. With his hand on the small of her back, he guided her to the door and out.

They walked in silence until they'd left his office area. On the way down the stairs, his gaze remained transfixed to the natural sway of her ass in that skirt. All he could think about was taking her up against the wall, those limbs wrapped around his waist as he pounded into her. So deep he could feel her heartbeat.

'I'm not on any kind of birth control'. Her statement did something he didn't think would ever happen. Take his mind from thinking about sex with Arissa Wright. What if she was pregnant? Well, they'd get married of course. Then if he had to, he'd spend the rest of their days convincing her how much he loved her.

He tripped. Only his reflexes saved him from falling down the remainder of the stairs.

"Are you okay?" she asked, whirling around to face him.

Heart pounding erratically, he nodded. "Must have missed a step."

Her gaze moved up and down his body as if needing to ascertain it for herself. "Okay."

I love her. A woman he'd not known for very long then had been separated from for a few months. He loved her.

"Where are you parked?" he asked as they pushed out into the warm sunlight.

"In the main lot."

He reached out and stopped her. When she faced him, he cupped her face in his palm, his fingers playing in her hair, and teased her bottom lip with his thumb. "Call me as soon as you get your schedule, Arissa."

She blinked, slow and languidly. "I will."

He moved slowly, giving her a chance to back off. She didn't. Her lips met his halfway and he groaned at their kiss. Electricity spiked through him and just like that, he forgot everything but her.

"Have a good day, Deiter," she whispered against his mouth.

"You too, Arissa."

He stared after her until he could no longer see her. Then he hurried off to class so he wouldn't be late. He couldn't wait to hear from her. And couldn't wait to see what came of her possibly being pregnant. If she was, wonderful. If not, well, there was always next time.

Chapter Nine

Arissa groaned and shed her gloves before tossing them to land inside the trash bin. That was it. The final patient of hers today. She strolled from the exam room and readjusted the stethoscope around her neck.

For the time being, there was a lull in the hustle and bustle of the ER. And being the pragmatic woman she was, she was going to take advantage of it and get her ass out. It didn't take her long to change and grab her things.

"Night!" she called out as she passed the desk.

"Bye, Arissa. Have a great one!"

She waved over her shoulder and stepped out into the twilight that bathed McKingley in a gentle glow. Placing a hand on the back of her neck, she tried to rub out the kink. She'd been working here for two months now and had settled into her rotations and routines well.

She was still dating Deiter and things were going well there, if she thought about it. She wasn't pregnant. When she had told him, she could have sworn there'd been disappointment in his gaze.

They didn't get to spend tons of time together but what they did was cherished. But today was her Friday and it was his as well, so they were heading out of town to spend their weekend in Santa Fe.

The sound of sirens made her pause before she shook her head and continued on to her car. Deiter was going to come by and pick her up, she just had to call him and let him know she had finished work.

Activating her hands free she called him and waited for him to pick up.

"Hello?"

What the fuck? This wasn't his voice. It belonged to a woman.

"Hello?" the woman asked again.

"May I speak to Deiter, please?" Arissa questioned in a cool tone.

"He's in the shower right now, can I take a message?"

Shower. Her eyes burned and she blinked a few times before she could formulate a sentence. "Just tell him Arissa called."

"You're Arissa?" the woman sounded pleased, which only pissed her off more. "I've heard about you."

"Lovely for you." She disconnected the call.

Damn it! And damn him for constantly reminding her she had no right to be jealous. True to his word, he never said a thing anymore when men touched her. She could see how it upset him but he never said a thing. But...*this*...her being the one who had to watch as other women rubbed up against her man. Damn well pissed her off! But all Deiter did was shrug and say, "It's the same as you and your male friends." Then that was the end of it as far as he was concerned.

"Not as far as I'm concerned," she seethed.

She drummed her fingers impatiently as she waited for the gate to open at Deyon's. *I really need to get a place of my own.* Once she'd parked, she stomped inside and slammed the front door behind her.

Thankfully, she knew she wouldn't have to face anyone. Jackson was still at the hospital for his shift. Deyon would be at her store—she had been working late. Grumpy and cranky, she went up the steps to her apartment and headed directly to the shower and took a short yet refreshing one. Delivering a half-kick to her packed suitcase, she made her way to the kitchen and looked for something to eat.

When the doorbell rang, she jumped. Her hand was on the knob just about to open it—she had been heading out to her car to get her cell she had forgotten. Since no one could get in without someone letting them in, she opened it figuring it was Deyon or Jackson. Deiter stood there with a sexy half-grin on his handsome face.

"What do you want?" she snapped.

"A hello would be a good place to start." He arched an eyebrow. "Are you okay?"

"Me? I'm fine. Why wouldn't I be?"

He leaned in for a kiss and she pulled back, retreating up the stairs. The sound of him following her came to her. In her living room, she faced him.

Deiter frowned and sighed heavily. "What the hell is going on, Arissa?"

"Not a damn thing."

"Are you ready to go or are you going to act like a baby?"

"Baby? I'm not acting like a baby."

"Okay then. I'll go and cancel the trip to Santa Fe, since you don't seem like you want to go."

"Why bother cancelling it, why don't you just take the bimbo who answered your phone while you were in the shower?"

He muttered in German before he reached out and caught her up in one arm. "I've had just about enough of this," he growled.

She struggled to get free. "Put me down damn you!"

He did. Dropped her on the couch like a rag. "You are something else, Arissa Wright," he said, his words clipped, accent prevalent highlighting his anger.

"You're one to talk."

"I've told you repeatedly you don't have to worry about anyone else. I want you. However, you seem so keen to believe the worst of me. And I don't know why. I've never given you any reason to do so. Hell, I even stand there and let those fucking friends of yours put their hands all over you when what I really want to do is smash them into bits of bloody pulp. But I don't. Because *you* told me you don't 'do' possessiveness. So how come it works for you but not me?"

She stared at him, lost in the fury of his eyes. "I don't have men answering my phone while I'm in the shower."

"How do I know that? I've called you and had Jackson pick up the phone."

"You know because I said so!"

"I'm supposed to believe you but you don't have to believe me?" He shook his head. "Not fair, Arissa."

She got to her feet and stood toe to toe with him. "Yes!" she screamed. She was being irrational and she knew it. But when that woman had answered his phone, all she could see was red.

Deiter shoved his hands in his pockets and shrugged. "I don't know how else to prove myself to you, Arissa. I love you but it's not good enough for you. You want me to be okay with other men touching you, *my woman*, and not question it. But the rules are different for me? I just don't know. I'm leaving now. I'll be at Kell's if you feel like talking. I'd love for you to come, there's someone I want you to meet. Otherwise, I'll...see you later." He pivoted around and went down the stairs rapidly. The shutting of the door below echoed in his wake.

She couldn't move. He'd said he loved her. Then left. No, surely it was a ploy to get her to come after him. She hurried to the window and peered out. No sign of his vehicle. He had left.

Arissa screamed in frustration. *What the hell is going on with me?* Hell, if she'd not got the news she wasn't pregnant, she may just begin wondering if she was, given her extreme mood swings as of late.

What's it going to be? Let the best thing yet in your life get away? Or swallow some of your damn pride and go after him?

Moments later, her engine started as she turned the key. Her bag for Santa Fe was in the trunk just in case. She didn't want to lose him and she really had to be much more considerate of his feelings when it came to her male friends.

She drove as fast as she could to Kell's. Her mood didn't improve any when it took a while for her to find a parking spot. Even after she had secured one, she debated going in or remaining out.

"Why am I chasing after him? He's the one who left me."

Because you're the one who acted like an utter ass, her brain informed her, a bit too gleefully, she thought.

"I'm not the one who has women answering my phone."

Get over yourself Arissa Wright or you're going to end up alone.

With a mutter at her subconscious, she climbed out of the car, locked it then walked towards the entrance. She enjoyed Kell's but hadn't been there in a while.

As she entered, she saw Martin the owner standing behind the greeter's podium. "Hi, Martin," she said.

"Miss Arissa," he replied with a grin. "Lovely to see you tonight."

"Thank you." She glanced over the crowd but didn't see Deiter. "I'm looking for someone—"

"Deiter Schneider," he interrupted. "We were told to expect you. I'll take you to the table."

She was expected? With a deep breath, she followed the still-handsome older man through the tables to one by the window, offering a lovely view of the place across the street.

"Here you go," Martin said.

Arissa looked down and found a petite woman with shoulder-length blonde hair sitting at the table. "Are you sure?"

"Of course," Martin claimed with a smile. "Can I get you a drink?"

"Tea please," Arissa replied.

Left alone, she put her attention back on the woman who watched her with a cool gaze. There was no invitation to sit down. She sat anyway. "Where's Deiter?" she asked.

"He'll be back," the woman's response fell like ice. "I had pictured something more when he told me about you. But I guess I was wrong."

She bristled. Who the hell did this woman think she was? The voice was identical to the one who'd answered his phone. "Excuse me?"

"All he talked about was how much he wanted us to meet and how much I'd like you. Well, he was wrong. I don't like you at all. You've hurt my brother for the last time. Do it again and I promise you, they'll *never* find your body."

The words were delivered with deadly promise.

"Arissa." Deiter spoke softly beside her. She turned her head and drank him in. Was it possible for a man to get even more handsome in less than an hour?

"Hi, Deiter. You said you wanted me to come, so here I am."

"I see you two have met." He sat beside her, close but not touching, and she missed his touch. "Arissa Wright, meet Marlis Schneider, my sister she works for the German military. Sis, this is Arissa Wright, a doctor."

Sister. The woman who'd answered his phone was his sister. She swallowed and gave the woman a small smile. "Nice to meet you." And military so...yeah crap, that threat was most likely a promise.

Marlis' smile didn't reach her eyes. "Likewise." She'd officially made an enemy of the sister of the man she loved more than anything.

She loved him. That's why she'd been acting like this. Because she'd fallen in love with him. *Duh!* Her subconscious added. Or at least just realised it. One glance to the man beside her made her sudden joy falter. He may not want her anymore, not after her behaviour.

Deiter sneaked peeks between his sister and Arissa. Something had happened while he'd been in the restroom. Honestly, he'd not believed she would have even arrived here. Not after the tantrum she'd thrown at her place. Nevertheless, here she sat.

While their food was delivered along with Arissa's drink, he asked Marlis in German, "What's going on between you two?"

"Nothing," she replied.

"So," Arissa began, "How long are you in town for, Marlis?"

"I'm leaving tonight, which is why Deiter wanted us to meet."

He glared at his sister for being so harsh with her response. Arissa stiffened a bit, as if embarrassed. He realised then she knew it had been his sister who had answered the phone.

"Oh, I see."

Arissa turned to him and licked her lips. Damn but he wanted to nibble on that plump lower one. He could feast on her mouth and never get bored.

"I'm sorry, Deiter," she said.

"What for, Arissa?"

"How I acted. You were right. I wasn't being fair. It's not right I expect you to not react when a man touches me and you not let any woman touch you. I guess...well, I don't know what I was thinking, but I know it wasn't right or fair."

"And?" he asked.

"And I love you."

His heart thudded loudly in his chest. She'd actually said the words. He wanted to pull her close and ravish her but he had to know she trusted him and believed him.

"Do you trust me?" he questioned.

"Yes."

He stayed silent for a moment until a sharp kick under the table snapped him from his thoughts. His sister glared at him. *Hmm, maybe she doesn't dislike Arissa after all.*

"Do you believe my words when I say there is no one else for me but you?"

She licked those delectable lips again and got up from the seat only to climb up on it.

"Get down from there, Arissa," he said, reaching for her.

She batted his hand away. "Can I have everyone's attention please?" she called out.

"Oh no, you don't have to do this." He captured her hand but all she did was squeeze it.

The room fell silent and every pair of eyes focused on their table. "I'm sorry to interrupt everyone's dinner but I wanted to say something. I'm Arissa Wright."

A few people called out greetings to her which she replied in kind.

"This man here," she said, tugging him to his feet, "is Deiter Schneider. He teaches at the university. We were supposed to go away to Santa Fe this weekend but I acted like...well, to be blunt, an idiot so I came down here to ask for his forgiveness." Arissa held up her hand to silence the cheers of 'forgive her' and waited until they complied. "I met him on a cruise and my life changed that very day. I don't know why I've fought my feelings for him, but we'll just put it back to that I was an idiot. Bottom line, I love him." She tilted her head down and met his gaze. "I love you, Deiter. With everything inside me."

He lifted her from the chair, thrilled when her arms closed about his neck, and kissed her. He poured every ounce of feeling he had into that one kiss. The room around them erupted into cheers and when he ended the kiss, he stared into her eyes, eyes that were a little shiny.

"I love you, too, Arissa Wright."

"Does this mean we still get to go to Santa Fe?"

He laughed and kissed her again. "Yes, crazy woman. We're still going to Santa Fe."

The rest of the meal, he fed them both from his plate and always touched her. Part of him felt like dropping to his knees and asking her to marry him but he didn't. She deserved a special and romantic proposal. They took his sister to the airport. He wasn't quite sure what Marlis said to her when she said goodbye — Arissa wouldn't tell him. They left her car at Tarak's and headed in his Durango for their weekend.

* * * *

Santa Fe

Arissa walked with Deiter as they explored the art exhibits. They had to head back to McKingley today, but for now, she was just happy to be with him. The calls had come after they'd departed for Santa Fe — her family asking her if she was engaged after the display at Kell's. She'd laughed and told them all no. But deep down, she wanted the ring. She wanted to be engaged to this man.

His arm was around her and she felt cherished, there was no other word for it. They'd barely left the hotel room on Saturday, instead spending time reacquainting themselves with one another's body. Truth be told, that's how they spent this morning as well. Breakfast in bed took on a whole new meaning. But she'd wanted to see this exhibit so he'd put on some clothes and come with her.

"Are you hungry?" he asked in her ear.

"A bit, yes."

"There was a place outside that I think would be fun. Or we could go to the cafeteria here."

"Outside," she said with a grin. "Cafeteria food isn't ever a good thing to me."

"Right behind you," he replied.

They found a place that sold funnel cakes and so she promptly forgot about good nutrition and had him get her one. He came back with two, one for each of them. Hers had powdered sugar on it and his had cinnamon sugar. They ate leisurely, sharing with one another.

Finished with that, they walked along and took in the rest of the art show. It was a huge event and there was just so much to see. They held hands as they meandered along. Eventually he guided her back to the hotel room where they packed up their bags.

"Are you sure we can't say for one more night?" she groused, not even remotely ready to get back.

"We could, but I think a few people may come looking for us. Like your patients and my students."

She groaned and latched her suitcase. "Fine, then." Grabbing the handle, she said, "I'm ready."

"Arissa?"

She dropped the luggage and spun around to see what he needed. "Yes?"

Deiter stood right there.

"What?" she asked.

"We can stay another night if you want."

She slid her arms around him and kissed him. Lord, she loved kissing this man. He tasted so damn good. And intoxicating.

"We have jobs waiting."

His dejected sigh made her laugh. "If you insist, woman."

"No, you're the one who pointed that out first. I was content to forget it but now that you've reminded me..."

"Oh, blame me."

She grinned. "I just did."

He kissed the tip of her nose. "One more thing."

"What's that?"

Deiter removed her arms from around his neck then sank to one knee before her. He licked his lips and stared at her. "Arissa, I know you deserve something romantic and I should be doing this on the deck of a ship during a sunset or something, but I can't go another day without knowing if you'll be my wife. You know I love you, I have I think since the day I met you."

She couldn't move. Her limbs had frozen. All she could do was stare and blink at the man who was reaching into his pocket for a box. He withdrew it, opened it then offered it to her.

Her jaw trembled and she nodded. "Yes. Oh God, yes, Deiter, I'll marry you."

He pulled the ring free and slipped it on her finger. As he got to his feet, she stared at the ring. The ring centre was a faceted amethyst set in a starburst pattern, flanked by four rows of brilliant diamonds on each side. The band was a braided design in white gold.

"It's absolutely beautiful, Deiter," she whispered in awe.

"Yes, you are," he said, cupping her face in his hands and kissing her.

With a groan of surrender, she gave herself up to her German. The road may have been bumpy but things were now going great. To top it all off, this man holding and kissing her as if she was his world was the best thing yet.

About the Authors

McKenna Jeffries

McKenna Jeffries has loved the written word from time she picked up her first book. Soon she was creating tales of love and family.

Although McKenna used to make up stories she never thought to put them on paper until...she realised the stories would keep filling her until they were written. Since then she's been writing and sharing her books.

There is always some new story floating around her head. An itchy feeling in her fingers fills her until she can get a piece of paper to write it down.

She writes because it's a love affair. Writing is in her blood and she enjoys taking readers on a journey.

Aliyah Burke

Aliyah Burke is an avid reader and is never far from pen and paper (or the computer). She is married to a career military man, and they have a German Shepherd, two Borzois, and a DSH cat. Her days are spent sharing her time between work, writing, and dog training.

She can mostly be found reading — anything from thrillers to sci-fi to horror. However, her first real love will always be the world of romance. When writing her goal is to write stories with a heart of romance, a troubled road to reach happiness, and more than a hint of happily ever after.

Both authors love to hear from readers. You can find their contact information, website details and author profile page at http://www.total-e-bound.com.

Total-E-Bound Publishing

www.total-e-bound.com

Take a look at our exciting range of literagasmic™
erotic romance titles and discover pure quality
at Total-E-Bound.